WHEN HE
VANISHED

A TOTALLY ADDICTIVE THRILLER WITH A
BREATHTAKING TWIST

T.J. BREARTON

First published 2019
Joffe Books, London
www.joffebooks.com

Please join our mailing list for free kindle crime thriller, detective, mystery, and romance books and new releases.
http://www.joffebooks.com/contact/

We hate typos but sometimes they slip through.
Please send any errors you find to
corrections@joffebooks.com

We'll get them fixed ASAP. We're very grateful to eagle-eyed readers who take the time to contact us.

©T. J. Brearton

ISBN: 978-1-78931-114-3

For my mother
(But don't read too much into it, haha)

PROLOGUE

We're alone on the highway except for the headlights trailing far behind us as we pass alongside a frozen lake, silver in the moonlight. Beyond it are dark mountains, stars hanging above their jagged peaks.

"Sometimes I think I'm afraid to feel good." John holds the steering wheel with one hand. It's the first thing he's said in ten minutes, but the silence has been comfortable. If we're having a problem in our marriage, at least right now everything feels distant and manageable.

"We all have that." I pick at something lodged in my teeth and can still smell the garlic and cilantro from our dinner date. "You know, it's called something. A negativity bias."

"I tell myself if I feel good — let my guard down, you know — bad things will happen."

I reach out and touch his hand. "You should feel good. We're doing okay. Right? This is it. This is life."

He doesn't say any more.

After eight years of marriage I've come to accept that John isn't going to change much. He's a kid from North Country poverty, a troubled home, and considers stoicism part of his success — if you don't talk too much about your problems, maybe they'll just go away.

"Is there any gum?" I ask.

"Glove box."

As I load a piece of spearmint gum into my mouth I can just see the steep rocky face of Poke-O-Moonshine in the dim light. A few houses — cabins, really — occupy the private land between the road and the state-owned mountain. Their lights flicker behind the evergreens, smoke snakes from their chimneys. Winter wants to stick around for a few more weeks.

We crest a rise on the southbound side of the interstate and after a few seconds the vehicle behind us does, too. There's not much to this area; it's a protected wilderness ranging six million acres — a lot of beauty and solitude, just the way John likes it.

"So do we want to do this or not?" I ask.

"Spring break?"

"Yeah — but you tell me. You're the one who's been doing all the work on it."

"It's good, yeah." He seems distracted for a moment, then he says, "The snow's gone over there — buds are popping on the trees."

"And if we're not going to Arizona . . ."

"We're not going to Arizona," he says with finality.

"All right. I guess it's settled."

John takes the wheel in both hands and grows pensive. I start thinking about our dinner, about all of the things we discussed — and the things I didn't quite dare to. But I'm bolder now, maybe because I'm thinking of visiting the lake house for the kids' spring break — how happy they'll be — and maybe I can see it: a chance at our own *real* happiness. And I want to go for it.

"John?"

"What."

"I don't want you to get upset at me. But I think, you know, baby—"

"I know what you're going to say, but I'm not depressed. I don't feel depressed."

"Honey, it's not a bad thing. It doesn't mean you're weak or anything. To see somebody. If you wanted. Obviously something's going on. It would be just to *talk* . . ."

He doesn't seem to be listening, like he's tuned me out, which is frustrating. Then I notice that the vehicle behind us is closing the gap, and at a good clip. I have to raise a hand to shield my eyes from the headlights glaring off the mirror.

We've been traveling at the same speed for some time and haven't slowed up any. I know this from my habit of checking the speedometer, which stems from my mother and her lead foot; I've always been a bit of a backseat driver. And we're in the slower traffic lane.

"You ever get this idea you're not who you think you are?" John asks.

The question distracts me from the gaining vehicle. John has a restless mind, but maybe it's not as random as it seems. Maybe he's still talking about how he feels, digging at something, trying to get to the bottom of it.

"I mean, like, you have an image of yourself — a mental projection. *This is me, what I'm like, who I am.* You forget your flaws. You're trying to do the right thing, but you have these . . . limitations you're not always aware of."

"That's what makes a good person," I remind him. "We all have flaws. A good person tries to do the right thing anyway."

"What's the thing that poet says? *You can't touch your own fingertips.*"

"That's what you have a wife for," I say, and the smile feels twitchy on my face. But I give him another pat on the arm, thinking it's not unusual to have one of these *what-does-it-all-mean* seminars with my husband. I know John is haunted, that he's seen too much of the world, seen too much in people, and the knowing makes him nervous. But if I'm honest, he's been going through something more acute for weeks, now. When I tried to pick through it at dinner his answers were shallow, lacking detail.

"What is he doing?" John says, glancing at the rearview mirror.

The lights behind us are brighter. My hand's been hovering to shield their reflection, but they've moved out of range because the vehicle is closer.

"Go around me," John says into the mirror. "Why's he riding my bumper?"

I get my bearings: we're between off-ramps, at least ten miles of nothing between Exits 33 and 32. "Maybe he's having a problem."

"Okay — now I think he's backing off."

The lights blasting in seem to dim a little at the same time they reappear in the mirror on my side of the car.

"Weird," I say, quietly.

After a moment, John says, "Listen. You don't need to worry about me. I'm sorry I said anything."

I forget the other vehicle and face my husband. "Don't be sorry you said anything. That's not how it works. But it's a two-way street — you say something and then *I* might say something, and if it's not exactly what you want to hear it shouldn't make you sorry."

"So you think I need to go see a therapist because I'm afraid to feel good? You said everyone feels that way."

"I said it's negativity bias. But the trick is to get right with it."

"I was being figurative. I didn't mean . . ."

I glance in the mirror then turn around. The vehicle behind us has drawn closer again — dangerously so, cruising along just one or two car lengths back. "What is this guy doing? Really, John — maybe he's having trouble."

"If there was a problem he'd flash his lights, not tailgate me."

Once more, I raise my hand against the reflection and peer into the night, hoping to see signs for our exit. Nothing yet. Maybe two or three miles to go.

"What the hell . . ." John sounds as worried as he is angry, adding to my anxiety. "He's fucking with us!"

"Maybe he's drunk . . ."

John takes a hand from the wheel and gestures. "He's got a whole open lane. He can go around us."

"Is it police?"

"Those aren't cop headlights. I don't — no, it's not a cop."

The whole thing is souring the enjoyable dinner we just had. "Let's just get home. Okay?"

"That's the plan."

It pisses me off a little. John and I don't get much time alone and we really needed tonight. Something is up with him — up with *us* — and we were just starting to get at it. Mid-life crisis? A belated seven-year itch? I rub the back of my neck and watch the lights in the mirror, then close my eyes.

Maybe the tension lately is normal — nearly a decade of marriage, two full-time careers, two kids, a house, bills, everything that happened with John's family — it adds up. But I can't shake the feeling there's more. Something hidden, lurking in the distance he keeps.

Our car suddenly goes dark. No more glaring lights behind. Nothing.

John risks a glance backward. "Where did he go?"

I twist around, too. The vehicle is no longer behind us.

Then I see it still cruising along; it hasn't gone off the road, it's just faded back a ways and the lights are off. It's an SUV, something big. "Maybe he lost power or something? Could be an alternator thing." I'm chatty because I'm nervous. "Remember that little Volkswagen I showed you pictures of? That happened when I was—"

"I think he's getting closer again. God, how does he see anything?"

"Probably because of our lights in front of him. And there's a little bit of moon."

"Not much. Jesus — what is the *deal?*" There's real fear in his voice now, something rare.

Maybe it's a game. If not someone drunk then probably a couple of kids, daring each other to drive without lights.

John stomps the gas suddenly and the Subaru lurches forward.

"John . . ." I watch the gauge as our speed climbs. The SUV seems to be keeping pace. My temperature drops, muscles tense. "John . . . *John* — he's keeping up with us so he can see. It's a couple of kids or something. Maybe you should slow down." We're doing ninety.

My husband ignores me.

Ninety-five. "*John*! Slow *down*!"

A road sign informs us our exit is in one mile. The SUV is running in time with us, matching our acceleration, keeping to our lane, driving blind.

The headlights blast on again. I flinch at their reflection and stare ahead at the oncoming highway, praying that we reach our destination safely — *come on, come on, come on* — but I can't stop myself from imagining the sudden wreck as John loses control of the Subaru, which veers into a series of flips, tossing us around inside like stuffed animals until John's skull cracks against the glass and my legs snap in the twisting metal, everything thundering and shattering and scudding along until we grind to a halt, engulfed in flames.

John slows finally, but he's not turning on the blinker. The green sign for Exit 32 floats toward us. It's getting close, then closer, then the exit lane opens up.

"John . . ."

At the last possible moment he hits the brakes and jerks the wheel and we swerve into the exit lane. The SUV goes rocketing past and I let out a pent-up breath. There will be no violent car wreck ending our lives and orphaning our two children.

John celebrates with a whoop of excitement. "There! There you go, baby! There you go!"

He slows to a stop at the end of the exit ramp. From our spot I can see the interstate continuing south and the red taillights come into view beneath the bridge spanning the road. The SUV keeps barreling along, cones of headlights stabbing the darkness. The next exit is another long distance away, at least ten more miles. Unless the driver decides to make an illegal U-turn at one of those crossover places, it isn't coming back.

"Maybe it didn't have anything to do with us," I say, but my heart is pounding.

John gets going with a right turn. He's not saying anything, just driving and checking the mirrors.

The tension seems to dissipate as we pass the Department of Public Safety where the county jail and sheriff's office are located. "That was crazy," he says at last. Then he looks at me and wags his eyebrows. "I always did know how to show you a good time on a date, though, right?"

I try to keep a straight face but the relief is strong. I don't know whether I'm mad at him, the SUV or myself for getting so riled up. Probably all three.

He gives my hand a squeeze. "You all right?"

"I just want to get home."

He nods. "I'm sorry."

After another deep breath, I feel myself calming. John's no adrenaline junky, but all the excitement took the focus off of his own issues and, in that way, he's probably grateful for it.

A gas station and truck stop roll past and then there's nothing but trees again. We travel the last five miles home theorizing a bit more about the mysterious driver and in the end we agree that wild kids are the best explanation. People do random things. You get used to your life, the daily humdrum and routine, but, at any moment, something can always happen.

* * *

We should've called the police. That's what's on my mind the moment I blink awake in the middle of the night. Even if it was nothing more sinister than a couple of kids, it was still dangerous. The driver could've hurt someone — if only himself and any passengers. But neither John nor I got a look at the license plate, and dark SUVs are common.

Eventually I worry myself enough to get out of bed, drink a glass of water and check on our children. They're older now, well past the point where a mother worries about sleeping babies, but it comforts me to hear their soft sounds, to see the glowing stars still stuck to Russ's wall from when he was placed in the Science Fair. Melody's room smells like her new perfume, something we got at the mall in Plattsburgh. Since I'm up, I pee, and only after another half an hour staring at the dark ceiling do I manage to find sleep again.

It's the last good sleep I'll get for days.

CHAPTER ONE / THE STRANGER

Saturday, March 23rd

"It's the menstruation crustacean," my seven-year-old says. His dark bangs hang in his eyes and he tilts his head back and forth and repeats the odd phrase in an off-key song. "It's the men-strayshunnn crust-ayshunnn . . ."

"Russ!" Melody snaps. "Knock it off!"

They're at the breakfast table, Russ with a giant bowl of cereal, my preteen daughter with uneaten toast and a reddening face.

"Why is it in the girls' bathroom?" Russ asks.

"Mom . . ."

I'm about to intervene when someone knocks on the front door. It's early, so my first guess is the guy who comes around every spring hoping to blacktop our driveway. Or it could be the solar panel people, who've been making the rounds, picking up where Jehovah's Witnesses left off.

A red pickup sits in our driveway and an unfamiliar man stands on our small front porch. He sees me standing in the window and raises a hand in greeting. He's middle-aged, with a short crew cut and pockmarked skin. He gives me a big smile and I open the door a few inches.

"Hello?"

"Hi — sorry to just drop in on you. I'm Bruce Barnes. I'm John's friend from way back. You must be his wife, Jane?" He sticks out a hand.

I give the truck a more careful look, then open up the rest of the way and talk over the quick handshake. "That's right. Come on in."

Bruce Barnes scrapes off his boots on the welcome mat and steps into the house. The kids fall silent at the breakfast table and stare openly.

He waves at them and grins. "Hi, guys."

Melody offers a weak smile and focuses on her toast. Russ waves back at the man and keeps watching us.

"John's just working," I say, closing the door. "I'll go get him. Here, let me take your coat."

He shrugs off the winter parka and hands it to me with a concerned frown. "I hope I'm not interrupting him. Does he write in the mornings? He probably writes in the morning, doesn't he? I should've known."

"Most mornings, yeah. But don't worry about it. We interrupt him all the time."

Bruce's eyes are electric blue — though he's excited to be here he seems genuinely contrite. I find myself warming to him right away, but then I typically warm to most people.

"He works weekends, too, huh? Man that's dedication. I always knew John had it in him, though. Even when we were kids he was always writing stories or drawing pictures in his notebook. I used to draw too, you know? Comic-book type stuff . . ." He's following me in to the house as he talks and edges a bit closer to the table to address Russ. "You like Batman?"

Russ answers with a mouthful of Frosted Flakes. "Yeah, Batman is great! I like Spider-Man, too, though. He's my favorite."

"Spider-Man is cool. I would look at the comics, you know what I mean? I'd study them and try to get the

10

muscles right. Muscles are hard to draw. Feet too, I was always terrible with feet and I'd try to hide them in a bush or something. You must be a good artist if John is your dad."

I haven't left yet. Our sudden guest is gregarious, but he has a way with Russ, who's beaming like Bruce Barnes is himself a superhero. Bruce looks John's age, thirty-eight, though he's losing a bit of hair. He could be a modern rancher or homesteader the way he's filling out blue jeans, a crinkled button-down shirt, and thick work boots.

He must catch me looking because he jerks back and points to his feet. "Oh, man — should I take these off?"

"No, please — don't worry about it. Snow is mostly gone and the ground is still frozen — no mud yet. Let me just go get John, okay? I'll be right back."

I finally move down the hallway, listening to Bruce talk to the kids and realize in my haste that I never introduced them. Bruce does it. "So you must be Russ, right? And you're Melody?"

My son cackles. "No, *I'm* Russ and *she's* Melody . . ."

"How old are you?" Bruce asks. "Twenty-five?"

"I'm seven!"

I knock on the study door. "John?"

"Just a minute . . ."

"There's someone here to see you. Bruce? He says he knows you from way back."

Behind the door, John's chair squeaks as he gets up. I twist the knob and enter to see him peeking through the window blinds at the woods in the backyard. "What's he doing here?" John says. Then he turns to face me and I feel the smile dwindle on my lips.

John heads toward me, his brow dented, his mouth forming a grim line. He's not particularly pleased to hear about our visitor; either Bruce isn't a close friend or there's something between them.

I follow him into the living room.

"Hey!" Bruce sounds ecstatic. "There he is!"

"Hey, man." John crosses his arms after a quick handshake. He takes a step back. "What are you doing here?" It's a friendly question, but there's an edge in John's voice.

"Well, we're moving back up here. Me and Rainey."

John gives me a sidelong glance and speaks to Bruce. "Uh-huh. Wow. You, ah, missed the snow, huh?"

"Nah — it's a work thing." Bruce catches my confusion. "I lived in Florida for the past eight years."

"Oh," I say. "Very nice."

John remains uncomfortable, maybe a little nervous. When he glances at me again, something flickers in his eyes before he turns back to Bruce. "You were just outside Jacksonville or something. Is that right?"

"Yeah, actually right in the city. But, ah, you know — Rainey's family is up here, my family is up here. It's all about family. We're staying with them for a bit while we're finding ourselves a place. Anyway, look at you, huh? Your two kids are growing up, your lovely wife . . . that's just great, man."

John is silent as Bruce barrels on. "So I was just coming through, and I recognized your house from the pictures online. And your car. I thought, you know, give it a chance, maybe just pop in and say hi."

Over at the dining room table, Russ has lost interest now that the conversation is back in adult territory. He bends over and slurps up some spilled milk.

"Russ." Melody grimaces. "That's gross."

"What? I'm not wasting it."

"You don't have to conserve every drop."

"I'm the menstruation crustacean . . ." Russ slurps more.

Melody grunts and takes her empty plate and glass into the kitchen. She's five years older than her little brother — twelve going on twenty.

My attention returns to our guest. "Bruce? Get you something?"

"Probably too early for a cocktail, huh?" John flinches when Bruce claps him on the shoulder. "Ah, I'm just kidding. Just kidding — I'd love some coffee. If it's not too much

trouble? Don't make a cup, I just mean if you have some
or—"

"Not a problem. I just made some. How do you like it?"

"Extra milk, extra sugar."

I start to move away as Bruce puts both hands on his
hips and looks between us. "You guys — you're both the
picture of health. I mean — I shouldn't assume anything
though, you never know. Everything okay with you? You
heard what happened to Andy Potter?"

Curiosity roots me to the spot as John nods. "Yeah, that
was sudden." He must see the question in my face. "Andy
went to school with us. He, ah—"

"He was a great guy," Bruce cuts in. "Great guy. He
passed away a few years ago. I mean, so young. Had a very
rare thing. Very rare cancer I guess."

I've never heard John talk about Andy Potter before. A
friend who suddenly died of cancer at a young age? Maybe
they weren't close either. I keep thinking about the way my
husband seems affected by our sudden guest: tentative, the
way he tends to be around new people. But Bruce isn't exactly
new, not if they shared a childhood. Bruce is a little taller,
and he does look older, like life has been a little rougher on
him. From this angle I can now see a tattoo poking up from
his white shirt collar.

Bruce shakes his head, still mourning the loss of their
mutual acquaintance. "Yeah — just tells you . . . you gotta
take life by the horns. You gotta live every day, you know?
Carpe diem." He snaps out of it and smiles broadly again.
"Just like John. God, man, I am so proud of you. You really
did it, you know?" He turns to me. "I don't know how much
this guy has told you, but we used to hang out a lot when
we were kids. I always said to him, 'You gotta put me in a
book one day, right? Make me a character!' And the fact that
he went on and became a writer . . . We didn't have a lot of
kids in our graduating class — what was it, about a hundred
and fifty?"

John swallows. "Yeah, about that."

13

"And I'm not saying anything bad about anyone. I mean, everyone has their path and they're on their own time clock. You can't envy, you can't mock. But — anyway, I'm rambling. I'm just proud of you, man."

Things get quiet again and I can feel my husband's continued discomfort. "John, you want to show Bruce around while I get him that coffee?"

His eyes alight on me and then he looks away. "Sure."

"Oh, that'd be great," Bruce says. "Love to see where it all happens. Is that cool? Can I see the office? The man cave? The *atelier*?"

"Yeah, sure."

"Let me get that coffee for you." I slip around the corner into the kitchen as they move down the hallway.

Melody remains by the sink, wearing a frown. She keeps her voice low. "Mom? Who is that?"

I grab a mug from the cabinet. "Just a friend of Daddy's, apparently. What's this thing about the menstrua—"

"How long is he going to be here?"

"Mel, don't worry about it. Be nice."

Russ carries his bowl and spoon from the table and lobs them up into the sink where they crash against the other dishes. Melody jumps away from a splash of water. "Jeez! Russ! God you're such a baby."

I put a hand on my daughter's shoulder. "Mel, take it easy. What's the matter?"

"I'm going to my room." She shrugs me off and strides out of the kitchen.

Russ lingers, looking up at me. "Mom, can I have a snack?"

"Can you have a *snack*? You just had breakfast, bud."

"I'm still hungry."

"Fine. Sit back down. I'll make you some eggs."

"Can I have a snack instead?"

"Russ . . . eggs or nothing."

He sighs and sulks his way back to the table, yanks out his chair and gives me a wounded look over his shoulder.

First I fill the coffee, listening in as John and Bruce move through the house. They've gone down to John's office, Bruce's voice booming as he continues to praise John for all of his success. Then I add the milk and sugar and stir. "Just sit there," I tell Russ. "I'll be right back."

John's door is halfway open, but I knock. "Here you go, Bruce."

He wheels around with that enormous grin and crosses the room. "Oh, thank you, thank you." After taking a drink he nods with approval. "Perfect. Look at this place, huh? I'm sure you're used to it by now. But, man. This is cool . . . this is cool. Hey, John, how do you work with all the windows? Does it distract you?"

John's study is a corner room of the house. What was once part of a large back porch has been weatherproofed and remodeled, but the big windows remain, overlooking the forest and the mountaintops beyond. The large blinds are closed now, morning light glowing around the seams.

"Yeah, you know, I stare out sometimes." John catches my gaze again. It's evident he's hoping this comes to an end soon. Poor John, my introvert. I give him a reassuring smile.

Bruce sips the coffee and browses the bookshelves. One shelf displays John's suspense novels. "So much that goes into these, huh? I gotta admit, man, I keep meaning to read your stuff but I just never get the chance. Which one should I start with, huh? Which one is your best one? Or is that always the one you're working on now?"

I start backing out of the room. "I'm going to go make Russ something else to eat — he's going through a growth spurt, eating non-stop. You boys have fun."

"Man that kid is the spitting image of you, John," Bruce says. "And Melody, too."

John and I share a quick, knowing look — Melody is not John's biological child. "I'm sorry," I say. "I should have introduced you . . ."

"Oh yeah — no, that's okay. They saw my ugly mug."

"Well — thank you — okay. Have fun."

Walking back to the kitchen, I figure Bruce can't have been keeping very close tabs on his friend's life after all if he thinks Melody resembles John.

The thought is knocked aside — Russ has dumped the salt onto the table, where he swirls it around then sucks on his finger. "Russell, come on, buddy. What is it with you and eating off the table?"

I lose track of the background conversation as the men move on from the study and go upstairs. They creak over the floorboards above my head while I cook the eggs and talk to Russ about making messes.

John and Bruce thunder back down the stairs. "I'm going to show him the basement," John says out of view.

I plate the scrambled eggs and serve them to Russ and walk into Melody's room. By the time I finish untangling some preteen drama about little brothers and not being allowed a cell phone, John and Bruce are back by the front door.

"Well this has just been great," he says. "Again, I'm so sorry to barge in. I just — you know — I get it from my mother. Big personality, right?" He gives John another swat on the back, then draws him into an awkward hug. "This guy . . . He's always been the quiet one. Now you know, right? He was writing all these books in his head."

I smile, still trying to unpack whether John is merely put out by the intrusion or whether there's something more to the way he seems to shrink against Bruce's embrace. "So, Bruce, what do you do? Or what were you doing in Florida?"

Bruce's whole demeanor changes and his words take on a grave tone. "Oh, I was on the job down there, ma'am. Law enforcement."

"Wow. Okay. Is that what you'll be doing up here?"

"Oh, no, ma'am. No . . ." He glances at John, defensiveness shading his eyes. "John doesn't talk about me, huh? Well, I guess he's just writing it all down." He winks then suddenly lifts his shirt above his waist. "No, ma'am, I was shot." There's a gnarled scar on one side of his exposed abdomen.

A clatter of cutlery, a thump, and pounding footfalls precede Russell's arrival. "Oh, no *way* . . ." I catch him by the arms before he touches Bruce. "Holy crap! You were shot by a bullet?"

"Russ," John says. "Language."

Bruce nods somberly. "That's right, little man. Took one right in the gut." He tucks his shirt back in. "Yeah — that was it for me. I think, you know, you take your chips and you know when to leave the casino. You know what I mean? That's as lucky as one guy's gonna get, because it could've been a whole lot worse. I'm not going to tempt fate, no way. So . . ."

The moment hangs suspended and no one seems to know where to look, except Russ, staring in awe at Bruce's clothed stomach. I finally break the silence. "It was nice to have you stop by, Bruce. I hope you settle back into the area without too much trouble."

John snaps out of it. "Yeah, if you need anything, you know, don't hesitate."

Bruce pumps John's hand with a firm grip. "That's great to hear. Look, I know it's been a long time, but friends have to stick together. Right? Friends are like family, and we go back a long way."

John edges toward the door as Bruce takes one last look around, almost wistfully. "Well, so nice to meet you, Jane. And you, big man. And give my best to your daughter."

"I'll walk you out." John opens the door.

"Sounds good, partner."

I see Bruce's parka hanging from the coat rack and pluck it down. "Bruce . . ."

"Oh! Jeez. My God — see? I'm still living by Florida standards. I don't know how I'm going to get used to this again. At least the winter is ending, right? I'm getting here at just the right time. All part of the plan." He smiles at me one more time and John shuts the door behind them.

"He was shot! Mom, did you see that?"

"Uh-huh . . ." I let Russ go and drift to the window to watch John and Bruce in the driveway. They reach the car and stand around and Bruce laughs about something. I wonder if Bruce picks up on John's reticent behavior and decide probably not — he seems the type of person living in his own world, oblivious to certain social cues or maybe just ignoring them. Full of life, and like he said: *big personality*.

After sliding into the driver's seat, Bruce takes one last look at our house, and when I feel his eyes on me I almost jerk out of sight — but I wave and he waves back. Then he reverses the truck down our long driveway.

John returns, rubbing his arms from the cold.

"Well," I say, "*that* was something."

"Yeah." He removes his boots.

"Dad!" Russ is still mooning over Bruce's scar. "Your friend was shot with a bullet!"

"Uh-huh."

"How did it happen?"

John clears his throat. "I don't know, buddy."

He starts past us but I block his path, put my hands on his shoulders and look into his face. "You okay?"

"I'm fine. Listen, I was right in the middle of a chapter so I'm going to try to get back to it before it's lost. We can talk in a little bit, okay?"

I know it's best to let him be so I give him a quick kiss. He moves off down the hallway and I hear the door to his study close.

Back beside the window I watch as Bruce pulls into the road and takes off. Something tells me it's not the last we'll be seeing of him, whether John likes it or not.

CHAPTER TWO / THE PAST

"He invited himself to dinner."

John's elbows are on the table, his mouth pressed against his hands. It's been two hours since Bruce's visit.

"What's the story with you and this guy?" I sit down beside him.

"What do you mean?"

I give my husband a look over the lip of my cup of coffee to convey how obtuse that is. "I mean, John — I don't know. Is he a friend?"

"I guess we were."

"Okay . . ."

Maybe he's not ready to talk after all — he avoids eye contact and chews on a knuckle. I get up after half a minute and saunter into the kitchen. "Melody has piano in an hour. I'm taking Russ grocery shopping so you can have some peace and quiet — make up for some of the time you lost this morning." I peek in the refrigerator to remind myself how much butter is left.

"What should we do?" John says.

I lean against the fridge once I've closed the door. "Well, I mean, I think that's up to you, babe. I don't know this person and you don't seem to want to talk about him. What did he say? How did he invite himself? 'I'm coming to your house again for dinner, put the fucking kettle on?'"

John cracks a smile that vanishes an instant later. "No. But this guy . . . you know he's — he walked me into it. Said we should get together again . . . life is short . . . blah blah blah."

I move a little closer. My back has been bothering me lately so I brace against the kitchen counter for support. "When?"

"Well — I was like — I thought about putting it off, saying, 'Maybe next weekend.' Then I could say we're busy. But then he'd say, 'Okay, how about the weekend after that?' It will just keep going on and on."

"Just him?"

"He said he wants Rainey to meet you, thinks you two would like each other."

"That's his wife? Or girlfriend?"

"I don't know, honestly. Maybe they're married — I think we just have to do it and get it over with." He looks away. "You don't know this guy."

"And you're not helping in that department. So I'm not sure what to tell you. Unless you want to talk to me and tell me what's going on. Otherwise I'm just going to roll with it."

John stares through the windows at an early spring snow, softly falling and clinging to the trees like wet sugar. Russ's TV plays in his room, burbling cartoon voices. We debated at length whether or not to get our seven-year-old son a TV. I came down against it but John made the executive decision. Melody is still in her own room, brooding over who-knows-what.

"I didn't have a good time with Bruce when we were kids," John says at last. "You know — the way it was with Bruce was like one week the light would shine on you, you'd hang out constantly — he treated you like you were his best friend. Then another week and you'd be in his shadow and he acted like you didn't exist. There was no in-between."

Okay, I think, that's something. Bruce was a jerk when they were young. I can see that, being that he's so energetic and outgoing, it might have taken some years to get under control. And kids are raw and uncensored in high school, the empathy taught in kindergarten displaced in a confusion of adolescent hormones.

Plain Jane.

The two words grab me as I refill my coffee — two words I haven't heard put together in a while. Aside from a few bad apples, I liked school and had good friends. John was an outsider and the whole school experience left a bad taste, though he's never gone into specifics. I've been to one reunion so far — the ten — and my twenty is coming up in three years. John graduated high school at seventeen and would've had his twenty-year reunion last summer, but he never mentioned it, come to think of it.

I draw closer to him and put my hand on his shoulder. "Well the light is shining on you this week, honey. So let's make hay. We'll show them a nice time, and then he'll move on to someone else, right?" A playful bump with my hip doesn't seem to rouse him out of it. Though it does test my mobility and I can feel the inflammation settling around the base of my spine, near the sacrum.

John finally stands and pushes in his chair. "He threatened to kill me once."

"What? Why?"

"Because he was a bully."

"How old were you?"

"Twelve, thirteen — something like that."

"Did you tell anyone about it?"

"After a week of it I told my parents. Well, my mom. She knew his mom so she called her up and they talked about it."

"Did it help?"

"It went from him saying he was going to kill me to him calling me a momma's boy, calling me a pussy, all of that. Oh and get this . . . we had two — count them, *two* — African-American kids in our school. One of them was named Gerard. One day after school, we're in Bruce's cousin's car — his cousin is driving — and we see Gerard walking down

21

the street, and Bruce rolls down the window and yells out, 'Hey! Blackie! How big is your dick?'"

"Ah, man . . ."

"Yeah, but then there's this . . . a couple weeks later and they're the best of friends. Bruce and Gerard."

"It sounds like — like an authoritarian kind of thing."

"Exactly. He intimidates people and then offers friendship. And they take it because . . . small school, I guess."

"Because it's better to forget the insults and be praised," I think aloud. "Better not to live in fear of someone but think of them as on your side."

Plain Jane. Plain Jane is insane.

I shrug off the internal voice. "Does he have brothers and sisters or is he an only, like you?"

"He had a half-sister. I don't know what happened to her."

"It sounds to me like a kind of pathology." I'm still thinking it through. "You abuse people then pay them special attention."

I'm glad John is finally talking because I knew there was something hidden beneath the surface. But it still feels off, like he's covering the real problem.

Or maybe I'm conflating his past with elements of my own.

"And in the meantime," John is saying, "I'm on the outs. No one is talking to me — Bruce, his cousin, or even Gerard, who I was always friendly with. They're all writing shit on my locker, calling me John Gayboy instead of John Gable. Fun stuff like that."

"You never got the school involved?"

"No."

"I guess those were different times."

He shrugs. "Yeah. I don't think kids get away with that stuff today."

Probably not. Russ has never been remotely bullied, at least that I know of. Melody is in the seventh grade and so far

22

there have been no real problems with other students. Even the minor things are nipped in the bud.

"Did Bruce ever actually hurt anybody?"

"He never really got into actual fights — he'd talk his way out of it. I think he learned it from his mother's boyfriends. We didn't know it at the time, but his mother had a couple of abusive guys. There was one week that Bruce wasn't at school, and when he came back he had a broken arm."

My hand floats up to my mouth. I pull it away after a moment of silent horror — and now I'm *definitely* mixing my own story with John's, with Bruce's.

"It doesn't excuse anything," John says.

"No — it doesn't excuse anything. But it makes some sense of it. You know, if he had abusive men in his life when he was a kid, then lashed out at others, he pulled the same stuff on them."

John looks at me, probing, but then he lowers his gaze. "Yeah, he pulled it on kids he thought were weaker. Like me."

"John . . ." I take his hand, try to draw him close. He's like a live wire, electric current running through. "Hey, hey, honey. It's okay. We don't have to do anything you don't feel comfortable with."

A tear slips down his cheek. "You must think I'm pathetic."

"Absolutely I do not. That's ridiculous."

At last he embraces me and I bury my face into his neck. "You're a good man. Someone from your past is just stirring up memories."

"I love you." His breath pushes against my hair. "I'm sorry."

"I love you too. And you don't have anything to be sorry for," I say, with more coming to mind. "How about this? We have them over tonight. Feed them some grilled chicken. Make polite conversation. We say it's been nice to catch up and send them on their way. Done."

John shakes his head. "It won't end."

"We do it tonight, bang-boom, and you're off the hook, no week-long anticipation. And if he says he can't, then you're safe for two weeks. What?"

John is giving me a look. "Safe?"

"You know what I mean. I just mean you're in the clear."

He lets go of me and smacks the back of the chair with the heel of his palm, slamming it against the table. "Fuck!"

The move startles and frightens me and I take a step back. "John . . ."

"Why can't people just leave me alone? What is the frigging *point*?" He stalks out of the room and down the hallway, his last words muffled when he encloses himself in his study. "I was fine. My life was *fine* . . ."

I've never been co-dependent and I'm not going to start now. Clearly this is beyond social discomfort, more than John's general disfavoring of small talk and get-togethers. It's about childhood victimization. It's what Bruce does to his sense of security, somehow, as a man — but it's not about me, not about my own trials and tribulations as a kid.

Plain Jane's life is a runaway train!

Plus there have been our own challenges afoot, getting older with two jobs and two kids, trying to keep the marriage spicy — and I suspect a trouble spot with John's work that's been going on for a few weeks, maybe even a couple of months. It's just not the best time for him, and now here comes this unexpected complication.

I need to soldier on, keep to my own track — always the best plan.

First, gathering the reusable shopping bags, I continue to prepare for the trip to the store. I drag Russ from his room and into his winter boots and parka then step in front of Melody's door, face to face with the homemade mailbox that's been Scotch-taped there since we first moved in. Heart stickers and My Little Pony stickers adorn the manila file folder that's stapled to form a pocket for leaving notes. In the midst of everything, my baby girl is growing up, going through her own difficult almost-teenaged times.

I rap my knuckles softly against where her name is written in pretty handwriting.

"I know," Melody mutters from within her room. "I know — I'm coming, hang *on* . . . "

Maybe Bruce saw something beyond physical appearance. Our teenaged daughter resembles John in other ways: sullen and temperamental.

When she opens the door she gapes at me and says, "What? Mom, what?" and I realize I'm grinning.

You have to find the humor in life where you can.

CHAPTER THREE / PARANOIA

Fresh snow covers the evergreens and melts in the sunlight flashing between cotton-white clouds as we drive into the sleepy little mountain town. The hospital where I work looks typically indifferent; two nurses are huddled together out front, smoking cigarettes. After a few turns we drive alongside a row of small houses and stop at the much larger house at the end. John calls the early Victorian home where Mel takes her piano lessons "the mansion," and it's looking every bit regal today with its lighted windows and twinkling garlands of snow.

"Time to make the donuts," I say.

Melody doesn't respond or move.

"What's the matter?"

She pushes my hand away. "Nothing."

There have been signs she's getting her first period — but talking about it in front of her brother would mortify her. I try to catch her gaze but she's looking out at the piano teacher's house.

"Who was that guy, again?" Melody asks.

The question is so out of line with my thoughts it takes me a second. "A friend of your dad's — well, someone he knew from high school."

"He was weird."

"Mel . . ."

"He was loud."

"He had a bullet hole in him!" Russ makes a shape with his fingers and thumbs, about the size of an orange.

"Melody . . ." I'm still hoping she'll look at me but she grabs the door handle.

Colette, Melody's piano teacher, emerges from the house. I wave and she waves back.

"Okay." It's more a sigh coming out of me than a word. "I'll be back in an hour. And, Mel, if you, you know . . ."

She shoots me a look. Though my daughter has a rebellious streak, she's otherwise been sweet her whole life, so the fire in her eyes unnerves me. My mother tried to prepare me for this but I never really listened. *When it happens, you'll know. You turned into a woman overnight.*

No I didn't, Mom. No one turns into a woman "overnight."

"Just please don't be late," Melody says. "I don't like hanging out in there. It smells like mothballs."

"Melody Grace Gable." I've finally snapped, defaulting to a stock reprimand. Whether I agree with her views on womanhood or not, I'm becoming my mother. "I don't know what your deal is today, but you need to make an adjustment, okay? Take a deep breath and let it out. Realize how fortunate you are to—"

"Okay, Mom." She shuts the door behind her before I can get in another word. The regret is instant, my words ringing in my ears. Melody walks up to the house where Colette opens the door and ushers her inside, looks back and gives another wave.

Colette and her giant Victorian house with its steep roofs and black shutters in our otherwise economically depressed little town, with her cedar hedgerows running the front walk toward the pillared porch and bright red front door. All alone in there, her headhunter husband only home about three full weeks of the year. I know this not just according to local gossip, but because their nephew is my ex-husband, Marcus Gainsborough.

Making Melody Colette's great-niece.

"Mothballs," Russ laughs. "Moth*balls*. Do moths have balls?"

I lower my hand. "Russ."

Driving back through the narrow streets and into town, I'm struck with a pang of nostalgia for a younger Mel, missing those big brown eyes and that gap-toothed smile. Where has my spunky, sweet little girl gone? I realize that teenagers swing between moods, but it still sucks.

The town is tiny, not much more than the grocery store, drug store, hardware store, diner, gas station, and a couple of bars. I open the backseat to help Russ out of his booster seat and he stares up at me. "Did you see that bullet hole the man had?"

"It wasn't a bullet hole. It was a scar."

"It was *awesome*."

I'm hauling him out and closing the door. I happen to glance over to the street where an SUV is rolling along, not moving very fast, perhaps even slowing. Its tinted windows obscure the interior but I feel something — someone — looking out at me.

"Mom."

The vehicle gains speed and continues down the street.

"Mom?" Russ is tugging on my arm. "Can I get a Tasty-tea?"

"Um, we'll see, honey." I keep a hold of Russ by his shirt, watching the SUV until it's out of sight, feeling sure it is the same one from last night but knowing there's no good reason for thinking that; it was dark and I only really saw the vehicle from the rear.

I'm slipping into paranoia, hunting for secrets. Melody's dislike of Bruce, John's palpable anxiety — both family members are having an effect on me whether I like it or not. I grab a shopping cart and push through the automatic doors.

* * *

28

John's text comes in the middle of the soup aisle. *I called him. They're good for dinner tonight.*

I text back *Great* and start adding things to my mental shopping list.

Bruce doesn't strike me as vegetarian but I decide to check with John anyway. He says he doesn't know, causing me a pinch of frustration. *Can you find out for me, honey?*

The other question is whether or not to get alcohol. John doesn't drink, I seldom do, but I might need a glass if my husband is going to be ornery for the next several hours. And our guests might enjoy it. *Would you be okay if I got some wine?*

I form a recipe — some rosemary for the chicken legs, fresh parsley, a side of rice, a side of broccoli. The phone buzzes again on my return to the produce section. *No not vegetarian. Wine is fine.*

Riding the front of the cart, Russ leaps away and runs down an aisle. I text John back: *You sure?*

Grocery stores don't sell wine in New York State so if John is truly all right with it, I'll take a trip to the liquor store at the other end of town. I catch Russ ogling the sugary cereals with cartoon characters beckoning. "Hey, get back on your horse, mister."

"Can I have these?"

"That cereal is made out of cookies, Russell. No."

We're not food fascists. John grew up in a family perpetually on a shoestring budget and a father who was rarely around, so his mother did what she could. We're both health-conscious but we don't judge; we just want our kids to eat decent food. If I followed every health or diet fad I'd be crazy. This week, red meat is good for you; next week it causes cancer. Lectins are bad, meaning tomatoes and beans . . . except tomatoes are high in vitamin C and beans are a staple diet in nearly every country U.S. doctors once mined for the healthy blood plasma. Excess sugar gets stored in your liver and turns to fat . . . but if you're a vegan then you're blowing lines of it in the back of your hemp automobile. You can't win.

The grocery store is small like the rest of the town. I have a line of sight out to the parking lot and the street beyond — I don't know what causes me to look out there, maybe just movement catching my eye, but I see it again — or, I think I do: the same SUV driving slowly, and now it's going in the other direction.

"Mom," Russ whines. "You never let me have anything *fun.*"

I drag my attention back to the shopping and to Russ. "That's not true, mister."

"Yes it is. All you think about is homework and food and clothes and giving me haircuts."

"I think about other things, too, kid."

"Like what?"

Like stalkers in SUVs.

"Like how you need a bath."

He freezes and looks up at me with exaggerated wide eyes. The scream starts low in his chest. "Nooooo!" It rises to a crescendo before he takes off in a run.

His comedy lifts my heart and I start after him, almost running with the shopping cart, and round the corner into the next aisle where the laughter dies in my throat as someone says, "Gotcha!"

Russ has run into the arms of Bruce Barnes. "Mom! Look who it is!"

A lock of hair has fallen across my forehead and I push it aside. "Hi."

Bruce ruffles Russ's hair in an oddly old-fashioned manner. *Good boy, slugger.* But his grin is disarming as always. "Fancy meeting you here, ma'am."

"I'm just picking up a few things for tonight, actually."

"Oh, great. I just got off the phone with John. You guys are really so nice. Thank you for inviting us over to dinner." If there's any hint of irony, Bruce tucks it away somewhere his eyes can't betray. "John said you were going to figure out something to eat but I wanted to get a dessert." He's got a basket with him and looks down at its contents. "Couldn't decide whether you guys like ice cream or—"

"Ice cream!" Russ hops up and down.

"—or cake," Bruce finishes. "So I got both."

"That's very thoughtful."

"I figured this was a special occasion. Who knows when we're going to get the chance to do it again — right, Russ? You've got to live in the moment."

"Right," Russ says. "Can I see your bullet hole?"

"Russ," I say, "come here."

He gives me a mopey look and drops his shoulders as he shuffles toward me. Bruce is unfazed. I start to form the words to say goodbye and he tilts his head. "So what do you do? You're a nurse here in town?"

"Nurse practitioner."

"Oh yeah?" He raises his eyebrows in a way signaling he's unsure what it means.

"I have some of the responsibilities of a physician. I oversee a small staff right now. I'm mostly focused on the older patients at the hospital."

Bruce nods. "That's great."

I want to ask him about the SUV. Want to ask him so bad I'm afraid I'm going to blurt it out Tourette's-style. But if he's in *here*, and the vehicle is out *there*, they're obviously unconnected.

Unless the driver of the SUV is his girlfriend, or wife — he hasn't said yet — Rainey.

Silly, I tell myself. No reason to think that at all — except that Bruce seems to show up after each SUV sighting.

Twice. It's happened twice. And the first time a whole night passed before Bruce appeared.

As I start thinking again how I need to invest in a tinfoil hat, I feel a tug at my arm. "Mom . . ." Russ is whispering. Apparently a lowered volume makes begging more acceptable. "Can we have *both*? I think it's a good idea. Ice cream and cake . . ."

I ignore him, focused on Bruce, hoping to be unobvious as I try to see the rest of the tattoo that emerges from his collar. Is it a prison tattoo? Why was he shot? What happened? Is Rainey his wife, girlfriend, mistress, or parole officer?

"Is your — is Rainey with you?" My awkward question is meant more to elicit information about the nature of their relationship than whether or not he's involved in strange highway chase scenes.

"No, I'm going to head off to go pick her up in a little bit — just have a few things left to do around here. That's why I came by your place. I'm looking at houses for sale."

"Oh yeah?" At least the answer eliminates the possibility she's driving around with tinted windows. "Seen anything you like?"

"Ah, one or two. You certainly get more bang for your buck out here, that's for sure. Be nice to get something with some good acreage, you know? Settle back into the quiet country life. After city living, you know . . ." He flaps a hand and glances at Russ with another grin. "Anyway, you guys probably need to get going. I'll get out of your way."

After he nods at me and walks past I get a whiff of something, like motor oil, like boats, and then he turns and walks backwards a few steps. "Looking forward to tonight."

"So are we." My smile is real but I'm thinking about Bruce buying property in our town. Won't John be pleased.

* * *

By the time I finish up the shopping, Russ is practically climbing my body, talking incessantly about Bruce, bullet holes and ice cream. Bruce is nowhere to be seen as the clerk bags up my items. I didn't see his pickup truck when we entered the grocery store and I don't see it now.

He's left, or is leaving, Florida for reasons unknown, though it could have to do with the scar on his stomach, like he said. I have no reason to disbelieve that the shooting happened. I've seen more than one gunshot wound and the scar has the right characteristics: a darkened dip on the skin, almost like a birthmark, with more texture indicating it's at least a few years old, the skin stretching around the harder tissue as Bruce perhaps packed on a few middle-aged pounds. But when he told me he was looking for property it felt like a lie.

CHAPTER FOUR / THE DINNER

"So . . ." Bruce's blue eyes shine with candlelight. "Here we are." He raises a wine glass. "To family and friends, one and the same."

"Hear, hear." Rainey is dark-haired and dark-eyed, a kind of tough look to her, wrinkles starring her eyes. I find her pretty in a natural way; she doesn't wear make-up or jewelry and is dressed in a simple black V-neck sweater and jeans. If anything, she looks a little underweight, like she recently got over a bad illness. Bruce is in the same clothes from earlier; the white shirt has acquired a small dark stain on the lower sleeve. John raises a glass of Pepsi and the four of us toast then sip.

The kids are tucked away in Russ's room with a movie playing — I've already fed them. And I've tried to anticipate our music needs and put together a Pandora station that I guessed Bruce and his lady friend might like. Waylon Jennings sings about holding Bobby McGee as Bruce gives John a sidelong look. "You don't drink, Johnny?"

John stabs a floret of broccoli with his fork. "Not for twelve years."

"Good for you. Good for you, man." Bruce sets down his glass and takes hold of Rainey's hand. "You know what they say though — a glass or two of wine each day is good for the heart."

John pops the broccoli in his mouth and looks at me. I find myself regretting the wine. Five minutes into dinner and it's already a tender spot.

I take over. "How did you two meet?"

"We actually met on the job," Bruce says.

"You were both in law enforcement?"

Rainey nods. "It was my company."

"Oh yeah?"

"Security company."

"Wow, okay. I see. It was — did you own it, you mean?"

Bruce answers. "She ran the whole thing. She was the eyes and ears. I mean if that company was anybody's it was hers. You got some people sitting in a boardroom somewhere miles away? No, it ain't their company. We're the ones on the street. We're the ones dealing with the day-to-day. And if it wasn't for Rainey . . . I don't know."

I'm looking at them but keeping watch on John in my periphery. I imagine what he's thinking as he takes another bite — Bruce saying they were in law enforcement is misleading. People hear that and they think: *cops*. But I also know there's pride in a badge, whether it's for public good or for a private firm. Putting your life at risk is putting your life at risk; pride is understandable.

"Well that's very nice," I say. "So no plans to do something like that up here?"

Bruce frowns, shaking his head. "No, no. That chapter of our lives is over." He eyes John. "Right? I mean isn't life like a book? You finish the chapter, you turn the page. Done. Like you — you had your drinking chapter. Is it okay if I ask about that? You just — you had a hard time with it, or what?"

I wonder how John will respond. He tends to be pretty matter-of-fact about his past drinking, but it's also highly personal.

"Yeah I had a hard time with it," John says. "I think I stopped just in time. Before it got any worse."

35

"Before it got any worse," Bruce repeats. "Smart. Well, that was always you, John. You always knew what to do. Bang-boom, you cut it out. Good for you."

I sense my husband biting his tongue. Across our many talks about his alcoholism, he's never given me the impression there was anything bang-boom about quitting.

I jump in again. "So how was the property hunt? See anything you like?"

Bruce takes a drink, blots the corner of his mouth with his napkin and glances at Rainey before answering. "I saw a couple of places that were all right. Not what I'm looking for, though. We want a fresh water source, for one thing. And it's got to have some arable land."

"Oh, I see. Yeah. You want to be able to live off of it?"

"Yeah, want to be able to raise crops. Hunt. Things like that, you know." He takes Rainey's hand again and gives a squeeze. "Right, hon?"

Rainey's dark eyes flit between me and John. "How about you two? How did you guys meet?"

John answers ahead of me. "Well, the old-fashioned way, I guess. We had a mutual friend who introduced us. We went out on a couple of dates, then I met Melody and we just — you know — we took it from there. The rest is history."

Bruce looks a little embarrassed. He'd commented before on the resemblance between John and Melody; now he knows they're not blood-related. But he handles it with a knowing nod. "That's great, that's great. Instant family, huh?"

"Yeah. Exactly. A joined family is an instant family."

"How was that?" Rainey asks. "Was it hard to pick up a relationship with a child in the middle?"

I have a prepared answer and put my hand over my husband's to silence him. "Well, you know, I think it's always going to have challenges, but I think when a man has a son or a woman has a daughter it's a little easier than it might be otherwise."

I watch Rainey, expecting this logic to resonate among polite company, but she becomes distant. We've just stumbled

36

into another briar patch: Bruce and Rainey have their own story. Only, they're not talking about it and a silence slips over the table.

I aim for safer territory. "Who's your . . . um, financier on the house buying? We used Carrie Seward over in Lake Placid. She was great with it. We were able to close on this place in a hurry."

Bruce and Rainey exchange uneasy looks. So far this dinner is all elbows and knees. And it's so rare we have company.

"I don't, ah," Bruce says. "We don't really . . ."

"Oh," I nod quickly. "You're just looking."

Or maybe they're millionaires and don't need financing. You never know with people. But middle-class folk like John and I had to get pre-approved for a mortgage before a realtor would even bother showing us around.

"Yeah, we're just seeing what's out there before we get serious about anything like that," Bruce says. His eyes find me and I catch a hint of something — chagrin? Maybe not quite. It's possible that these two are the opposite of millionaires and that maybe credit approval and house-buying isn't really even in the cards for them.

"My mother was left a house on Lake Ontario," I say. "My grandfather bought it cheaply, way back in the day. On Henderson Harbor. John and I got married there."

"Really," Bruce says. "Lake Ontario, huh?"

"It's a little place, not winterized," I explain. "We call it the lake house but it's not much more than a camp. John's been doing lots of work on it lately. It took some damage this winter. Lots of storms, and then the lake was up — washed away a good section of the lawn."

"Wow," Bruce says. "Still, must be nice to get away. Change of pace, anyway."

"It is. It's nice to have."

"That's what we're looking for." Bruce's voice holds a tremble. "A change of pace. Big time." He turns and looks at Rainey and I'm suddenly aware of the tears in his eyes. This innocent little dinner, and it's like everyone has shown up with gaping wounds. "Rainey is sick," he says softly.

"I was diagnosed two months ago," Rainey follows.

Both John and I have stopped eating, just listening. I seek John with a sideways glance but he's fixated on our guests.

"We really struggled at first with the diagnosis." There is pain in Rainey's face. "But we decided to take it, to make the best of it."

I'm dying to ask what sickness they're talking about. Cancer? Something else? But it's like John and I have faded into the anonymity of a watchful audience.

"When something happens that's life-changing," Bruce says, "then you have to change."

I feel as if my heart is being squeezed. John pulls his hand from mine and finally looks at me.

What the hell did we get ourselves into? is written on his face. First it's awkward comments about drinking, then clandestine house buying — and now this bombshell. But I give John a little encouraging nod and touch his leg beneath the table. *It's all right.*

There is a commotion coming from Russ's room — like Russ and Melody are arguing. I'd chosen a movie I thought would keep their attention equally and set them up with popcorn and drinks, but the bond is unraveling.

Bruce and Rainey remain eye-locked with each other and no one says anything for a good fifteen seconds — an eternity. The door to Russ's room bangs open and someone thuds across the floor — probably Melody — and another door slams shut. Rainey finally looks off in that direction and smiles in a sad way.

It's got to be cancer. Just like that friend of theirs — Andy something. Just like John's own mother.

I consider getting up to deal with the kids, but I don't. I'm rooted to the spot. The kids can deal with their own problems for the moment.

"That's terrible, Rainey. I'm so sorry . . ."

She nods and looks down at her food. Then she lets go of Bruce and picks up her fork, spears a piece of chicken and eats it. I have to force myself to stop staring. Whatever it is isn't affecting her appetite. So not ovarian cancer, I guess. But I'm no oncologist.

The whole thing suddenly strikes me as bizarre. While it's ridiculous and inappropriate to doubt them, and I'm usually no cynic, I can't help it. As if any minute now our table guests are going to pass around a cup and ask for donations. Something. Bruce just showing up, mentioning the passing of a mutual friend, inviting himself to dinner, now dropping a bomb about Rainey's unspecified morbidity. There is an air about the two of them even if this story is true — and why wouldn't it be — there's some hidden agenda in the telling, some scheme. As if Bruce decided to share it after finding out I was a nurse practitioner.

I quickly banish these thoughts. People experience tragedy — the most awful things. I should know; I have patients at the hospital whose life stories would be rejected by Hollywood for being too incredible. John's own past is heartbreaking and I have a few sad things trailing me, too. The wine is just getting to my head, my judgment affected by the strange events of the past couple of days.

"We don't make it a big thing," Bruce says at last. "We're just grateful for what we have, glad to be back in the area where we both grew up."

Another silence develops. Even the kids have gone quiet.

"This is delicious, by the way," Rainey says.

"Oh, this is great," Bruce adds.

At last the levee breaks and Russ's door crashes open again with a bang. "Mom?" He's headed this way.

I push back from the table. "Excuse me."

"Sure," Bruce says.

Melody's bedroom door swings open as I stalk down the hallway. My daughter stands there like she's been counting the seconds until authority arrives, about to burst as she jams a finger at Russ. "He had his hand down his pants. While we were watching—"

"I did not! I had an itch!"

"Mom, he was touching his balls."

"All right. Quiet. Both of you. *Right now*. I told you, we have guests . . ."

Bruce calls from the other room, surprising me. "It's all right! I do that!"

And he and Rainey cut up laughing.

* * *

John is washing dishes as I put two plates in the sudsy water. "Well. That was interesting."

"Holy shit, right? I was waiting for them to ask us to sell Amway or join their cult." If anything, he seems relieved.

"She's sick? Did Bruce tell you what it was? I never got a moment alone with her. Did she say anything when you were showing her your office?"

"No. And I didn't, you know, feel . . ." He wipes his hands on the rag hanging beside the sink.

I rub at his lower back. "Well, at least when we said goodbye, nobody invited themselves for another dinner." It's a joke, but he's not laughing.

"I just . . . I mean . . . is she terminal? The way they were acting . . . But what do you say? Can you ask someone how long they have to live? How do you ask that? I can't believe I didn't even know she was sick."

"Why would you? You haven't been in touch with him."

"Yeah . . ." He clears his throat. "Just something you'd think you'd know."

I move away and grab a dishrag, soak it and wring it out. John is acting funny again; there's still something he's not telling me.

"Well I guess some people are just different," I say. "They have a different way." I use the rag to wipe up the counters. "They seemed nice enough, though."

John tuts and gives his head a shake. "I was waiting for that."

"John, everything we talked about — his mother's abusive boyfriends, his need to be the center of attention — he's a sad man. And now he's with a woman who's sick with something. They had to shutter their business, it sounds like. They're back up here, starting over."

"That's one way to look at it."

"What do you mean? You think they're lying?" I almost hope he does.

John studies the floor. "Maybe you're right. You're probably right. But I'm sorry if this sounds like I'm being the asshole now — I really don't want to see them again."

"That's fine with me. We invited them in, showed them hospitality. There's no more obligation."

"Sounds like an ad," he says, cracking a smile. "Bruce and Rainey . . . try them for free, no money down, no obligation to buy."

"Stop," I say, but feel the humor tugging the corners of my mouth.

John sweeps me into a hug and spins me around, just lifting my feet from the floor. When he sets me back down, we stay wrapped up in each other's arms. I can feel the muscles in his back, the knobs of his spine as I run my fingers over his shirt. I've never once considered John a weak person and the extent of his suffering doesn't change my mind, only makes me think that whatever it is he's not completely sharing, or can't, is bigger than I understand. With time, I figure, it will come together.

"Maybe he was looking to bury the hatchet," I say as John lets go. "He might not even consciously remember all of what happened with you guys. He probably has a different picture of high school than you do — remembers things how he remembers them. But maybe somewhere inside he realizes he's done you wrong. So he shows up, he flatters you, he praises you . . ."

"Nah, I think it's like you said. We did our part. Let's leave it." He gives me a peck on the lips and starts away. "I'm going to get to work. Maybe get some actual writing done this time."

"Good luck." He's probably right. Better to let the whole thing go. I'm not the type to believe in omens — not literally, anyway, not after I escaped the cult of my mother — but if that dinner wasn't an indication of a relationship better left untended, what else is? And the way Rainey was looking around my house, like she was planning to crib my decorating . . . or the way Bruce took so long in the bathroom . . . They were too familiar, too comfortable too soon, even for my tastes.

Anyway we have enough going on in our lives to keep us plenty busy. It's Saturday night and I have a shift tomorrow from noon until midnight. John has a deadline for a new book and he's been struggling with it. *Keep things simple,* that's our motto. After a bit of a rocky start we learned to pace ourselves, make some sacrifices. I had to let some of my old relationships wither a little. John learned to trade his beloved solitude for community interaction in order to be married and have a family.

I finish cleaning up the kitchen and my mind swings to work and what's in store. One of my patients has Lewy body dementia. Another has Alzheimer's. We just got two new people admitted to the ward. It's going to be a busy week.

* * *

Just before bed, I hear John on the phone in his study. Melody is in her room, sprawled on her bed with her headphones on and swinging her feet. Russ is playing with Lego and I get him dressed in his pajamas and we go through the ritual of brushing his teeth. Somehow he manages to spit more saliva on the bathroom mirror than he gets into the sink.

I usher him into his father's study for a goodnight kiss. John has his back to us, but turns around, puts his hand over the mouthpiece. For a moment I see something in his eyes, just a hint of something unfamiliar. It's gone in an instant and he says, "Hang on a sec," and sets the phone on the desk beside him. Still in his chair, he leans forward and spreads his arms and Russ leaps at him. John catches him and goes sprawling back, banging the desk, and he starts roughhousing with our son, nipping at his neck and growling in his ear and making him roar with laughter.

"All right, all right . . ." I hold out my hand. "Come on, buster."

"Night, Dad. Love you."

"Love you too, buddy."

Russ pads over to me, yawning. I take his hand and he starts to lead me out of the study and I look back at John. I half whisper, half mouth, "Who you talking to?"

He shakes his head and sticks out his lower lip, a dismissive face. *It's nothing.*

Then I'm pulling his door closed, tucking Russ into bed. *Weird.* Not that my husband and I are privy to every single detail in each other's lives, but we're pretty damn close. And if he's having a talk with Bruce, either to let him down gently or because he's getting suckered back into something, it's odd he didn't give any sign.

I knew early on that John was a contender for being my partner because of the way he was so open with his life. I didn't want secrets like I'd had with Melody's father, Marcus. I didn't want drama, but transparency. John was an open book, honest and straightforward about his recovery, about his doubts and his dreams. We like a lot of the same things: movies, books, shows. We vote along the same lines, have similar religious views, all the necessary ingredients for compatibility. But I've never really seen that look in his eyes before, and as I give Russ a kiss on his forehead and turn out his light, a coldness forms in the pit of my stomach.

CHAPTER FIVE / THE WARD

Sunday, March 24th

It's evening when Selma often gets disoriented. Sometimes she wanders around the hospital looking for her husband. Her husband died three years ago. Tonight, though, she's sitting in her chair by the window as the daylight fades.

"Selma?" I set the clipboard down on her bed. "How are you feeling, dear?"

I call her that because she calls me it, too — it's her preferred salutation for just about everyone she meets. *Oh, hello, dear.*

She is lit in the soft glow of the window. I stand beside her a moment wondering if she's aware of me. An unfinished game of solitaire shows on the laptop on the corner desk. Our patients are encouraged to play card games and use computers (with certain limitations — Twitter recently sent one octogenarian into panic-like paroxysms). They're encouraged to read, do crossword puzzles, play games. Seeing the half-finished cards on the screen, I wonder if Selma is having some sort of episode after all, perhaps triggered by an inability to focus.

They were Henry and Selma Ford, from Morrisonville, about an hour north, where she taught fourth grade for almost thirty years. Not wishing to induce thoughts of Henry if Selma's fugue is unrelated, I ease down beside her, mindful of my lower back. "Selma? It's Jane. How are you feeling?"

What do you see out there? I want to ask, but don't. Being haunted by government-looking SUVs is my problem, not something I wish to transfer to anyone else, especially when I've spent years routing the conspiracy-theorist inside me.

Selma has a small, pretty face. Her upper lip sprouts a couple of corkscrew gray hairs she calls her "whiskers." I see her chest rise and fall as her hands grasp the chair arms, bony knuckles protruding against papery skin. She is somehow redolent of sea air.

"Mrs. Ford?"

At last she blinks and regards me with faded blue eyes. I don't see recognition in her face, but that's okay — Selma almost never remembers me. I stick out my hand for her to touch, if she wishes. "Hi, Mrs. Ford. I'm a nurse. Do you know where you are?"

She keeps looking at me until someone moves past the open door. A male patient shuffles along, mumbling under his breath. Another sundowner; it's almost five o'clock and the sun sets in half an hour. Things are about to get their busiest — the time when, as John once put it, the patients at Hazleton Medical wander like acid-trippers at a Grateful Dead show.

Knowing I can't linger — there's too much else to do tonight — I bring my attention back to Selma. "Mrs. Ford, you're at Hazleton Medical Center. My name is Jane Gable. Can I get you anything? Do you need anything?"

She keeps looking at me with those milky-wet eyes, but she's not really seeing me. Who knows what face she conjures out of mine, what memories she's living in.

Selma's dementia is mid-staged but it's advancing rapidly. Sundowning, or "late day confusion," is considered a symptom. The full-spectrum light beside her bed keeps the room well lit through late afternoon and evening. That way, patients hopefully skip disorientation and get solid sleep when the lights go out. Selma seems peaceful as she turns her wrinkled face to gaze outside again.

"Well I'll keep your door open, Mrs. Ford. Okay? If you need anything, I'm just outside."

I take up the clipboard and make some notes: when I was here — 5:11 p.m.; what sort of state Selma was in — peaceful but unresponsive; and I check to make sure she's updated on all of her meds. As I'm writing, Selma mutters a few soft, unintelligible words.

"What's that?" I move closer.

"A nice man." She's still looking out of the window.

I bend down to track her line of sight. Poplars line the sidewalk and a gray house with brown shutters sits across the street in the abandonment of late afternoon. A green car rolls slowly past.

"You see someone out there, Selma?"

"He was nice, always nice when he visited. A nice man."

Her voice registers just a tick above inaudible. Despite her diminutive size, I know Selma can turn up the volume when she needs to; a fourth-grade teacher has to be able to speak above the din of an unruly classroom.

"He was a nice man? Do you mean Henry? Or your son, Adam?"

Her wrinkles deepen into a frown then relax. She's not talking about either of them — or she doesn't know. Speaking of loud voices, I can hear the patient from the hallway, and it sounds like he's getting worked up. With a soft pat on Selma's bird-boned shoulder I start to leave and she grabs my hand, turns her head and looks up with that dreamy expression. "He is a nice man but he has a trouble."

Intelligence outshines her opaque eyes. Sometimes it's prudent to follow the thoughts of a patient, even if they seem delusional, because they aren't always such. I lean closer, whispering, "What trouble does he have?"

She has a hold of me with her left hand. She raises her right arm in the air, trembling slightly. "He has a trouble with this."

The way she's holding her arm out she might be talking about a former student struggling with penmanship. It wouldn't be the first time she's recalled her teaching days.

I lower her arm gently to her chest. A crooked finger stays pointing in my direction. "Well, I'm sure you'll know what to do," I say.

Apparently it's the wrong response. As new wrinkles cut through the brittle skin, tears bubble up in the saggy pouches beneath her eyes. "No. He won't." Her lower lip shudders and she shakes her head. "He won't listen."

"But he's a nice man," I assure her. "Remember? A *nice* man. Maybe he had trouble when he was young, but that's over now, right?"

"He wants to protect his family."

The words are like nettles pricking my scalp. I see my husband the way he was last night, sitting on the phone in his study, looking at me with the eyes of a stranger. Obviously I'm conflating one thing with another. Even if there was the most remote chance she means John, Selma taught school in another district and would have no cause to know him.

Unless . . . Well, there was the one time John found my cell phone and brought it to me at work. But he wouldn't have come into one of my patients' rooms to shoot the breeze.

I'm losing objectivity. The psychologists call it transference. "Let me get you a glass of water, Mrs. Ford. Would you like that?"

But she won't let go. The patient in the hallway is getting louder, too. I know who it is: Edward Cormack, a seventy-nine-year-old with Alzheimer's, and I need to get out there. Another patient shuffles past the doorway with a look of alarm. A nurse follows quickly after, talking in soothing tones. We're heading toward the critical hour when the aged flower children are fully peaking, lost in the thrall of Jerry Garcia's long strange trip.

Selma is shaking her head, grasping at me. "He loves you."

"He loves me?"

I stare back at her, the anxiety crawling through me now like tight packs of termites, even as my rational mind protests the emotional response — *this has nothing to do with me*. I run through the locked-in elder care ward at Hazleton Medical. None of my patients know a thing about my personal life, beyond the fact that I'm married and a mother.

Selma blinks at last, as if returning to the present from some faraway place. "I'm sorry. I'm not who I think I am."

The words strike a chord that rattles through me: wasn't John talking about something similar?

Coincidences stacking up, I free myself finally from her grip and move to the bathroom. I fill her a glass of water, drink it myself, fill it again. When I step back into the room, Selma stands beside her bed with a worried, watchful look. "Who are you? What are you doing here?"

I have to go through the whole routine again: reintroduce myself and tell her where she is. We're back on familiar ground and the anxiety starts to drain off. I urge her to sit back down but she's not having it. She wants to leave. We're not allowed to physically restrain the patients at Hazleton, nor would I ever want to. We only intervene if they're going to hurt themselves. But Selma is scurrying out of the room now and I quickly set the water down and chase after her.

* * *

Ten minutes later, our wayward male patient is in restraints, spit bubbling in the corners of his mouth, eyes gone pink from stress and fatigue. A nurse named Caitlin gives him his injection and his body almost instantly puddles. In five more minutes, Nurse Jagger and an orderly named Beaumont attempt to coax another patient back into her room, but she's insistent that she's lost her wallet in the vending machine and if she gets somebody to help her turn the machine over, it might just shake loose. As I pass through the lobby with a fake wallet from a stash we keep behind the front desk, I notice the bank of monitors, cycling through the cameras on two hallways and each of the eight rooms on the ward. The cycle just happens to be on Selma's room and she's in her bed. After I leave the placebo wallet with Jagger and Beaumont, I check in on Selma. She's awake, having a moment of clarity, and knows where she is. She remembers that her husband passed and she has two grown children, a son and daughter, who live far away.

"Selma? Do you remember what you said to me a little while ago?"

"What, dear?"

"Do you remember I was in here earlier and we talked?"

She gives me a blank look. I get her comfortable with a book and exit her room with the door ajar.

While I'm in the coffee room feeling my aches and pains, Caitlin walks in. Her forehead shines with perspiration and she washes up at the sink then pulls a juice from the fridge — the kind she likes, called *Naked* — and guzzles half before swiping a hand across her mouth. "Phew. That was a good one."

"He's going to be fine."

"I know but it's Renita who gave me a chase over the whole damn hospital. I haven't gotten that much exercise in years. I'm telling you we got to put rubber tabs on the bottom of those slippers, slow them right down."

I smile at Caitlin as she vents. I have a good staff here; they all have big hearts and are dedicated to what they do. At some point each of them realizes, like I did, that in order to get through it you have to be able to poke a little fun at the patients and at yourself. If you take it all too seriously it can drag you down.

She gives me a look. "How you doing?"

"I'm good." My phone is in my hands and I set it down on the table next to me.

"Mrs. Ford give you any trouble?"

"No, she wasn't any trouble." *She just said some things that I can't shake.*

Caitlin stretches. "I'm going to do the bed check."

"Thanks, Cate." I look at the phone once she's gone. Tonight is no different from any other night, things patients say no different than at any other time.

But I've texted John twice now, just to see how he's doing, and he hasn't responded.

CHAPTER SIX / THE DISAPPEARANCE

When Melody turned twelve, I considered her ready to babysit. John thought it was too soon. "Let's give it one more year."

"Come on," I teased, "kids used to take care of each other on the farm when they were seven, eight years old. Arthur Miller's father came here from Poland when he was just a boy and had his own business going by eleven, right? You're the one who told me that."

It was like that for me, too. I was already cooking and cleaning by age nine. My mother had different men in her life as I grew up and I was alone with my younger half-brother and half-sister much of the time. By eleven I could prepare a three-course meal and feed them.

When I said as much to John he correctly pointed out, "Yeah but that pressure you faced caused a rift between you and your mother."

Ding-ding-ding . . . Tell him what he's won, Vanna.

Now, even if sometimes I feel guilty, like I'm sheltering her, keeping her from growing in self-reliance, I remember that Melody ought to have a childhood. I never really did, and I was about to commit the same mistakes my mother had.

It works out fine. You just have to find a balance, like with our diet; there's a place bestriding lofty ideals and devil-may-care eating. And there's a place for kids in between spoiled entitlement and expecting too much too soon. It's not *Little House on the Prairie* times anymore and childhood goes quick enough as it is.

She's asleep now in her room. I check in on Russ next — he's half out of his covers and flopped over the bed at an odd angle but sleeping like a log. The room smells faintly of chocolate and boy farts.

I check the study for John but he's not in there.

The queen-sized bed in our room is still made from the morning, so I flick on the basement light and go downstairs, calling his name softly. Sometimes he'll take a break from writing by doing some woodworking, but he hasn't had anything going for a few months and there's nothing to indicate a new project: no fresh scent of pine lumber in the air, no sawdust, no trace of the joint on which he'll puff occasionally.

I return upstairs to check his study again and my heart does a little somersault when I find his cell phone sitting beside his computer.

John takes his phone everywhere he goes. We joke about how kids who used to leave the house with nothing grew into adults afraid to go fifty yards without a device linking them to every imaginable support and convenience.

He's got to be around somewhere. Our nearest neighbors are a quarter-mile away, a family expecting their first child. He's a correctional officer at the county jail and she's a waitress at the local diner. We had them over for lunch once, but it wasn't an obvious fit as far as friendly couples go — about as awkward as Bruce and Rainey.

Who knows — maybe it's us?

John wouldn't be at their house unless it was an emergency and, if so, he would've let me know.

The door gives a long, low squeak as I lean outside. "John? Honey?"

This time of year, early spring, even warm days can dip below freezing at night. I grab a light parka from the coat rack to wear over my nurse's uniform.

So as not to disturb anyone's sleep, I've parked in the driveway, avoiding opening the garage door. The area light trips on as I walk to the car, flooding the driveway in a white wash. It takes me back to the other night: the SUV tailgating us as we sliced through the dark at speed, lights blaring.

I cup my hands to the garage door windows to find it empty of John's Subaru.

He's gone.

Maybe he just went out for milk and eggs? Or he had a writing breakthrough, took a quick run to the convenience store for a Pepsi. But it wouldn't explain why he hasn't responded to my texts for the last four hours. Even if he'd been in the midst of a writing frenzy and hadn't looked at his phone, he'd have checked it and responded before leaving the house, surely. But then why leave the phone behind?

The cold starts sinking into my skin. There's another possibility — he's out drinking something else, something he's not supposed to be. The theory makes sense of his abandoned phone. There are two bars in Hazleton, one at each end of the town — if he's at either one of them, he doesn't want to be reached.

Returning to John's study, I pick the phone up and look at it. Notification of four missed texts, all mine, sent over the course of the night — and a missed call bearing my number from a half hour ago. To bypass the home screen requires a password.

That stops me cold. As far as I know, John's never used a password. I've always been able to use the phone if needed. The last time we went on vacation I scrolled freely through his pictures, comparing them to the ones I'd taken. Now I can't get in. With mounting guilt, like I'm spying, I try John's birthday. Then the kids' birthdays, mine, even his late mother's. No luck.

Scattered over the wall-length desk are piles of papers, manuscripts and notebooks, plus a printer. It looks more like a standard office than a writing den, but then John has never been much of a pipe-smoking, wingback-chair kind of writer.

As long as I've known him he's gone about the business of writing with a kind of blue-collar work ethic, a sense of routine and order to balance against the vagaries of creative inspiration and spontaneity. Or something. I've never quite been able to fathom John's process, or any artist's process, for that matter.

Nothing in the paperwork provides a password clue. The notes are mostly gibberish, things out of context mixed with ruminations on current events and the publishing business. One note has the name *Bruce* written on it, with a number. Would they have met for a late night drink? There's no way John would abandon the kids and not communicate with me about something like that. If he's with Bruce, he's hiding what he's doing. But it's after midnight, not an appropriate time to call someone I barely even know.

I stick the number in my pocket, replace John's phone and walk out of the study, leaving the door open. Moving down the hallway I triple-check my phone that John hasn't tried to contact me. The last text I have from him is from more than twenty-four hours ago: *No not vegetarian. Wine is fine.*

I put it away. I need a shower and I need to sleep. If he's gone to one of the local bars or met up with his old high school classmate, there's nothing I can do about it right now. The kids have school and Russ will need help getting ready for the day. When I have my late shifts like this, John handles the morning, only it doesn't look like he's going to be able to take care of business tomorrow.

A lump of resentment forms in my throat as I strip off my uniform. John has always been a good husband. We both grocery shop, we both look after the kids. I tend to deal with Melody more closely — either because she's my biological child or because she's the female or both — but John was hands-on with Russ from the beginning, performing diaper changes and midnight feedings with the best of them. He does dishes, he cooks, he cleans floors. We both do. But I know sometimes he resents that while my work schedule is something of an immovable object, his routine is the more mutable one; he's the flexible parent for dealing with sick kids and snow days.

There were times I thought John might leave, times every family struggles with a squalling infant, messy house and diminished sex life, but I haven't worried about that for a few years — I figured we were through the worst of it. No more loaded diapers and colicky tantrums from Russ. No more night terrors from Melody, sleeping in the bed between us, all elbows and knees.

Not that everything falls on John's shoulders — there are plenty of times that I stay home with sick kids. I attend doctor's appointments. I help when the kids are off on school breaks. But if my husband is running out in the middle of the night, not telling me, leaving his phone behind, leaving his *two children* behind . . .

I'm growing angrier as the minutes pass and catch myself rehearsing different versions of the conversation I'm going to have with him when he shows up. What gives him the right to just take off? So he's struggling, maybe with work, maybe with the unanticipated arrival of some old high school crony. And maybe that's stirred up some emotions in John, I can sympathize with that. But this is still inexcusable. He knows I would understand his needing some time to himself. I probably would have given him leave if asked; the hospital where I work is only a few minutes by car, and I'm the one who thought Melody was old enough to babysit in the first place.

I need facts, but the emotions are bubbling up regardless. The more the water beats down in the shower, the less inclined I am to forgiveness and the more I feel betrayed. It's my usual night to wash my hair. Typically I'd go through the ritual with the door closed, drying and straightening, then into bed by 1 a.m. It can take some time to wind down after a shift like the one I just had, and I might read. But tonight I pin my hair up, wash the critical areas and hop out to towel off. I don't want to be in the shower when John pulls in the driveway. I want to be ready to give him hell.

* * *

The drain makes a sucking sound with the last of the water and with it goes my anger. I towel off and dress in sweatpants and a long-john shirt. The shower has helped clean away my resentment, but what remains is deep worry.

Perhaps I've been naïve. John could be having a harder time than he's let on, getting mouthfuls of the water he's treading and I haven't noticed.

It's time to figure out what to do.

He doesn't really have any friends locally, so there's no one I can call. The numbers on our fridge are for plumbers and electricians and general contractors. He's an only child, and alerting his father and stepmom would be premature.

I remember the glint in his eyes last night, hunched over his desk, talking quietly on the phone, that spooky, unfocused look he got when I interrupted him, the intense reaction he had to Bruce showing up.

I take out Bruce's number and stare until deciding against it for the second time. I've got to exhaust everyday things before I go texting or calling someone I barely know. Perhaps John has left me a note somewhere. I flip on the kitchen light and check the counters, the junk drawer, the dinner table. On the fridge is a small dry-erase board with a reminder to buy dish soap and one about Melody's piano recital at the end of the week.

Melody . . . Could it be John left her with some kind of instruction? Perhaps she saw or overheard something — it's worth waking her up. Only I find myself standing in the living room, staring out the window at the dark night.

God, John. If you're drinking . . .

I know what chronic alcoholism can do to people and it's not something I want in my life or in the lives of my children. He's slipped up twice before: once while I was around and once on his own. He struggled to forgive himself and get back on track. What am I going to do if he comes home in a few minutes, or another hour, smelling like a distillery? If he's had a drink (and driven), what sort of recourse do I have? Take the kids and leave? We'll have to have a serious talk at least and John will need treatment.

We chose this spot when John's book, *Edge of Night*, struck it big. I'd completed my master's and been working at Samaritan Hospital in Troy, but we wanted Russ to grow up out of the city, and I got the position in Hazleton at the hospital. Our house has a hefty mortgage, but it's beautiful and near to my job and the school. So we moved. We've had our bumps and bruises in the three years since, but nothing major.

God, John . . . why?

There are voices coming from down the hallway.

* * *

It's Russ, mumbling to himself in his sleep. After tiptoeing into his room I push him back fully onto his bed, tuck the covers around him and leave.

John must have given Melody a message to deliver when I came home. No matter what, he's not this irresponsible.

"Mel? You awake?"

She rolls over in her bed.

"Mel? Honey?" I hesitate to ask her point-blank. If he's instructed her to say something, just rousing her should do the trick. I sit down on the bed and stroke her shoulder. "Mel, it's Mom. Is everything okay?"

She faces away from me. "Huh?"

"I thought I heard you talking."

She says nothing, then mutters, "Probably Russ. He's been farting, too."

"Okay, honey. Sorry. Anything . . . anything that you want to tell me?"

"What?" She props up on her elbow.

"Everything go okay tonight?"

"Um, yeah. I think so."

"You think so?"

"Yeah. I read my book. Listened to music. No phone, you know . . ."

"Did Dad have any trouble putting Russ to bed?"

"I don't think so."

"And he came in and kissed you goodnight?" I'm dangerously close to letting the cat out of the bag.

"I don't know. I was asleep. I just passed out." She sits up fully. "What's going on?"

"Everything's fine, honey. I'm sorry I woke you."

"Are you mad at Dad?"

I can see her face in the light sneaking through the partway-open door. "Why would you think that?"

"I dunno. You seem mad."

"No, honey. Everything is all right." I ease her back down and plant a kiss on her forehead. "Go back to sleep. We'll talk in the morning."

"Okay . . ." The word sounds sarcastic.

I linger in the doorway. *Come on. Your dad told you something, left some instruction, some explanation for his absence. Please.*

But less than a minute later, Melody is snoring.

It's 12:55 in the morning. I need sleep. Our bed is cold and I rub my feet together for warmth. The book I'm reading is good but after picking it up I realize that I haven't comprehended a word of the last two pages. I stare at the ceiling, take a deep breath and close my eyes.

A few minutes later, I'm looking at Facebook on my phone. John hasn't posted anything in a week. I perform a fruitless search for Bruce Barnes, scan John's friends but only find a Bruce with a different last name with a picture of a hockey jersey for his profile picture. I try Rainey Barnes with no luck.

The time is 1:16.

Dammit, John.

This is so unlike him. John is a homebody. His family is his refuge. Russ's sporting events, working on the house, tending to a few enduring friendships all keep his troubled soul busy when writing doesn't. He's a good partner. I love him and I want him to be okay.

1:41. Eyes are getting heavy at last but I can't sleep. No missed calls or texts. Time drags on, and I'm looking at the clock at roughly fifteen-minute intervals, watching when the digital numbers switch from 2:01 to 2:02.

John . . .

Honey . . .

Where are you? What are you doing?

And why do I feel like I've done something wrong?

CHAPTER SEVEN / PANIC

Monday, March 25th

Someone crackles a plastic bag in the kitchen. The bedroom is cool but there's a warm pool of sunshine where my feet touch down on the floor.

"John? You there?"

7:42. I've overslept. There are no calls or messages, just fading dreams of my husband lying in a ditch beside his wrecked car. His side of the bed is cool to the touch.

I enter the kitchen still toeing into one of my slippers and wrap my robe around my waist. Russ has made a mess of cereal on the kitchen table but he's feeding himself, at least. It looks like he's attempted to get dressed; his T-shirt is inside out, tag sticking up in the back. "Mom, where's Dad?"

"He'll be back soon, honey."

Russ considers this and pours some milk into his bowl — a bit too much, and it slops over the sides. His cereal is not a normal child portion, but a mound meant for a weightlifter.

"Russ, go easy on that."

"Maybe he's with his friend looking at the bullet hole. They could be taking pictures."

"Yeah, maybe." I reach for the coffee only to pull out an empty decanter. John is usually the one who sets up the coffee on my work nights. I take it to the sink and run water, talking over my shoulder at Russ. "Did you see Dad talking to his friend last night? With the scar?"

He says something unintelligible around a mouthful of cereal.

"What's that, honey?"

He swallows, sticking out his chin like it's a load of rocks going down. "They were talking outside," he manages.

I halt in the middle of removing yesterday's soggy grinds. "Dad was talking outside with his friend? The man with the scar?"

He shakes his head, ready for another bite. "No. It was a lady."

"A lady?"

"I heard them talking in the driveway when I was in my bed. Dad and the lady. She looked like a superhero."

"She looked like a . . . Russ, who are you talking about? The woman who came to dinner?"

"No, not her."

"Did she have dark hair?"

He shakes his head. "Huh-uh. She had, um . . . yellow hair."

I try to think of blonde women I know and a few faces come to mind, no one that John would have over to the house late at night.

Sitting down across from Russ, I give him a careful look. "Honey, are you sure? Last night a woman with blonde hair was outside, talking to Dad?"

He looks woeful. "Maybe it wasn't last night."

"Then when?"

"I don't know. Um . . ."

"Recently?"

"Yeah, *recently*." He's testing out the word.

"Did you — when she was here — did you hear anything they said?"

61

"Huh-uh." He shakes his head again, spoons in some more Frosted Flakes. His bedroom is at the front of the house. It's still springtime and cold at night so his window is closed.

"Russ, can you be sure, though? You saw a blonde woman talking to Dad? Did you recognize her? Where were they standing?"

"On the porch. I saw from my window."

"Did Dad know you saw him?"

Another no, indicated by a flop of the bangs in his eyes. He needs a cut.

"And you don't know who she was."

"Nope."

I get up from the table and continue the coffee ritual on automatic pilot — fresh filter, a scoop of grinds, normal things — wondering who in the hell she could be. I feel like I'm riding a bike with loose bolts and screws, ready to come apart with the next bump.

With the coffee started, I hurry off to Melody's room, surprised to find her still in bed. "Mel, honey. We overslept."

"I didn't," she mumbles. "I'm not going to school."

"Are you sick?"

"Mom. I'm not going."

I glance around her room with a feeling about what's going on. Her pajamas from the night before are poking out of her closet laundry basket. It's happened. My daughter has gotten her first period.

"Listen, honey, I'm so sorry . . . I'll be right back. I have to get Russ to school, okay? We're late. But we're going to talk."

She murmurs something else and turtles deeper into her covers.

I run a toothbrush over my teeth, splash some water in my face. In the bedroom I pull on a pair of jeans, a fresh T-shirt and a sweatshirt. Russ's cereal bowl clatters in the sink when he lobs it in. "Go pee!" I call. "Brush!"

Five minutes later I'm clicking his seatbelt and then banging out of the driveway after a quick peek in our empty garage. A morning frost grays the lawn. We get to school with one minute to spare.

"Mom?"

"Uh-huh."

"What's the menstruation crustacean?"

The words are so garbled it's like he still has cereal in his mouth. But they're vaguely familiar.

"The what?"

"The men-stru-ation crustacean. It's a thing in the, um, girls' bathroom. A big lobster thing and you can get the cheese sticks out of it."

"When were you in the girls' bathroom?"

"Skylar showed me. She's in middle school."

"That's what you were talking about at breakfast the other morning?"

"Yeah."

And now I get it. Hazleton is a small rural village where all the kids go to one school. He's talking about the tampon dispenser in the girls' bathroom where the seventh graders go.

"Those aren't cheese sticks, Russ." I snap him out of his car seat and help him to the sidewalk, put his backpack over his shoulders. "Stay out of the girls' bathroom. I love you." After a kiss, he goes running inside and through the front doors just as the bell rings.

One of the other parents, Karen Dewitt, sees me and walks over. "Running late?"

I nod and shiver.

"Us too," Karen says.

Like me, she has two kids in the school, though they're closer in age and both boys. She's active in the community and runs the school yearbook club. There's a subtle tension between us that I've never quite understood, except maybe because John and I are transplants and the Dewitts have been locals for several generations.

"Cold today," I say.

"Spring is coming." She gives me a closer look. "Everything all right?"

"Oh yeah. It's just ah — you know, Russ just told me about the thing in the girls' bathroom. He thought it dispensed food."

Karen smiles but the humor doesn't travel to her eyes. We stand just outside the loop where the buses drop the kids off. The crossing guard ushers a few latecomers across the street.

I can't lose it here, not now, but I'm starting to panic. I have no idea where my husband is and apparently there's been a woman at my house. A friend? Someone else? I've kept my emotions at bay and got Russ where he needed to be, but I can feel the pressure mounting, the backs of my eyes stinging with tears. Karen's husband is a sheriff's deputy with the county police. I occasionally see him bringing people in who need to be hospitalized for mental health reasons.

But — cops? What if John is having an affair?

I heard them talking in the driveway. Dad and the lady.

"Jane?"

"Sorry," I say, and get moving toward my car, parked on the street. "Rough night, rough morning."

Karen keeps step with me but doesn't say anything. The morning is bright and crisp, a vividness that suddenly assaults my senses. When I reach my car, Karen is still there and I lean against it. "I'm having a problem." It's a struggle to meet her eyes.

Her voice is soft. "Oh. Okay. Listen, I, ah . . . I don't have any girls . . ."

"It's not — I mean, yeah, Mel just got her period, but that's not ah . . . everything's just happening at once."

"That's how it works, right?"

We've known each other for three years and worked the school consignment sale together. I decide that Karen is the nearest thing I have to a friend outside of work. But I'm just not ready to say anything yet. John could show up. He could be home already. The last thing I need is a scandal about my family in this little town where we've lived so far in relative peace and quiet. "It's not a . . . I'm making too much of it," I say to Karen.

Her hand is on my upper back and I wonder who's watching; the school is right behind us, all the classroom windows facing the street. Here it is, everyone, the moment you've been waiting for — the trendy couple from out of town, the divorcee and the alcoholic writer and their happy little joined family are finally crumbling! Gather round, y'all, and see what happens to the ones who don't stick to their roots. Gather round!

I turn to face Karen and force a smile. "I'm okay. Thanks."

She's dubious, I can tell, an aura of friendly skepticism around her, unsure whether she should let it go.

"It's probably just the day," she says. "My mother used to tell me that — 'It's just the day.' Right up there with other sayings like 'This too shall pass,' which probably doesn't help."

"No, it does. I appreciate it. Thanks, Karen."

"All right. I'll see you later, okay?"

"Okay."

I almost call after her but don't, reminded that Karen is a veritable community switchboard and I don't want rumors about my husband. There are a few things I can do on my own first.

Back in the car, I text Melody: *You okay?*

I check my face in the mirror — eyes are bloodshot, dark circles beneath. Hair is a bit frazzled but otherwise I'm just another working mom who had to hustle a little this morning. Time for a pep talk with myself: everything is going to be okay. John is going through something and, while his behavior is a bit scary, he's a sane and rational man. He would never jeopardize his family, his marriage. And he would never cheat.

Oh no?

He's too introverted. The only socializing he does is through me. I can't envision it.

Then what about his drinking? Remember the weekend you left with the kids and he spent the entirety of it drunk and depressed?

That was years ago. Before Hazleton. Before he was published and truly working as a writer.

Maybe a call to his agent is in order. There could be more to his work problems than I know about.

What about all the time he's been spending at the lake house?

Well, he's been clearing debris, making repairs and, occasionally, as it's a four-hour drive, he'll spend the night. So maybe he went back there for some reason and just didn't tell me.

Yeah, or maybe that's where he meets the blonde woman. Until she finally shows up at our house, desperate with love and carrying his child.

My phone jiggles with a reply from Melody: *I want to throw up.*

I write back. *I'll get you something and be right home.*

A car horn blatts, the sound going right up my spinal column. I'd started to pull away from the curb without looking and now the motorist is glaring at me as she drives slowly past. The crossing guard gives me a worried look. I raise my hand — *all good now, whoops* — and he lifts his own arm in a tentative wave.

Watch your shit, lady.

* * *

Mel ignores the egg sandwich I bought and takes the ibuprofen, then pulls the covers up over her head.

"I don't want to talk right now."

"All right . . . Just get some rest, okay?"

"Uh-huh."

I pause in the doorway. "Hon — I'm sorry — did anyone come over last night? While I was at work?"

Her finger pokes out of the white down comforter and just lowers it enough to reveal her eyes. "Who?"

"I don't know. Did you see anyone?"

"You mean those people from dinner?"

I don't know what to say. *Your brother says he saw a blonde woman.* Melody is too mature to just shrug that off and I don't have an explanation.

"Anyone," I say. "Did you hear anything? Your brother thinks he heard someone talking to Dad."

"He's probably just making it up."

"Okay. Get some rest."

Before I leave she says, "I think maybe someone pulled in the driveway, though — I saw headlights. It was pretty late."

My stomach goes gummy. "Last night? You sure?"

The covers lower some more. "It might've just been you, though. Coming home."

"You were asleep."

She makes a face that suggests it's all she knows. Then she furrows her brow. "You sure you're not mad?"

"I'm not mad — I don't know what you mean."

"You just seem it."

"I'm just trying to figure something out. We'll talk more in a little bit, okay?"

Back outside, the morning is still crisp and bright. Everything looks the same but different. The house is a natural wood color with sand-toned trim around the windows and doors and green shingles on the roof, but after three years it seems new and alien again, a place where strangers live; the windows that reflect the sky hide a truth inside.

People coming and going? The woman Russ saw, possibly a couple of nights ago, possibly last night. My seven-year-old is not the most reliable witness. My daughter sleeps on the other side of the house, involved in her own worries. But even if their stories are unclear, they're telling me what they believe is true.

The driveway beneath my feet is still just the driveway, weeds sprouting in the cracks, a scattering of acorns from the previous fall, but as I scan the asphalt for a stray cigarette butt or an empty dented can of beer I'm thinking about invisible tire tracks and footprints.

Circling around to the walkout basement, I find the door locked. I have to reenter from the front and descend the stairs. The recycling bins separate glass and plastic and I paw through both, finding nothing besides the usual soda cans and juice bottles. And then I'm standing in the doorway of John's study again, wiping my hands with a paper towel, giving everything a fresh look.

Beneath the long desk is a locked file cabinet. Beside it are shelves; stacks of paperwork on the top, some office supplies on the bottom. And the edge of something shiny — a glint of glass. I push aside a mug of pens and a tape dispenser.

The bottle of bourbon has about an inch of liquor left in the bottom.

"Oh, John . . ."

CHAPTER EIGHT / SEARCHING

In Hazleton, nearly everything closes early except for the two bars, open past midnight. I visit the Trailhead first, just a couple miles out of the town proper. At nine o'clock in the morning everything looks closed and locked. A lone pickup truck sits in the lot.

I get out and burrow into my parka and smell dirt and sawdust riding the air. When the whine of a power saw splits the silence, I follow it around back where a man is up on a ladder.

"Hello . . ."

He shields his eyes from the sun as he looks down at me. "Hi — help you?"

"Are you the owner?"

"No, ma'am."

"Is the owner here?"

"No."

"You wouldn't happen to have his number, would you?"

The guy gives me a long look then climbs down. He's in his late forties or early fifties, dressed in coveralls. He dusts off his hands as he walks toward me and I take an inadvertent step back. "Ray is in Myrtle Beach with the family," he says. "Everything okay? Something I can do?"

I put on another smile. "Oh — everything's okay. I'm just looking for someone. He might've been here last night." *He'd be the miserable writer drowning his guilt. Maybe the one with a superhero-ish blonde.*

The man gets a knowing glint in his eye. "Gotcha, gotcha — well, I don't really know the staff here. I think maybe RJ was working the bar last night, though. You know RJ? You could try him."

"Thanks. You wouldn't happen to have his number?"

"Um . . ." He pats at his pockets. "No, don't think so. I know where he lives, though."

"That would be great, if you could tell me."

He gives me RJ's address and then looks me up and down. "Sorry for your trouble. Hope you find who you're looking for."

"Thank you."

Five miles to the north side of town is The Knotty Pine. With darkened beer signs in the windows, this bar is also locked up, no one around, no cars in the driveway, just an overflowing garbage bin wafting foulness. I don't expect to see my husband passed out on the floor, but I'm braced for it as I cup my hands and peer inside.

The place is empty. I get back in the car.

Marty Spicer's number is actually in my phone. John's agent is not someone I've talked to beside the one time we met in New York shortly after John was signed on, so I'm happy I had the presence of mind to record his contact info. But I'm expecting to leave a voice mail — don't agents and those types start the day around 10 a.m.? It's not that yet.

"Hello." Marty has picked up.

"Mr. Spicer? Ah, Marty? Hi, it's Jane Gable. John's wife. I'm just—"

"Jane! How are you, darlin'? Good to hear from you."

At least he sounds like a morning person.

"I'm okay, I'm okay — ah . . . this is a bit weird to be calling."

"What's going on?"

"I'm just . . . I don't know what the ethics are involved here, or if there's a certain confidentiality with your clients but — I'm just going to come right out and say it. Has John been doing okay?"

"Something happen?" His voice is tinged with concern.

"You know, it's one of those things . . ." The more I talk the sillier I feel. It's one of those things? One of *what* things? Drinking and extramarital affairs? "I think John's been having some . . . maybe it's trouble with work, but he won't really talk about it. I'm sorry to bother you about it and it's probably fine. Just how writers are, right?"

Marty chuckles. "Well let's just say that the rest of us socialize blame but writers think everything bad is their fault. Masochists, all of them."

My own laughter sounds like a horse's whinny. "Yeah, right. And — I don't mean to break any sort of confidence, but I was wondering if . . ." I let the question hang in the air. I'm sure Marty knows what I'm driving at but I just can't bring myself to ask.

"Well," he says, "yeah, to some extent John's work is a privileged matter. But I'm sure you know we send him quarterly statements. So . . ."

Not a bad idea. I can check John's paperwork, see how things have been going. But that's not really why I've called, is it? I've got to tell someone or I'm going to scream. And John's agent is the safest person — out of town, barely connected to us.

"I don't know where he is, Marty. Right now I don't know where he is, and it's not like him to do anything like this. I think he might be drinking. He could be . . . I was just wondering if . . . you know, pressures from work — if he's said anything to you."

Marty is silent, just the rumble and squall of the city in the background. "How long has he been, ah, gone?"

"Since last night. I was at work, and when I came home he wasn't there. He'd gone, and left our two kids in bed. No message, no nothing." *Keep calm. Keep your voice measured.* "He didn't respond to my texts all night. In fact, he left his phone at home. It's password-protected, same as his computer — I don't know, maybe he was working on something top secret?" Another loose laugh flutters forth. I've become batty, unhinged. What's happening?

Are you mad, Mom?

"Jane, writers can really put themselves through the mill." Marty brightens a little, as if we're back on comfortable ground for him. "You know, for months they can just be deep in the cave, things can seem hopeless. But John's always managed to come through."

"Yeah, right. Exactly. Really this is probably just nothing and I'm being . . . It's been a lot with kids and work and . . ." I trail off, reluctant. Marty hasn't responded to the comment about John's drinking or whether they've talked, perhaps because that's precisely where the line is drawn.

A heat grows around my face and neck. I need to apologize for bothering him and go home and deal with this on my own.

His next words come over somber and serious. "I'll tell you, Jane — John and I haven't really corresponded much lately. He's sort of drifted away, to be honest. I mean I think it's been, ah, yeah, it's been close to five months or so since we even emailed, let alone talked."

It sends finger-like chills down my spine. "I thought, though — I thought he had a deadline? For a new book? He's been in his office working non-stop."

"Well, whatever he's working on, it's not through me. The last deal we had was with Lake Union, and that was . . . uh, *Edge of Night*."

"You don't have a book contract for anything right now?"

"I've been waiting. Waiting to see what he comes up with. But like I said, you know, it's been a while. We just had the one book deal. *Edge of Night* was a standalone. They've been ready, though. They'd pay an advance, even after *Edge* didn't perform all that well. I mean, that wasn't really John's fault."

It's a barrage of information. "*Edge of Night* didn't do very well?"

"Well the thing is . . . you sort of got this marketing lottery. Either you get all the spots or you get none of them. It was just bad luck with *Edge* and . . . You know, I wanted him to stick with his series, the other thing he was doing, but he wasn't into it. I think he tried to write a sixth book, but it wasn't coming off. So he had *Edge of Night* and I think he put a lot of pressure on that one to really perform well. It just got kind of swallowed up. It happens. I've played it laissez-faire because you hold any writer's feet to the fire and they just throw you a rough draft."

Swallowed up. Part of me wants to give Marty a few choice words — he's acting like these were all things beyond his control, but he's taking his fifteen percent to advocate for John, not just shrug his shoulders and play it "laissez-faire" when John's career is floundering.

In the beginning of John's series, I monitored sales, just for fun. It was exciting to watch the reviews come in and see the sales rank inching up on Amazon. He'd been trying to break into the business for so long. The day his first book cracked the top ten, we celebrated — we made love on the porch and drank sparkling grape juice like it was champagne.

"Listen, Jane, I'm so sorry — can I call you back? I'm about to step into a meeting."

"That's fine, Marty. Thank you so much for talking."

"Hope it helps." He pauses and the city traffic noise is gone, but I hear the chime of an elevator. "I'm sure everything's going to be okay. All right? Sometimes people just need to rejuvenate. Blow off some steam. But hey, when you talk to him, tell him to give old Marty a call, okay?"

"Yeah, will do. Goodbye, Marty."

I set the phone down on the passenger seat and smooth back my hair, looking out at the dark and gloomy bar in the empty parking lot. Rejuvenating with a fifth of bourbon. Great. Blowing off a little steam with some woman or maybe some old high school classmate.

I have no idea what to do now. Just wait for him to show back up? It's still early. Probably he's on a couch somewhere at the home of one of these mysterious friends, sleeping it off.

The idea makes me feel lonely, like I've suddenly lost my husband. Not because he isn't physically around, but because this isn't the John I know. Even if he's slipped up before, this feels more callous, even dangerous; he's never abandoned the kids like this. Wherever he is, when he wakes up he's going to feel utter despair, I'm sure. But he's going to feel even worse when I get a hold of him.

The phone vibrates beside me and I grab it, expecting the apologetic texts to start rolling in. But it's not John. It's Melody. And my breath catches in my throat.

Mom, someone is here.

CHAPTER NINE / CRITICAL TIME

I'm driving too fast, imagining the strange SUV parked in my driveway, its doors opening, people getting out. I can feel their bad intentions even if I can't picture their faces.

Or maybe it's John who's finally arrived home — he's disoriented, even hurt, careening into the garage and alarming our daughter. I glance at the phone but she still hasn't responded to my frantic replies: *Who is it? Are you okay?* The next time I look, I nearly go flying into a ditch and jerk the wheel to correct myself at the last second.

Heart pounding down the road to my house, the driveway rolls into view with a vehicle parked halfway along its length. Though not the SUV, thank God, the green car is still vaguely familiar. I jam the brakes, block it in, and hurry to my front door.

Halfway up the walk, I trip on a dislodged brick and go sprawling. My knee scrapes over the hard ground, and my palms grate against the sand John spread around on a recent icy morning.

When I scramble back to my feet too quickly, the hasty movement contorts my back the wrong way. The sensation is instant: the cold slip of a disk, the muscles surrounding it seizing instantly in protest and protection. I let out a frustrated yelp of pain.

Now I've done it.

Then I'm clawing my way along the railing, up the porch steps, lurching my way through the front door.

Karen Dewitt stands stunned, mouth hanging open. She lunges for me and circles an arm around my waist to help me stabilize. "Woah there! My God, what happened?"

"I fell." It takes a moment, but here it comes: feeling like an idiot, petrified and clumsy at the same time, like one of the Three Stooges if they'd starred in a Hitchcock movie.

"Here, sit down, sit down."

"No — sitting is no good." My words hiss through clenched teeth. I know from experience to lie flat on my back, so I reach for the ground. Karen intuits my plan and helps ease me down. "Clumsy . . ." I gnash my teeth some more and stretch out; the knotted muscles are reluctant to release their fresh chokehold.

I stare up at Karen and then Melody slips into view. "Mom — what are you doing? Your back . . ."

"I'm okay." I try to speak in a normal voice. "Hi, Karen. How are you doing?"

Karen doesn't know what to do with her hands or body and sort of wiggles around a moment before sitting in the chair next to me, trying to look everywhere at once. "I just came by to . . . You were so, ah . . . this morning . . ." It must seem to her now that the trouble is my back. Either that or I'm having some sort of mental episode. But before I can explain, Melody speaks up.

"Mom? Where's Dad?"

I catch Karen's gaze then turn my head to see my daughter looming on the edge of my vision.

It's time to come clean.

"I don't know, honey."

"You don't *know*?"

"No."

"Is that why you were asking me all those questions?"

"Dad wasn't here when I got home last night."

Karen looks more perplexed than ever, vibing indecision — she's not sure if she should leave or stick it out. Gradually, gingerly, I bend my legs and bring my heels back towards my butt. Then I draw my knees toward my chest to loosen the traumatized muscles. "I don't know what to say. I'm a little embarrassed, to tell you the truth. My husband, John — you know John — he went out last night while I was at the hospital."

She's silent.

"I don't know where he went. I'm sure everything is fine."

I ease my legs flat again and check the palms of my hands — little drupelets of blood pepper my skin. But my knee is worse; I can feel thick threads of blood circling around to the underside of my leg, sticking to the denim. I manage to roll over and get myself half-erect. Both Karen and Melody move beside me, their gestures tentative, like birds. The moment I feel their hands, the tears come. I let them fall this time. There's no use in trying to keep it all in anymore.

"I don't know where he is."

"Honey," Karen says. She's gone blurry in my vision. "You need to talk to someone. Maybe you need to call the police."

"I'll get you some Band-Aids and stuff, Mom." Melody lets go of me and heads out of the room.

"And some shorts too please, honey," I call after her. I'll be a bit cold but it's the best thing while my knee is like this.

Karen helps me up. I've managed to alleviate the worst of the back seizure — now I need to be careful. She keeps an arm encircled around my shoulders as I walk into the kitchen and turn on the tap. The soap stings my cut hands.

Standing beside me, she whispers, "You weren't kidding. Bad day, huh?"

"I know. I'm so sorry about this," I say, starting to tug down my jeans to reach my cut knee. Karen is certainly seeing a lot more of me today than she'd bargained for. I manage to push them down with some effort, and I grab a washcloth to wipe up the blood around my leg, making every movement slow and deliberate.

"Here," she says. "Give it to me."

I only let her because all the angles are making my back worse. Now there's a woman I know slightly better than the post office ladies down on her knees, dabbing at me with a bloody washcloth. While I'm in my underwear.

Melody comes back and hands the bandages to Karen, thrusting a pair of shorts into my hand. When I glance down a minute later, I catch Karen looking at me. "I think we got it."

"Thank you," I snuffle, trying to wriggle into my shorts. I take a tissue from a box on the counter and wipe my eyes, blow my nose. Melody is squinting, confused. "So that's why you're acting all weird? Because of Dad?"

"I'm sorry, baby, I know you're having a tough—"

"Dad went off somewhere?"

"I don't know. I think maybe he . . . It's possible he left last night, maybe to spend some time with his friends. Or someone."

The quivering of Melody's lower lip is a surprise. "Well, what did you expect?" Her voice trembles on the edge of yelling.

"What does that mean?"

She glances over at Karen who has drifted away to sit down on one of the stools beside the kitchen island.

"Never mind." Melody storms out of the room. The house windows rattle when she slams her bedroom door. I look to Karen but her eyes dart away again. What is she thinking now? Good Lord . . . A wayward husband, a disheveled wife, an emotionally overwrought daughter. What a picture. I was never one to care much what people think, but that seems to be changing fast.

"This is the first time I've ever been in here," Karen says. "You have a lovely place."

Her segue, with such convivial delivery, makes me laugh. "It's a mess. Thank you."

Her eyes slide back to mine. "Kids will be kids. Girls will be girls. Sensitive. I don't have any girls, but I know."

I move a little closer, still leaning against the counter in the same spot I was yesterday morning, talking to John while he sat at the table.

"Have you been . . . has everything been okay?" Karen waves her hands quickly in the air. "I'm sorry, it's none of my business."

"We've been fine. Everything has been fine."

Except for that tugging at the back of my brain, ideas about a blonde lover, a group of friends, a persistent SUV. But what is Melody upset about? Karen is right: kids can be sensitive, Melody especially. She could have picked up on John's recent anxiety, particularly about his visiting schoolmate. They have a special bond for which I've always been grateful. And *little pitchers have big ears*, the saying goes, so maybe she overheard something between John and me, thinks I pushed him into meeting with Bruce or something. She blames me for what's happened.

"His phone is here," I tell Karen, "but his car is gone." Saying these things reminds me that I haven't checked his phone yet this morning. Even with the screen locked there would be indications of new texts, and those typically show up as a number, at least.

"So what do you want to do? I think you can't be too careful. Let me call Matt." She digs for her own phone.

But thinking about her husband — the deputy — freaks me out.

"Hang on a sec, okay?"

Karen stops and regards me coolly. There's a look in her eye I've seen before — a look I'm sure my own patients have seen in my eyes, too. It's the expression of someone who no longer trusts you to be the author of your own story. Karen sees a woman standing in front of her, or rather leaning and in pain in front of her, and she's determining how much control she needs to exert. But she sets the phone on the kitchen island beside her and folds her hands in her lap.

I reach into my pocket for the Post-it note with Bruce Barnes's number on it. Karen is still watching me closely so I stumble through a recap of recent events. "The two of them together — it's the only thing I can think of." On the other hand, would John have really gone drinking with a guy he could hardly bear to be in the same room with? After he told me he wanted to be over and done with it all? Bruce seems unlikely, but it's still a call I need to make.

"What about the hospital?" Karen asks.

"I think if John was brought in I would have been notified right away. Even if he was missing his ID, someone there would have recognized him and called me." This is true, though I omit how I spent the night picturing John half-dead in a wrecked car, then dreamed of him still alive in some shallow grave.

"Maybe one of the other hospitals in another town?"

For just an instant I want to leap across the kitchen and wipe the somehow smug look of concern right off of Karen Dewitt's face. But she's only trying to help, and I'm either a fool or suffering denial for not even considering other hospitals. "Good point. But let me just . . . I want to try his friend first, you know? I'm not sure I can handle a . . . I mean . . ."

The sentence won't complete itself. No, I'm not ready yet to find out John is some unknown subject in an emergency room. Not ready to hear that, despite all efforts, we're very sorry, but he expired last night around 3 a.m. due to the blood loss and head trauma of a violent car crash. And by the way, ma'am, it's our duty to inform you that his blood alcohol content was three times the legal limit.

I tap in Bruce's number, get it wrong, start again, steadying my hand. Melody comes loudly out of her room and moves into the bathroom. She closes the door forcibly but at least doesn't slam it. My poor daughter. She's going through something new and potentially frightening and I'm preoccupied. The anger flares up again — anger at John for putting me in this position. Even at Bruce Barnes for showing up, whatever his intentions, and even if he does have a sick wife or girlfriend or whatever. Since he knocked on my front door Saturday morning, nothing has been the same.

The line is ringing. I wait for what seems like a long time, trying not to stare at Karen, who sits primly and patiently like she knows all of this is in vain, that I just need to suck it up and call the cops. Maybe she's right. Maybe I just have to face it. It's not that I have any problem with police — I'm the first to yell at the TV when some character in a movie isn't dialing 911 — but it's the same problem as calling emergency rooms. I'm not ready to face how *real* it all becomes the moment they get involved: the inexorable machinery that starts up, slow and methodical and completely out of your control; the eyes crawling over you; the neighbors looking in; the somber questions and the scribble of pens. You're no longer a special snowflake; you're just a case number, another sad story in a world of sad stories.

"Hey it's me," Bruce's recorded voice says in my ear. *"I can't get to my phone right now, but if you leave a message I'll decide whether or not you're worth calling back."* There's a pause, then Bruce says, *"Joking! I'm joking. I'll call you back because I have no life."*

There's a beep. I'm momentarily speechless, derailed by the self-deprecation. "Hi, Bruce, it's Jane Gable. John's wife. Listen . . . I'm calling because John went out last night and he hasn't come back. I'm just wondering if maybe you two guys are up to something, or if you know anything. This is really not like John. Be great if, um . . . I would appreciate a call back. Thanks."

I end the call and set my phone on the counter and look at it.

Karen's eyes are direct. She lifts her phone to show me the list of area hospitals and their numbers. "We can do it together. All right?"

I let out a long breath. "All right. Just a second." Hobbling down the hallway, I check to make sure Melody is still enclosed in the bathroom. "Everything okay?"

"Fine."

"I'll be right out in the kitchen."

"Okay."

Melody's flat tone hurts but I'll have to make it up to her later; I've put this off long enough. I make my way back by running the ridge of my hand against the wall so as not to smear any blood.

We start going down the list. Each call tightens my chest and ends with gushing relief: no one named John Gable has been admitted, not anywhere in the region, nor, for that matter, any mysterious blonde along with him. I google for regional car accidents and show the search results to Karen. "Nada," I say, triumphant.

"Other friends?" Karen asks. "Family?"

I tell her briefly about John's strained relationship with his father, his departed mother, and that his friends are far-flung. "We're from Troy. Well, I am. John grew up around here, but he went to college in Albany. That's where we met. We started out in an apartment — Russ was in our bedroom forever — then John's work took off and I found the job up here." I shrug. "You'd think in three years we'd have more friends but we've just been so busy."

"What about your own family?"

"They don't live here."

"In Troy?"

"One of them. My stepbrother. He and John have only met once. At our wedding."

"Well . . ." Karen sighs. "I guess now we just wait." Her brown eyes seem heavy. She's pretty in a hard kind of way, with no-nonsense straight hair cut to chin length and a small upturned nose. She's dressed in jeans and a cream sweater.

"I'm sorry, Karen, I just — you know? If this thing just turns out that he's . . . the idea of getting all kinds of people around and worried and he just shows up in an hour . . ."

She flips her hand in the air. "I understand. But I'll tell you what I know from Matt being a cop all these years — the first few hours of anything like this are the most critical."

"No, I know that, but . . . I mean, it's John. This is just going to turn out to be something that . . ." I take a few uneasy steps and look out the front windows, the edge of the main road visible from fifty yards away. "Like losing your wallet or something. You're about ready to cancel all your credit cards and then it just shows up."

She's nodding as if this makes all the sense in the world — or she knows that it makes absurd sense to me, the obviously unreliable wife. She says, "You don't think anything like this will happen, of course. That's the way it is, and John is a responsible person. Which is all the more reason you need to treat it seriously."

Her tone, the way she's looking at me, relights my defenses. "I *am* treating it seriously. I went looking for him this morning. I told you about it." I nod toward the phone. "We just called all the hospitals in a hundred-mile radius and I left a message with some guy he barely knows and practically accused him of being up to no good with my — where are you going?"

She's off the stool and gathering her phone with a shake of her head. "I've overstepped my place, I'm sorry."

I follow her to the door, but I'm still hobbled, moving too slowly to catch her. "No, Karen . . . *I'm* sorry. This has just been . . ."

"I hope it works out," she says, as she opens the door. "And I hope Melody is all right, too. Call me if you need anything."

I want to say something, but now I'm truly mortified by the whole thing — three years in this community and we've been the picture of normalcy. Well, maybe our lives are a little off the beaten path in a region where most husbands work construction, or at the jail, or are *in* jail, but we've managed to find our place and fit in. Now I'm clamoring after this woman, my back has gone out, I'm bleeding, my husband is missing, and my preteen daughter is getting her first period.

Karen gives me one last forlorn look, both disapproving and oddly disappointed, and closes the door behind her.

She's right. She's been right about everything and I've been too chicken to face it. I watch from the window as she maneuvers her car around mine — I forgot I'd blocked her in. Great.

If the situation was reversed I'd be advocating the same moves: call the police, don't waste any time. Saving us embarrassment if John shows up hungover and smelling of cheap sex shouldn't be the priority. And I've kept saying it's not like him because it's not. He would have called by now, somehow gotten word. It highlights the possibility he's injured, alone, trapped.

Karen's husband Matt is a local deputy but I want the state police. The 911 emergency center will know where to dispatch the call. I'm already keying the numbers and about to hit send when my daughter cries out.

"Mom!"

She sounds terrified. I drop the phone into my pocket and hurry away from the living room, using the wall to brace myself as I move stiffly down the hallway.

"Mom!" She's screaming now.

CHAPTER TEN / THE POLICE

There is blood in the toilet. We have officially arrived at our destination, ladies and gentlemen.

Her face is streaked with tears, her lips pressed into a grim line. It breaks my heart. This should be a positive thing. This is a step toward womanhood, a step toward possibly bearing her own children someday. And for some reason it's causing her all of this anxiety. I hover painfully and awkwardly as she gets herself under control.

It's not early — I got my first period about the same age — and we've prepared for it. My mother never said much, and when the first rust-colored blood showed up in my underpants I thought I was dying of cancer, so I've been conditioning Melody for a year. It's only recently she became so reticent, well before her adoptive father went missing.

She wants privacy again. I leave and stand staring at the closed door, wondering where I went wrong with her or what I've done. Fresh tears tickle my cheeks. Since the moment I encouraged John to have his old classmate to dinner, I've made one poor choice after another. I should've butted out, let John keep his distance. Or, at least, never brought up the wine. God, if Melody is right — if I had a hand in triggering John's alcohol relapse . . .

No. Don't blame yourself.

But who else is there? I have to take responsibility for my family role. I affect the emotions of my loved ones the same way I affect my patients. After all, that's part of the job, part of why I'm there, and I'm good at it. Why am I good at my career but so lacking in my personal life?

I wipe away the tears and move gingerly back to the kitchen and take out my phone again. No more bad decisions. The call to 911 is going through as I put the phone to my ear.

"911 emergency response — can I have your name and address please?"

"Jane Gable." I give her my location, looking out of the window. The sun is melting the frost on the grass and trees. At least that's something.

"What can I do for you, Jane?"

"My husband is missing. His name is John Gable."

* * *

The state troopers arrive in two vehicles, now parked in my driveway with the engines running. Having the state police here is not a comfort: they represent hard, final facts.

I know some of the state police assigned to Troop B because, like the local deputies, I see them coming and going from the hospital. These two, though, are unfamiliar to me as they come up the walk. They introduce themselves as Trooper Morse and Trooper Gorski. The male trooper, Morse, gives me a look.

"Ma'am, you all right?"

"I have a slipped disk."

Gorski stands a few yards behind him, one hand up on her utility belt. Her hair is pulled back in a tight bun and her eyes are starred with sun wrinkles. "Back problems?"

"A past injury and it gets aggravated every once in a while if I'm not careful."

Stop talking. It's a ridiculous thought — I've done nothing wrong — but something about police can make you feel guilty whether you're innocent or not. Maybe John and I have watched too many documentaries about coerced confessions and falsified evidence, people jailed for crimes they didn't commit.

Gorski gives me that cop look that's both imperious and indifferent as she judges the way I'm holding myself against the porch railing. She lowers her gaze to my bandaged knee. "And you got that from falling?" Her free hand feathers the air around her. "Out here?"

I nod. "We've been meaning to tear out these old bricks. I was rushing because my daughter texted me that someone was here and I wasn't watching my footing and I tripped."

Morse is a little younger, with a soft face and pleasant eyes beneath his felt Stetson. "Ouch. That's no fun. Is there somewhere else that would be more comfortable for you?" He glances over my shoulder at the front door.

I haven't asked them to come inside yet. Not sure why — maybe I just need to take things one step at a time, like wading into the ocean when the water is cold.

Before I can answer him, Gorski asks, "Who was here? Who caused you to rush like that?"

"Karen Dewitt. She's a local woman I know from the . . . she's my friend. I didn't know she was here. She got a new car recently and I didn't know it was her. She left a little while ago."

"And the fall?" Gorski points at my lower body. "That's how you got those scrapes on your hands, too?"

"Yes. I did."

Trooper Morse is near enough that I can see how long his eyelashes are. It gives him a harmless, almost babyish appearance. "You know about that bruise forming there on your cheek?"

My hand floats up involuntarily. "I must've hit my head, too — when I went down. Didn't even notice it."

Morse blinks those long lashes. "Ma'am, have you and Mr. Gable been having any trouble lately?"

"No. We're fine, everything's good."

"No, um . . . no getting rough — getting physical? Nothing like that?"

"Absolutely not."

"But he's never run off like this before, never left without telling you where he's going?"

"No — but it's not . . . He works from home . . . It's not that I always know where he is or what he's doing. He just . . . he doesn't do much. Much that's unpredictable, I mean."

"Uh-huh . . ."

"He might go to the store, run errands, that kind of thing — while I'm at work. And I don't know where he is for a few minutes, maybe. I work primarily from noon to midnight at the hospital and he stays home with the kids once they're back from school."

"But he left last night, you think, and the kids were home."

"That's — yes, that's right."

I don't think John has done anything illegal by leaving our almost-teenager alone with our seven-year-old but I'm not sure exactly where the law lands on child neglect and it makes me a bit nervous on top of everything else.

They ask me the expected questions about friends and family and about where he might've gone, and I tell them what I told Karen: there's nowhere, really, nobody. "Well, we have a lake house."

"Lake house?" Gorski's eyebrow goes up.

"It's just a camp. A seasonal place. John's been doing some work on it."

They drift a little closer as I explain where it is, our plans to vacation there for the kids' spring break, how John's been doing some repairs on it, but that the idea he went there in the middle of the night, unannounced, is highly unlikely.

Finally I ask, "Would you like to come inside?"

They exchange looks and silent communication. Morse gives me a smile and moves toward the door. I understand that Gorski wants to stay outside, maybe have a look around. Carefully stepping in, mindful of my back, I hold the door for Trooper Morse as he appraises my labored movements. "Boy, you really sprung a coil, huh?"

"It's not usually this bad."

"You said it's from an old injury or something?"

I lead him into the house. "It's always been a little glitchy, even when I was young. We went camping one year and I helped John take the canoe down from the car and something happened. I've been to chiropractors and massage therapists. The best I can do is just be careful with it." It's not the entire truth, but there's no need to discuss my last pregnancy with a state trooper.

"John's study is down here, and his phone is on his desk. I found it there when I came in last night."

We're moving down the hallway. Russ is still at school and Melody is in her bedroom with the door closed. I wonder how she's feeling with the police being here. Morse stops in the doorway to John's study but doesn't go in. "Did you look at the phone? Check to see any latest texts or calls?"

"Of course. Yes. But it's protected by a password."

"Uh-huh."

"Which made me wonder because John doesn't ordinarily keep his phone password protected."

"Oh no?"

"No."

Morse walks into the office, creaking over the floor. He keeps both hands on his belt as he looks around. "I'm not going to touch anything in here, and probably you shouldn't touch anything else, either. I'm sure you're in here a fair bit, but in case we need to have a close look at things, maybe keep the kids out. Leave everything as it is. Don't clean. Did you touch anything else, besides the phone? Move anything?"

Having Morse treat things so seriously brings relief after all: the process of getting John back is underway. At the same time, it feels overblown, like he's going to show up any minute and all of this about evidence and fingerprints is going to seem like high drama. We'll even laugh about it eventually. "I touched the phone, tried to get into it, and then

I looked around a little bit. I took a phone number that was written on a Post-it note."

Morse raises his eyebrows. "An important number?"

"Someone who recently came back into John's life. An old high school friend."

Morse stands there. His pants are gray with a black stripe down the legs. His belt supports a gun, a phone, a nightstick and a radio. The Stetson angles down over his brow. "Someone new in his life . . . Did you try to contact this person?"

"I did. I thought it was too late to call last night but I tried him this morning. Got the answering machine. His name is Bruce Barnes. He and his wife had dinner with us on Saturday night."

Morse takes a notepad out of his uniformed shirt pocket and clicks on a pen. "Barnes," he says. "Know how to spell that?"

"Ah, actually I don't. My guess would be B-a-r-n-e-s."

He gives me a look. "So this isn't a close relationship, then."

"No, not really. I just met him."

"And do you have that number for Barnes?"

"I do." I pull the crumpled note from my pocket and hold it out to him.

"Just hang on to that for now. And did Mr. Barnes call back?"

"No, not yet."

He nods a little and regards me with his big brown eyes, blinks those caterpillar lashes again. "And did you try the wife, too?"

"I don't have her number. I tried looking both of them up online but didn't have any luck."

"Okay."

I see something catch in his face. "So, your husband is predictable, you say. Tends to stay at home, doesn't have any history of this sort of thing, and the big change lately is that there are two new people who have come into his life." He puts the notebook away as the heat rises in my cheeks.

90

"They might not be the only people."

Morse waits as I build up the nerve. I tell him about the woman Russ saw and Melody's suspicion that a vehicle arrived the night John disappeared.

"Okay. So it could be the old high school buddy, could be someone else, this woman. Maybe whoever it is, you know . . . they get together, go out for a few drinks . . ."

"I actually went to two bars this morning. There was a roofer at the Trailhead who gave me a name. He said that someone named RJ was bartending last night. So maybe he's worth talking to?"

"Uh-huh. RJ?"

"Yes."

"Got a last name?"

"I'm sorry, no."

"I can find out."

"Thank you."

Morse looks around, chews on his lip. "Does John have a passport?"

"He does."

"Is it in here?"

"I haven't seen it."

"Just his wallet."

"Yes — his wallet was in the bedroom on his dresser. Why?"

"Well, you know, I'm thinking . . . your husband's not showing back up this morning . . . this old high school friend has come back on the scene . . . Something guys do sometimes around here is they take a run up into Canada. Go to the clubs."

It's not comfortable to contradict a state trooper, but there's just no way. "I, ah . . . yeah . . . I can't see John doing that. And I mean, they're not really even friends."

"Hmm." Morse looks unconvinced. He has *boys will be boys* written on his face.

"To tell you the truth, John wasn't really that happy about Bruce showing up."

Morse cocks an eyebrow, inviting me to say more.

"John says . . . well . . . Bruce picked on him when they were kids." I flinch at my own choice of words. John would hate the insinuation he was some kind of victim. But wasn't he? This stuff has got to come out. Now that a state trooper has put it like this, I feel I've been too dismissive of the Bruce thing, too paranoid about some blonde woman my seven-year-old might have dreamed.

And I've got to talk about the bottle, too. The drinking. So far I've made an effort to keep my gaze from wandering to where the Jim Beam sits on the low shelf, but I'm looking there now.

"Trooper Morse . . . John has been in recovery for twelve years. From drinking. But there's a bottle in here — I found it last night." I point to the bottom shelf.

Morse moves toward it. "Here?"

"Behind those things there." I can feel the dread in my stomach as he squats down and bends his neck for a look.

"So maybe alcohol is a factor after all," he says.

My voice sounds small in my ears. "Yes."

"He attend AA meetings, things like that?"

I shake my head. "He did for a time in the beginning but he hasn't in a while. Since I've been with him, really."

"Does he have any sort of record?"

"Like a criminal record? God, no."

"How about any DUIs?"

"Oh. Well, I think . . . maybe . . . but before we met. More than ten years. I thought after ten years . . ." I stop because a light has come into Morse's eyes and he's shaking his head at me.

"Doesn't matter in Canada," he says.

"I'm not sure I understand."

"Canada has different laws for DUI. They have stricter punishments. Your husband could have crossed the border, not known about that, and been detained. Happens all the time."

"Detained?"

"Because — okay, so you get a DUI in the U.S. and you pay your fine, maybe take a drunk-driving class, get it cleared up. But in Canada, like I said, it's a more serious offense. So they'll detain people and check them out — Border Patrol handles it. Then they either kick you back into the States or they can continue to hold you — they can prosecute you there."

I'm following along the line of thought, feeling this queasy mixture of relief and fresh worry over John being jailed in Canada. It's not a bad explanation — that someone gregarious and a bit pushy like Bruce convinces John to come out for a drink, John leaves his phone and wallet but takes his passport for ID, and before too long he's three sheets to the wind and agreeing to go to a Canadian club but gets stopped at the border and locked up.

"But wouldn't someone have called? A lawyer or something?"

"Maybe not yet."

The theory loses some traction for me.

Perhaps sensing my skepticism, Morse says, "Contrary to popular belief, there's no constitutional guarantee of a phone call from jail in the U.S. — same goes for Canada. What I'm saying, ma'am, is the border is forty-five minutes north of here and John is from the area. I don't know about him, but when my big brother was in high school, him and his school buddies would go up to Montreal, go to the clubs where they could drink. You know what I mean? This old high school acquaintance comes back into your husband's life, maybe it's to make amends, this and that — and they go hit the bars in Canada for old times' sake. It's just something to pursue. It's an idea."

The floor groans as Morse starts out of the study. I follow him back down the hallway as he peeks in on Russ's room and then pauses outside of Melody's door.

"My daughter," I explain about the closed room. "She's not feeling too well."

He hesitates before moving on. When we reach the living room, the front door opens and Gorski steps in. "Ma'am, do

93

you have the plate number handy for your husband's vehicle? Or maybe a copy of the registration?"

"I don't have the plate number committed to memory, but there might be a copy of the registration in John's office."

"Or maybe," Gorski adds, "If the vehicle is registered in your husband's name I can just look it up that way."

"Sure, that would be good. Thank you."

Gorski starts to push back through the door and Morse speaks to her. "We want to check with USBP, too. Just see if maybe he popped over into Canada. He's got an old D-dub on his record and he could be dealing with that up there."

Gorski looks around Morse at me. "You think your husband went into Canada?"

"I'm not . . . I mean, ah . . ."

"It's an idea," Morse says. "Here, let's step out for a minute. Mrs. Gable, we'll be right back."

"Okay."

They walk back to their cars. I'm about to go check on Melody when my phone vibrates in my pocket. My heart trills and I take it out. It's not someone in my contacts but I've come to know the number by now: Bruce Barnes.

CHAPTER ELEVEN / BRUCE BARNES

"Hi," Bruce says on the phone. "Who's this?"

"It's Jane Gable — John's wife."

"Jane! You guys are like the Jetsons. But I think that was George, though. George and Jane Jetson. Wasn't it?"

"Bruce, did you get my message?"

"No, sorry — I mean, I saw it but I haven't listened to it. What's going on?"

I have a hand on the front door, about to go outside so I can have this conversation in the presence of the state troopers, but the words jump out of me. "Bruce, I don't know where John is."

A pause. "You don't know where he is?"

"Is he with you, Bruce?"

"Is he with *me*?"

"John left last night at some point. His phone is here but he took the car — his Subaru — and he's gone. I thought maybe you two . . . maybe you got together or something."

Another hesitation, and I can hear noise in the background, like voices, the bubble of laughter — as if from a TV audience. "No," he says, "we didn't get together."

"So you haven't seen him? Not since the dinner."

"No, not at all."

"Did you talk on the phone? I thought maybe he was talking to you later that night, after dinner."

"Yeah, oh — yeah, we talked a little bit after dinner."

"Can I ask what about?"

"Yeah, yeah. Just the old days and whatnot. Talked a little about his work stuff. Stuff like that. Just catching up."

"Even though you'd just seen each other at dinner?"

"Sure."

I find this suspicious, but there's nothing more I can say about it and I have other questions for him. "My son says maybe he saw someone, maybe last night, maybe before that. And Melody thinks maybe . . . Do you know anything? Any reason why someone might've been here last night?"

He lowers the pitch of his voice. "I have no idea."

My mouth opens — then I realize I'm close to calling Bruce a liar. I barely know this person. Even if his recent appearance coincides with John's disappearance, it doesn't have to mean anything. "All I know is that I don't know where he is. He left at some point last night while I was working at the hospital. He left his phone, like he was in a rush."

Or because he doesn't want to be found.

"Jane, I would tell you if we got together. I mean, we've had no plans. Nothing."

Or because he didn't intend to leave at all — he was abducted.

Bruce says, "So he's like . . . missing?"

Carefully now, so as not to offend: "Is it possible maybe John misread something and *thought* you had plans? That you were going to get together? He went somewhere to . . ."

"Jane . . ."

"I'm sorry. I know . . . it's just—"

"I'll tell you what we talked about, okay? On the phone, later that night after we had dinner. For one thing, we talked about the writing slump he's in."

My mind is reeling. John talking to someone he barely knows or trusts about his writing seems far-fetched to me. On the other hand, maybe he sought a fresh perspective, an outsider's opinion. And I know it's true from my talk with

John's agent, Marty. Although why he had to call Bruce that very night to talk about it I don't know.

"Happens to every writer," Bruce says with an expert's tone.

"What did he say?"

"I told him stories take as long as they take. He was putting too much pressure on himself, psyching himself out. He thought maybe he needed to shake things up. Break out of his routine."

"And do what?" My volume has risen. John talking about all this with someone he ostensibly dislikes instead of me makes me angry. "What did he say he was going to do? Did you encourage him?"

"Hey, Jane, I didn't tell him to do anything. I just agreed, you know? Maybe the same thing, day in and day out — he's going back to the same well and the well is dry. That's what happens."

I close my eyes and take a breath. Making enemies with Bruce won't help. And there may be a deeper element here that warrants empathy: John's complex feelings about their past. When I speak again I'm calmer. "But did he say anything specific, Bruce, about what he might do."

"No. I mean, he made some allusions."

"To what?"

"Hard to tell. Just little things I picked up on. Listen, Jane, you know — this is what I do. I mean this is in my wheelhouse, my field."

The conversation has shifted, Bruce eager to put his purported law-enforcement skills to work. Whether he's skilled or not, the cops should talk to Bruce. I open the door, still on the phone. Gorski is sitting in her police cruiser, doing something out of sight. Morse paces at the end of the driveway, talking on his phone. He sees me and waves. I start toward him, walking like a scarecrow come to life.

"I'm with the state troopers," I tell Bruce.

"Oh." He makes no effort to conceal the disappointment in his voice.

"Would you come talk to them? Tell them what you and John talked about?"

"I mean like I said, he didn't say anything specific."

"Please, Bruce." I stop halfway to the driveway.

He sighs again. "Yeah. All right. They're there now?"

"Yes. They're here now. Can you come over?"

Nothing from Bruce except more background noise. I'm not so sure it's canned audience laughter anymore. It sounds like something else, maybe an engine trying to start, not turning over. Finally: "Okay — give me a few minutes and I'll be on my way."

"Thank you so much, Bruce." I start walking again and it occurs to me that I've said things to the cops about him. I don't want to create bad blood, especially if he can help us. "Hey I just need to tell you — I told one of the state troopers that you and John — you had some rough patches in your friendship. When you were kids."

"Uh-huh . . . That's okay."

"But I also said I thought maybe you being here, dropping by . . . maybe it was your way of mending fences."

I'm almost to Morse. The air is crisp but warming up, and I catch the scent of moldering earth: spring smells. For a moment I'm filled with a kind of remorse, like a beautiful day is being squandered by all this drama. That sense is gone in an instant when I glance at Gorski's face. She's looking very serious, and I see her poking buttons on a computer mounted to her cruiser console.

Bruce is still talking in my ear. "Well, truth be told, you know, John had his moments, too."

"Say that again, Bruce?"

"It's a two-way street."

"What do you mean?"

"I mean, kids do shit. I wasn't the only one."

"John was a bully too?" The word just slips out and I regret it instantly. At the same time, my husband is missing. Too bad if some guy gets offended.

"John said that? About me? That I was a bully? That's a bit much."

The comment pricks me. And maybe I'm emboldened by being in the presence of two uniformed police officers. "He said you threatened to kill him, Bruce."

My words have grabbed the attention of Morse, who is snapping his phone onto his belt and giving me a concerned look.

"Yeah, well did he tell you the whole story?" Bruce says in my ear. "Listen, Jane. You're very nice, but maybe you don't know everything about your husband."

His words are cutting, and I feel like I'm getting a glimpse of the person my husband described, someone who would threaten assault, yell racial epithets out of car windows, scribble insults on school lockers. I need to be the bigger person here. Morse has homed in on me and is standing close, listening as I finish the conversation.

"Bruce, I'm sorry. That's all in the past and I'm sure you two could work it out. If you say you have no idea, then I believe you. But I thought maybe something between you might have upset him. I thought maybe he relapsed and went somewhere to drink. One of the officers suggested the two of you — or maybe just John — might've gone into Canada."

I wait for Bruce's response. I hear those voices in the background, but nothing from him. "Bruce? You there?"

"Sorry. Look, I'll call you back later. We'll get to the bottom of this."

"Bruce, I thought you were—"

"I'll call you back, Jane." The phone beeps that the call has been cancelled.

Morse is watching me expectantly.

"Well, that was the friend," I tell him.

"And? Sounded a little tense."

"I don't know what was going on. He seemed distracted."

"Maybe we should talk to him in person."

"He said he was going to come by. Then he . . . I don't know if he changed his mind."

"When you mentioned Canada."

I don't have any response to that. It's another mixed bag — a feeling of guilt and righteousness. Bruce might've had the best intentions by reaching out. If he was flustered by my call, that's understandable; I was partly holding him to account. But he is the anomaly in our otherwise routine life, and was evasive about what "shaking things up" meant. Why be vague? Because something bad happened and he's trying to protect himself?

Gorski steps out of her cruiser and slides her nightstick into her belt. She stands there a moment with her gaze flitting between me and Morse, as if she can't decide who to address. "Your husband's car has been located," she says, and my whole world suddenly feels like it's tilting.

"What? Where?"

"It's intact, no apparent damage . . ."

I take a lunging step and Morse grabs me because I'm unsteady on my feet. Gorski's face is leaking color, turning gray as I start running out of oxygen because I'm not breathing.

Her lips move in slow motion and her words reverberate deep in my eardrums. "It looks like there could be blood in it."

CHAPTER TWELVE / THE CAR

My daughter's door with the paper mailbox and its hearts and sparkles has become the gateway to a path I question walking. With everything that's happening, I need to keep my family together. Russ is safe at school surrounded by responsible adults; leaving Melody alone scares me. But if something has happened to John, I'm not sure I want her in the midst of some gruesome discovery. Gorski's statement echoes in my mind: *there could be blood in it.*

"Ma'am?" Gorski is in my living room at the end of the hall. "Ma'am, is there someone who can stay with her?"

I ease away from Melody's door, lowering my voice. "How about you or Trooper Morse? Could one of you stay and the other . . ."

She's already shaking her head. "Maybe in another situation, but I can't do that right now. If there's nowhere for your daughter to go, I can notify Child Services."

"No — can I just have a minute to think about this?"

"Sure." Gorski pulls her cell phone from her belt and checks it.

They're discouraging me from going but that's impossible — my husband's Subaru was found at an interstate rest stop ten miles away. Apparently another trooper who lays a speed trap in that vicinity responded to what Gorski called a "BOLO" — be on the lookout. The trooper rolled on through the rest stop and spotted the car right away. Gorski says they need more information before gathering a crew to search the area but I can't wait for whatever that might be — I need to go confirm the car myself.

My heart is beating so hard I'm having trouble hearing, but I have to go. Karen is the best option for Melody — no Child Services necessary — but I don't even have her number in my phone.

With Gorski looming and the sense of urgency turning the house into a pressure cooker, I finally find Karen's information at the bottom of a group email through the school and make the call.

"Karen, it's Jane."

"I saw the troopers outside your house when I just drove by — did you call them? What's going on?"

"I'm sorry I didn't take you up on the offer to talk to Matt. I just thought that state police, you know, had a wider reach . . ."

"Oh they're all connected. You learn that when you're a police officer's wife."

It's a subtle barb, one I can easily ignore. "They found John's car."

"You're kidding. Is he . . . ah, is it—"

"I need to go have a look at it. See if I — I don't know. I don't think Melody should come."

"Oh, no. Definitely not."

Maybe I'm wrong, but there's a tinge of excitement in Karen's voice. Like this is all transpiring on her favorite reality show.

"Karen, I'm wondering if you could—"

"Say no more. I'm on my way. Five minutes. Leave if you have to and I'll be there, I promise. The first few hours are the most critical so don't wait for me."

"Okay. Thank you so much, Karen."

"Go — go!"

We hang up. Gorski looks impatient but I still have to inform Melody. My lower back throbs as I hobble back to her door and knock. "Mel?"

Muffled response: "I'm sleeping."

"I'm so sorry, baby, I have to leave. But Karen is coming over to just hang out and—"

"Why do you have to go?"

"I just um, I need to see if um . . ."

I made myself a promise years ago never to lie to my kids, not even white lies. I don't want to become my mother, for whom fact and fabrication blur together. But this is needed.

"I just need to go talk to the police about Dad."

"I don't need a babysitter."

"I know, honey. It's just that with everything going on I would feel better. It's for me, okay?"

Silence. I glance toward Gorski but she's not there.

"Mom?"

"Yes, honey?"

"Where's Dad?"

"I don't know, baby. That's what I'm going to find out. I'll be back as soon as I can."

"Why did he leave?"

"Oh, honey . . ."

I open the door — at least it's unlocked — and find Melody sitting on her bed, fully dressed, hugging her knees as she leans against the wall.

She looks at me, those big brown eyes, the ones that I've been staring into since the day she was born. "Did you get into a fight about me?"

I take a seat beside her, ignoring the protest from my aggravated muscles and the urge to rush to John's car, and pull her toward me. "This has nothing to do with you. We're going to figure out what's going on and everything is going to be okay."

Yet I'm picturing the Subaru, the blood, my mind running away with one grisly scenario after another.

103

I kiss her forehead after another hug. Then I'm struggling to my feet, doing my best to hide it from her. Of all days to trip and fall. This is the worst it's been in months, maybe a year. Outside Mel's room, I run my hand along the wall as I limp away.

My purse is a small zip-up leather satchel sitting beside the coffee maker in the kitchen. Do I need anything else? Habit, I suppose, causes me to look in the mirror by the front door. I'm a total mess and getting messier. Streaked mascara, puffy red eyes, dried lips. Doesn't matter. Nothing matters but getting John back.

Maybe you don't know everything about your husband.

If Bruce Barnes has something to do with John's disappearance, he's going to be in a lot of trouble. Something is definitely not right between them, whether it's the past I know about or the past I don't. But that will be a job for the police.

Gorski opens the back door of the cruiser and helps me into the vehicle. A few seconds later we're on the road and racing toward the interstate, the same road where John and I had the incident with the SUV. And as we close in on the rest area I can see Poke-O-Moonshine Mountain in the near distance — we're actually just a mile or two away from where whoever it was turned off their headlights and chased us through the dark.

I want to tell Trooper Gorski about it. And I'll include seeing a similar vehicle the next afternoon outside the grocery store. But right now all of my attention is focused ahead as we go around the signs that announce REST AREA: CLOSED.

Weeds sprout through cracks in the asphalt. The bathrooms and welcome-center building is overgrown with ivy and peppered with mold. At the far end of the parking area, the image of John's abandoned Subaru feels suffocating.

Emotions roil to the surface as I struggle to breathe. When Gorski parks some fifty yards away, I haul myself out of the back of her cruiser. Gorski is there a moment later holding me up when I cover a sob with my hand and slump back. My husband's car is sitting at a shut-down rest area just ten miles from our home. This can't be happening.

"It's okay," Gorski says. "It's going to be all right."

It's what someone says when everything is falling apart. It's what they say when nothing is going to be all right ever again and there's nothing they can do about it. And I'm what the police are wary of — an emotionally wrecked woman making a scene. I snuff back snot and tears and steel myself. Gorski keeps an arm around me but I'm walking on my own. Screw my back. I don't care if I'm in traction for a year. I need to be strong now.

Walking to the car feels surreal. My life belongs to someone else and I'm watching from a distance. An unoccupied car is a prosaic thing, but here it is a sinister and lonely sight. That's John's car, and he's not in it.

The thought begins to play on a loop. *That's John's car and he's not in it.*

That's John's car and he's not in it.

He's drinking. He needed to shake things up.

He's not who you thought he was.

He's somewhere else, bleeding or dead, and your children have lost their father and you have lost your life partner.

That's John's car and he's not in it.

I always knew I was probably going to outlive him and have to spend a certain amount of time on my own, but not now. This is too soon. This is not right. This is—

A white van comes rolling past, startling me as it drives over the stalks of witch hobble blowing in the cool breeze.

"That's the crime scene unit," Gorski explains. "They're going to have a look at everything." She slows me down and her grip tightens. She's not going to let me touch the car or look inside.

"Everything is happening so fast," I say. "The trooper found it so soon after you made your call . . ."

"Actually a trooper working the previous shift already reported seeing it around 2 a.m. last night."

"Two o'clock in the morning?"

"That's right."

I think back to the interminable night before, my mind unable to shut off. Why had Melody thought I was mad at John? Her words from this morning ring in my ears: *Well, what did you expect?*

Am I missing something? Aside from the occasional tension between John and me over her upbringing, and whether or not Melody thinks I pushed John into meeting with Bruce and Rainey, is there something else? Why do I feel like there is and I just can't see it?

It's true that over the years there's been tension over our daughter. John is less authoritative, aiming to keep the peace. In some ways that's brought them closer together and positioned me as the bad guy. But I'm no martyr; I know it's a situation of my own making. She's my baby and I'm both protective and firm. It was just the two of us those first years, and you can't unscramble an egg.

Morse is up on the uneven sidewalk in front of the Subaru talking to another trooper, the one I presume was running radar in the area and responded to the BOLO. But I want to see the blood inside. I'll know if it's John's. I don't know how I'll know, but I'll know.

Gorski keeps a firm hold on me.

"Let me look."

"Okay. Just . . . easy."

I'm ten yards from the Subaru. Five. I can see in the windows. The unknown trooper points to something. Morse nods. They both look at me as Gorski stops me from getting any closer. I'm just a yard away, reaching my hand forward. We got the deluxe model of the Subaru when we bought it, which included beige leather interior.

"I don't see any . . ."

Gorski points — just a drop on the steering wheel, as if John drove the car with a cut hand or maybe a bloody nose. There's a bit more on the seat. It's an automatic transmission and there's blood on the shifter, a single smear no bigger than an inch. At least there's not much of it. At least there's that.

I see a notepad on the passenger seat, something written on the page facing up. I lean toward it, and I must still be reaching out unconsciously because Gorski grabs my wrist, eases me back.

Two people get out of the white van with *Forensic Services Unit* written on the side. A trooper greets them and they talk in low tones. Eyes dart in my direction. Morse drifts closer. "Mrs. Gable, is this your husband's car?"

"Yes."

CHAPTER THIRTEEN / BIG QUESTIONS

I blink away an image — Selma, holding up her arm, knobby finger unfurled toward me, accusing. *He loves you.*

It makes me think of Marcus Gainsborough, my ex.

I shrug Trooper Gorski's grip and check the abandoned vehicle's license plates. I never committed the numbers and letters to memory — who does? Maybe John, but not me. I couldn't tell you the plates on my Toyota either. But the numbers and letters seem wrong, just the same. A bright spark of hope ignites somewhere inside me. "Wait . . . maybe this *isn't* his car. Are we sure?"

"We're sure," Gorski says. "The vehicle identification number is a match. It's registered in your husband's name."

Of course it is — that's how she knew it was John's before they brought me out here. Morse looks at me with sad eyes, then turns his head. Another police car is coming into the rest area with an unmarked car following. Gorski takes my arm again and says, "Will you come have a word with us, Jane?"

The urge to look through the Subaru is almost overpowering. I want to read what's on that notepad and check through the glove box and under the seats and everywhere else. But the technicians are closing in. They'll do all that. I just need to be patient.

Deep breath. "Sure," I tell Gorski. "Where? Do I go to the police station now? Does anybody know anything yet?"

"Just come this way."

She helps me back towards her car, but at this point I'm doing fine on my own. All the walking around seems to be working out some of the kinks — imagine that. Morse moves away from us and meets with the newcomers. The trooper just arrived has black and gray chevrons on his sleeves. The person in the unmarked car hasn't gotten out yet. I can't quite see his or her face. Gorski is touching my head, pushing me into the backseat.

After we get situated, the passenger door opens and the trooper with the chevrons gets in.

"Hi, Mrs. Gable. I'm Sergeant Ferron. How are you doing? I understand you hurt your back?"

"I'm all right."

"Well," Ferron says, "this has been quite a morning for you, I'm sure."

Maybe I'll wake up and this will all have been a bad dream.

"We're going to look at a few different possibilities," Ferron says. "We'll search this area here, but right now it's looking like he might've gotten into another vehicle and left. Any idea who that vehicle might belong to?"

It's time. I tell Sergeant Ferron and Trooper Gorski about the SUV: how it followed from a distance, then sped up and rode our rear bumper; how the driver killed the headlights.

"Any chance you got the license plate?" Ferron asks.

"No. I wish I had. And I saw the vehicle again."

"You saw it again?"

"I think so. It was dark when it was following us, but the next day I was grocery shopping and I saw it on the road. Right in town. First it slowed a little, then it sped off."

"Did you observe the make?" Ferron isn't writing anything down, just looking in the mirror at me.

"I'm not good at knowing these things . . . Maybe a Chevy Tahoe? Or a GMC-something? I really don't know."

"Was it full-sized, or was it one of those compact SUVs? Like your car — a Toyota RAV is what we'd call a compact SUV."

"I know what a compact SUV is." The words are out before I have a chance to censor myself.

Ferron's eyebrows go up. "Okay, ma'am."

"I'm sorry — I'm so sorry. No, it was full-sized. Dark blue or black. And I think there was a brownish stripe down the side of it."

"From when you saw it on Saturday? Or on Sunday?"

"On Saturday. When I saw it from the grocery store parking lot."

"Okay," Ferron says. "Anything else that you want to talk about? Trooper Gorski tells me you and your husband recently had a former high school classmate over for dinner."

I go through it all again. I'm beginning to feel like an actor reciting lines.

Ferron says, "And you spoke to this . . . um . . . Barnes, who claims he has no idea where your husband might be and that they had made no plans to get together or anything like that."

"That's correct. Well . . . yes, that's correct."

Ferron shifts in his seat. He's a large man, I guess about fifty, a bit of hair growing out of his nose and ears. "Ma'am? At this point it's best to be as open about everything as you can be."

"I'm trying to be. I'm really trying to be. My husband's been having some issues with work."

"And what does he do exactly? Gorski said he writes – is he a reporter or something?"

"No. He went to school at Rensselaer Polytechnic but dropped out, just wanted to write fiction. He had a few books do well, and then one did really well and he got an agent. I spoke to his agent this morning and I guess he's been struggling. I think he talked to Bruce about it. Bruce said something like he needed to stir things up."

"Stir things up?"

"I don't know. Get out of the normal routine."

"Like take a trip?"

"Sergeant, I know how this looks . . . there's my husband's car — obviously he went somewhere. Or he started to go somewhere . . ." I have to pause, choke back the tears. "But I don't think that's what this is. I don't think John would just take off and not tell me. Not because of a friend, or even another woman. Something is wrong. Something is *very* wrong. There's blood in that car. John would never just leave me and the kids. No matter what."

Silence follows and I can hear Ferron breathing as I watch the people in white jumpsuits swarm the Subaru.

"Mrs. Gable, we're going to need you to provide some blood and DNA samples. Is that okay with you?"

"Yes. Anything."

"As we process the vehicle we're going to need to know which samples we collect might belong to you, and which might be your husband's."

"I understand."

"The last time you were in the car — in the Subaru — was that Friday night?"

I have to think about it for a second. "That's right."

"You had no occasion to be in the car since then."

"No. No reason to."

"So we'll have you come in and it will be a quick procedure, just a pin prick for the blood and we'll swab the inside of your mouth for DNA. It's called a buccal swab. That's okay with you?"

"Of course."

"Mrs. Gable, there is one other thing I need to ask you."

"Okay . . ."

Ferron turns to look at me directly. "Your mother is in jail?"

111

I swallow over the lump in my throat. But I had to expect this eventually. "Yes. She's in the women's wing at SCI Cold Brook."

"She's there for attempted murder."

It sounds horrible whenever someone says it aloud, conjuring the picture of a hardened criminal. "Second-degree, yes. Her lawyer tried to prove self-defense but he wasn't very good."

"When's the last time you saw your mother?"

"Not since the sentencing. So, a few years."

"You don't visit?"

"She doesn't want me to visit." *How is this relevant?* I want to ask.

Ferron lifts a hand, sensing my agitation. "I'm just trying to get the full picture here. This is what's going to happen — you're going to have an investigator assigned to this. Her name is Muriel Ridley. Trooper Gorski is going to—"

"Is she just a regular detective or—"

"She's from the Violent Crime investigation team. That's a unit with the state police."

"What about the Missing Persons Clearinghouse?"

Ferron studies my reflection for a moment. "You're a nurse?"

"Nurse practitioner, yes."

"The clearinghouse typically works with law enforcement on cases involving children and those involving vulnerable adults."

"My husband could be vulnerable."

He clears his throat. "Trooper Gorski is going to bring you to the barracks where you'll fill out the official missing person's report together, which will get the information to the clearing house, and we'll keep a hotline open for case intake and leads, okay? And then we'll draw your blood and tissue samples."

"Thank you."

Ferron keeps looking at me with his somber gray eyes. "Mrs. Gable, we'll do everything we can. As a nurse — ah, nurse practitioner — maybe you're aware that unless a person is elderly or under the age of thirteen, or suffers from a mental or physical condition, they're not designated as 'special category.'"

"I have patients with Alzheimer's and dementia and occasionally they leave their homes unattended. John may not be elderly or have a precondition but he's an alcoholic and he could be the victim of a crime. Could that make it special category?"

Ferron and Gorski exchange looks. Gorski turns toward me and says, "That's what we're trying to determine." Her gaze lowers to my hands.

It takes me a moment, but I turn my hands over, look at the cuts from falling on the front walkway, then think of the blood on the steering wheel of the car.

"What I'm saying," Ferron continues, "is that people over the age of eighteen, legally speaking, do not have to return home."

"My husband did not *leave* me!" I have to fight against sudden tears of angst and fear as I point through the window. "There is blood in the car!"

"I understand."

"I was at *work*. I fell this morning. After my husband — and the car — were already gone."

"Mrs. Gable, I think you're misconstruing what I'm saying. In an instance like this, when there are lots of emotions, it's hard for us to trust everything we think. We can get confused."

"What do you mean, confused? Why would you think I'm confused?"

There's something they're not telling me. Some piece I'm unaware of, and it's making me look unreliable, or worse — like I'm hiding something. Am I? I didn't say anything about my mother's incarceration because I didn't think it had anything to do with what's happened — not remotely. What else could I be missing?

"If you're not confused," Ferron says slowly, "maybe you could tell us why this person — Bruce Barnes — why we can't find any record of him. Why he doesn't seem to exist."

CHAPTER FOURTEEN / FUGUE STATE

I'm staring at bits of breakfast cereal on the table, the way they cast long shadows in the afternoon sunlight coming through the windows. *Small things . . . big shadows.*

He's not someone I just imagined.

No, Bruce was at this house, at this very table, eating a dinner I prepared, laughing with bits of food showing in his mouth. He was at the grocery store before that — people saw him. My *children* saw him. He's real and flesh and blood. Just maybe not who he says he is.

I'm not who I think I am. So said Selma Ford. And John's not who I think he is either.

I shake it off. The lack of sleep is getting to me and the past four hours have been a blur. In the first hour, I sat in the back of Trooper Gorski's cruiser and phoned Bruce to prove I wasn't confused or lying. Bruce's voice mail picked up: "*Hey it's me . . .*"

At least there was a working number and a man's recorded voice. After listening, Sergeant Ferron studied the screen and said simply, "We'll look into it."

I've memorized Bruce's outgoing message now, because I just keep hitting redial, thinking about the way Ferron was eyeing me. Picturing my husband's car at the overgrown end of a neglected rest area. Remembering those cracks in the asphalt, bunches of wildflowers poking through the fissures, the Subaru just sitting there, blood on the steering wheel, people in white suits circling like it might be fitted with explosives.

I managed to get through the buccal swab, blood draw and missing person's report at the state trooper barracks and return in time for Russ to get dropped off from school. Bounding away from the big yellow bus with his characteristic zeal, backpack manhandling him as it jounced side to side, all my worries and fears melted away for a precious few minutes. "Mom! I didn't go into the girls' bathroom today."

"Good for you, baby." And I kissed him on his forehead.

Karen has left to tend to her own children, but she promised to call me later, to come back if I need her. For someone who's barely registered as a friend, she's been a wonderful support. She doesn't eye me with suspicion the way Ferron or Gorski do, like I'm keeping secrets or losing my mind. My children are alive and well and I have the support of a local friend — these are good things.

I did notice a few looks from people about town as Morse drove me home from the barracks. People are undoubtedly starting to talk. There's no preventing that and I guess I don't care. At least, I shouldn't. My mother didn't raise me to worry about the opinions of others. *What other people think of you is none of your business,* she once said.

Ah, my mother.

It's one of those things you hear about: how when a person has an unstable upbringing they tend to become controlling adults. Growing up with Mom was pretty unstable due to a revolving door of subhuman boyfriends, drug abuse, and plenty of paranoid delusional thinking. I don't think I'm overly controlling as a result, but then I'd probably be the last person to know.

Melody is out of her room and her mood has improved. Teenaged moods come and go like the weather, and right now it's sunny and warm. She cooks pasta in the kitchen as I set the phone aside and open my laptop. I need to find evidence of Bruce Barnes and his wife or girlfriend Rainey before shoving my children in front of the cops to corroborate me. But I arrive at the same dead ends. It occurs to me that I've never seen the name Rainey spelled out. A Google search turns up several variations — Rainy, Raini, Rany, and more. The name could be short for something. Google says Regina, Katharina and various versions of Lorraine. I try them all on Facebook before giving up. Maybe John has it written down somewhere — like on that notebook in his car the police haven't shared with me yet.

And why haven't they?

Because I'm a suspect. Or at least what they call a "person of interest." No one's come right out and said it directly, but I can see it in their eyes. My mother is in jail for nearly killing a man. That he was abusive to her doesn't matter; for all the cops know, John was abusive to me, too. I have the same blood running in my veins; I've learned from the best. I must be a woman with reason to harm her husband.

Anyway, if John had more information about Bruce and Rainey in that notebook the police would have told me. They wouldn't have acted like my marbles were falling out.

I feel hollow. Russ doesn't even know his father is missing yet. Melody knows — just not about the car or the blood or the question of Bruce's existence. The dilemma to open up to her or keep her shielded forms knots in my shoulders and burns through my every breath. I don't know if I can handle her questions, her anxiety. This has been something I've tried to avoid all my life — instability in the household. Instead, a safe, familiar environment: routine, normalcy, a place for my daughter to thrive and become a well-adjusted adult.

When I first met John I didn't waste any time telling him about my little girl; I introduced them on our second date. Two men had already faded away after learning I was a single mom, so it became the obvious litmus test.

They warmed to each other quickly. He was a natural, like he'd been around small children all his life. He was funny and self-deprecating, a perfect balance of goofy and capable. He made faces and silly voices without infantilizing, and in the first week we were together he caught her in his arms before she could hit the ground after toppling over her chair.

Ladies and gentlemen — we have a winner.

Adoption happened when she was three; John formally became her father. In every sense but one, she is his daughter. I used to think a biological connection was the most important of all, but experience has proven otherwise — and Melody has had zero contact with her biological father. Now she's doing exactly what I used to do — cooking and cleaning like she can keep things on an even keel this way amid swelling uncertainty. I hurt for her, but I still can't say anything. Not yet. I need to know more. I need that stable ground beneath my feet.

A car engine gurgles into the driveway and I leave the table to peek through the window at the same unmarked car from the rest area. State Police Detective Ridley is blonde and pretty and about my age, thirty-five, wearing a gray pantsuit. We met briefly at the barracks; an introduction only, a prelude to now.

It's ridiculous to wish it was a man assigned to my case, but I do. I hate having a woman think my husband left me or judge my mother — or judge me, a daughter who at first followed in her mother's footsteps through reckless relationships and temperamental men. Until I met John — who now seems to have bolted at last.

It just took him a lot longer than most.

Stop. Pull it together.

I offer Ridley a smile and invite her in. "Can I get you anything?" We walk toward the open area that's our combined kitchen and dining room and I can't help but notice the badge and gun on her hip.

"No, thank you, I'm fine."

"This is my daughter, Melody. She's making some dinner for her and her brother, Russ."

"Hi, Melody."

Melody has changed her outfit and pulled her hair back and looks mature and pretty as she flashes a smile at the detective. "Hello. Mom, I'll just finish this up and take it into Russ's room. We'll watch some TV and eat."

"Thank you, honey."

"Good to have such a helper," Ridley says.

I'm eyeing the things Ridley's holding, including what looks like a yearbook from John's high school.

She says, "Let's sit down."

"Great."

We make small talk for another minute and Ridley compliments my home. Once Melody has plated up the penne and pasta sauce and walked out of the room with another pleasant smile and a knowing in her eyes that drills into my chest, Ridley sets out a small tape recorder.

"I'm just going to put this here. That way if I need to refer back to anything, I don't need to bother you. Are you all right with that?"

"Yes."

She clicks it on. "Monday, March twenty-fifth, 6:14 p.m., I'm here in Hazleton, New York, with Jane Gable. It's been approximately thirty-one hours since she last saw her husband, John Gable." She faces me. "When do your children say they last saw their father?"

"Bedtime. John put Russ to bed at eight o'clock. That's his usual time. Melody went into her room to read about half an hour later."

"And Melody — I'll speak to her too, if that's okay — but, from your understanding, Melody didn't hear your husband leave after she went into her room?"

"She had her headphones on, listening to music."

"She listens to music as she reads?"

"Sometimes."

"Did she come out of her room at some point to use the bathroom?"

"Yes. She says she came out around 9:15. The bathroom is right next to her room. She says she assumed John was in his study. The door was closed."

"And you found the door closed when you returned home from work . . ." Ridley consults her notes. "Which was just after midnight."

"Correct."

"So your husband could have been home when Melody used the bathroom."

"He could have."

"And after that, after she used the bathroom, she went right back into her room."

"That's what she says."

"Continued listening to music, maybe, while she read."

"Yes. I think so."

"So there's a two-hour gap between when a state trooper first saw your husband's car at the rest area and when you say you got home to discover him gone, at midnight. Was it right at midnight, or a little after?"

I take a sip of water. "My shift ends at midnight. It takes me maybe two or three minutes to get here from the hospital."

"So you came right home."

"Yes."

She writes something down then our eyes connect again. "And your son, Russ? He says he saw lights outside?"

"No. Melody says she might've seen headlights. The way they shine through the window."

"But your daughter's bedroom is not—"

"I guess she means in the living room."

"So her door was open?" Ridley reads something in my face and looks down. "I'll speak to her."

"It was Russ who said he saw his father talking to someone. His room is the one at the front of the house — he can see the porch; you know, the stoop."

"And he talked about a blonde woman."

"Yes. But he's not sure when."

"Okay, so Russ talks about the blonde woman he saw at some point. Melody saw the lights. Was she more specific about the time?"

"She just said it was late when she saw the lights. Definitely after Russ went to bed, so, after eight o'clock."

"Through the open door of her bedroom. In the living-room windows." Ridley's gaze holds on me before she looks at the legal pad and jots something else down. "All right. So what we're going to say, tentatively, is that your husband left the house sometime between 8:30 and midnight. That gives us a range of two to five or so hours that he could have been out, doing whatever he was doing, before depositing the car at the rest area."

"Have you learned anything from the car?" I've already been over all of these details with Trooper Gorski and I'm anxious to get to new information. Plus I don't like how Ridley is subtly insinuating that my statements aren't enough for her to go on. Her timeline is *tentative*, apparently.

"Just a minute on the car — we'll get to that. You've said John has a few friends, other than this person who you know as Bruce Barnes, but they're far-flung. Have you contacted any of them at this point, just to be sure?"

I take a breath and let it out slowly. "I have contacted John's friends, yes. He's not with any of them and he hasn't called them or anything. Not recently anyway. Have you found Bruce yet?"

She puts on a smile that's clearly meant to placate. "I know this has been trying and today has been a very long day. You rightfully want some answers. But I need to go through things in a certain order. All right? So nothing John said to any of them — the last time they *did* have occasion to speak, or correspond — would indicate plans to leave or anything like that?"

"I texted with two of them and reached out on Facebook to the third. It was hard to know what to say. But no, none of them had any plans with John. Nothing. That's why I'm

120

asking about Bruce. He's the person John *did* talk to recently, and they talked about, I don't know, something about John trying something new in his life. He's been in a work slump. A creative rut, I guess."

I know what she's thinking: that maybe this all has to do with some artistic whimsy gone awry.

It's not something I've discounted entirely, either.

"What about the lake house?" I ask.

"The place on Henderson Harbor?"

"Yes."

She nods, slowly. "We've had a trooper check it out. Everything is closed and locked. No one there." Her dark, smallish eyes fix on mine again. "And you told the state troopers that John wouldn't be with his relatives? They said you seemed fairly certain, but didn't elaborate."

I take another breath. "John's mother passed away two years ago. He doesn't keep in touch with his father and stepmother. We went out there . . . um, last year for a visit. John hasn't wanted to go back since then."

Ridley lifts a notebook sheet with her finger. "I understand John's father is Frank Gable. After his wife Katherine died — John's mother — he remarried and has since retired to Arizona." She looks up at me. "How about you — have you spoken to Frank?"

"I haven't."

She lets the paper drop and stares at me. "I have his number," she says with a flat quality. "I'll be in touch with him."

"I'm sorry. I'm not trying to be difficult. But I just know John is not with him. And if he was, Frank would have called me and let me know. We get along. John still blames Frank for how things went with Katherine. Her sickness, her passing. They didn't have much, and there was no health insurance. And when Frank remarried so quickly, John was . . . well, it's been difficult for him."

Ridley folds her hands on the table. "And what about your family?"

Here it comes.

"I have a half-brother and half-sister. My half-brother is overseas and my sister is in Iowa. I also have a stepbrother, but we're not in touch since my mother divorced his father. He's the son of the man she . . . We're not in touch. He lives in Troy, as far as I know. Yes, my mother has had problems. Both John and I came from . . . you know, I guess we came from troubled homes. And that's part of our bond."

Ridley absorbs all of this and then moves to the next topic with a bob of her head. "Okay. So, the car is going to take some time. Blood type will be quicker — later today or maybe tomorrow — but DNA can take a long time. You said in your statement that you can't think of anyone else who John has had in his car in at least several weeks. Just you, your two children and John."

"Correct."

"So once we eliminate the four of you, any additional DNA could point to a fifth person, someone else who's been in the car. But of course we'll need those elimination samples from your children. I might ask your stepbrother as well. Since you're not sure where he lives."

Her eyes acquire a smugness, like she's just caught me in something.

"Whatever you think," I say. The idea that my stepbrother could have something to do with this has entered my mind once or twice, revenge for my mother nearly killing his father. But that's too far out there for me to get a real grip on it as a possibility and Leland is too lazy anyway. And too inept from what I remember of him.

"Can we talk about your mother's case a little bit?"

"My mother took a plea deal," I say. "Self-defense was too hard to prove because she'd never gotten a medical report or called the police about the abuse. Not to mention that he has money, and I think there were threats of a civil suit if she proceeded with a trial."

Ridley frowns and shakes her head. "That's not right." She scribbles more notes in her pad.

"I'm not my mother."

Her eyes snap up and grab me. "I don't think I said you were."

"My mother grew up in a rough area. She learned to take care of herself. People then were taught and expected to deal with their own problems."

Like, you know, shoot them point-blank in the chest.

Ridley is watching me closely. Then she sets out the yearbook and slides it into the space between us. Lake Haven High School, 1995. My stomach has butterflies.

"Okay. Now we get to the Bruce thing." Ridley opens the yearbook to a page marked with a small pink sticky note and points to the picture of a young male amidst similar other photos of students. "This is Bruce Gramone. Is this the man who had dinner here with you and your husband?"

I only need to glance at it for a moment. "No. That's not him. Not even close."

"You're sure this man's last name was Barnes."

"That's what he said when he showed up at my door."

Ridley closes the yearbook. "There is only one other Bruce that went to Lake Haven High School, but it's a Bruce Stratford."

"He's not in there?" I fight an urge to start flipping yearbook pages.

"He might have missed school on picture day. But I have this . . ." She pulls a file folder out of her bag. I'm looking at redacted documents — police records or something with sections blacked out. She flips to a picture.

"That's him!" I tap the picture rapidly. "That's Bruce . . . *Stratford?* He said his name was Barnes. I'm sure he said that. When he first showed up."

Ridley calmly slides that photo aside, revealing another beneath. "This is Lorraine Barnes."

I stare down at it. The face is definitely Rainey's. The confusion takes just a second to sort out. "Wait . . . he took her name?"

"Here is a document showing that Bruce Stratford legally changed his name to Bruce Barnes less than two months ago — about a year after the signing of their marriage certificate. That's why Sergeant Ferron and Trooper Gorski couldn't find him in the system. Sometimes things are a little slow to filter through and some records with the Department of Public Safety, things like Social Security, don't always update right away."

"Okay . . ." I lean back, momentarily relieved. I remember the way Ferron and Gorski looked at me, like I had some sort of early-onset dementia. I replay the Saturday morning when Bruce came to the door: he introduced himself to me, but did he ever repeat his last name in front of John? It never came up. There would have been a discussion about it. My husband was likely still thinking of his old classmate as Bruce Stratford.

Or if it did come up and John didn't react, then he already knew.

"What about their security company?" I ask. "Does it say anything in the file about their security company?"

Ridley nods, picking through the papers. "It does. I have a business license from Florida . . . Night Watch LLC. It appears that Bruce Barnes — then Bruce Stratford — and Lorraine Barnes ran this company for a little over two years. They didn't have many contracts, just one overnight parking facility in Jacksonville, and Bruce worked at a bank for a while. There are a few others . . ." She's shuffling papers.

"And that he got shot?"

"There's a record of that, too. One of their contracts was for a company called Mango. They're a big restaurant supplier, lots of shipments coming up from South America, and Bruce was a security guard at one of the ports in Jacksonville. Apparently someone attempted to rob one of the shipments and Bruce tried to prevent it. There was an exchange of gunfire and he was shot through the abdomen."

So some of what Bruce has told me is true. I'm not sure if knowing what happened to him is a relief or not. "They said — when we had them over to dinner — that Rainey was sick."

Ridley's brow wrinkles and she shifts through some more papers. "I haven't found anything of that nature. Did she say what the sickness was?"

"No."

"Oh. I thought, with you having a medical background, you might have asked her."

There's an accusation there, another hint that the police think I'm unreliable.

"I respected their privacy. If they'd wanted to, they would have mentioned it."

"Well I'll have a look," Ridley says.

"They were both . . . they were strange."

"How so?"

I talk a little about how both John and I joked that we expected a donations cup to come around the dinner table, or that they were going to invite us into their pyramid scheme. How they stared into each other's eyes like Romeo and Juliet. The talking distracts me from the dread that's settling on my shoulders. I'm one step away from climbing into bed and not getting out. Falling into darkness and despair. But I can't. I have the kids. John needs my help.

"So here's what's going to happen." Ridley is putting the yearbook and the files back into her bag. "We're going to find Bruce and have a talk with him. It all sounds pretty bizarre to me."

"Okay."

"And we're continuing the search around the rest stop on I-87 where your husband's car was found. So far there are no signs of anyone — no blood, no trail. At this point it looks like he didn't just leave the car and go into the woods. But we're still looking. You've told us what you thought your husband was likely wearing. Have you gone through the shoes to get any idea of which ones he most likely had on?"

"I did. Everything is there except for his hiking boots."

"Are those waffle iron or honeycomb? The treads. What kind of pattern?"

"I don't know, I'm sorry — they're pretty old, though. They might be worn down."

"But you think they're hiking shoes."

"I think they're hiking shoes but that doesn't mean I think John went hiking." I'm walking a tightrope: on one side is the possibility of John being the victim of a crime; on the other is the possibility that it's all his own fault, that while drinking, searching for inspiration, something went wrong. I don't want to help the police to paint that picture, if only because it might distract or demotivate them.

I imagine laying my head on John's shoulder, the smell of aftershave on his neck, the warmth of his body, his green eyes staring into mine. I miss him — happy or grumpy, fat or bald. Throughout this whole ordeal I keep expecting him to be there, to turn to him, to share in this experience with me. It's like half of me has been cleaved away.

Ridley hands me a tissue. I didn't even realize I was crying. I'm not a big crier but since last night, I'm waterworks.

"We'll find him," Ridley says.

"Do you think he just . . . I don't know, what *do* you think?"

"Does John ever use anything else — or did he — besides alcohol, I mean?"

"No."

"No? Never a joint, nothing like that? Nothing harder?"

"Pot. Maybe once in a blue moon."

"Uh-huh. Well, as part of this . . . this idea to shake things up, as you put it, maybe he had an occasion. Because here's one theory: Your husband has some people come over to the house. Maybe they were pot dealers. Maybe something else. I know this is tough to hear, but this is the thing . . . We know that sometimes people can have quite severe reactions to combinations of alcohol and drugs. I know a lot of people today think marijuana is harmless, but especially if your husband hadn't been drinking for a long time, his tolerance would be very low. He might *think* he can handle a lot. We know that it can really affect decisions."

I consider these ideas, but it's still hard to wrap my mind around. "That wouldn't explain why his car was found where it was."

"If he's trying to get inspiration, he could be revisiting the area where you and he had the encounter with the SUV."

Why haven't I thought of this? In fact, I bet his little notebook contains thoughts on a potential story about it. I'm about to ask Ridley but she's still unspooling her theory.

"So your husband is there — I'm confident the blood and fingerprints will confirm it — but then something happens. Perhaps he's outside the vehicle and falls — similar to your fall — and he scrapes himself up. He gets back in the car to drive home, but the fall could have affected him cognitively."

"Was the car working? The engine? Did you test it?"

"One of the first things they did. Yes. Half a tank of gas. The engine turned right over. Everything in working condition."

"Wait . . . how did you test it? Did he leave the keys?"

"That's right. The keys were on the floorboard in front of the driver's seat."

"John usually tucks them up under the sun visor. I mean when it's in the driveway. He's lived up here most of his life and people don't always lock their cars. I lock mine. Force of habit."

"Right. Little things, little behaviors, are not the same. These abnormalities might suggest an addled state. Confused, your husband leaves the car behind. Then he flags someone down, hitches a ride. Either he doesn't know the way back home, or maybe he forgets. I've seen it happen. It's called a fugue state. You're probably familiar, as a nurse practitioner."

I nod, thinking, *or maybe he's running from someone and has to abandon the Subaru for his safety.*

"We're expanding the search, but it's tough. We're looking at a very wide search area. An area that's really impossible to cover." She has just articulated my concerns. "If he got in another vehicle right away, he could be halfway across the country by now. We just don't know." She reaches out and pats my hand. "But I think this is going to turn out all right."

The way she keeps spinning things positive makes me skeptical. I've never been part of an investigation, but offering hope to victims, or families of victims — is that the usual protocol? Why am I doubting everything and everybody involved? John would say I'm over-analytical. "Why do you think it's going to be all right?"

I can tell it's hard for her to say the next thing. "Because, Mrs. Gable, it's still possible that John has simply left. That he's not suffering any cognitive impairment — aside from perhaps the influence of drinking or whatever else. That he left the vehicle, left his phone and wallet behind because he doesn't want to be found."

"No."

She looks away. When our eyes connect again I can feel the rigidity in my spine. It's either disbelief or denial. I can't tell yet.

"There's one last thing we need to think about," Ridley says. "We need to think about how public we want to take this."

"How public?"

"Well, in situations like this, where it's not clear what the intentions of the missing are . . . You have a reputation here in this community. Your children go to school. You need to ask yourself what you want the world to know."

"How can we do everything to find him if we're not being public with it?"

"That's your call. We're going to work with the clearinghouse and John's picture and information will be out on the state police missing person's Facebook page. But there is some latitude — we can have a press conference right away or we can wait a little bit and see . . ."

She's asking me if I want the world to think my husband is a drunk who left his family. If I want to suffer, publicly, the embarrassment of a wayward husband chasing the muse in a sleazy hotel and passed out in puke. Or worse . . . dead.

"It's just . . . it could put a lot of pressure on you," Ridley says.

Maybe it's a test to assess my potential guilt. What do they say? The guilty fall asleep their first night in jail. How do they feel about press conferences? But over the time she's been in my house I don't get the sense Ridley is either on my side or convinced I've had a hand in John's disappearance. She feels neutral, unattached to the outcome so long as there *is* an outcome that allows her to close the book and move on.

"Let me think about it," I say.

She gets up from the table and puts her bag over her shoulder. She asks me to show her to the kids' rooms.

"Okay. But, you know . . . I haven't told them yet."

Ridley looks down for a moment then nods. "No, I understand that. I'll be discreet. I just want to ask about the things they saw."

Some small part of me thinks *do they need lawyers?* But that's just more protectiveness. My children have nothing to hide. Only, when Ridley asks for privacy and closes the door after introducing herself to Melody, I can't help but hover outside the room hoping to eavesdrop. *Are you mad, Mom? What else did you expect, Mom?*

It's just nerves.

Ridley takes ten minutes with Melody, about ten more with Russ. When she leaves Russ's room she starts straight for the front door. "I'll be in touch with updates. In the meantime, sit tight. You think of anything, you have my number. Call me anytime. Day or night."

"Everything go okay?"

She holds the door and gives me a look. "You have very lovely children. Very polite."

"Did they say anything that . . . Did it help?"

"I'm taking everything into account."

I catch her before she leaves. "Is it okay to go into my husband's study now? The troopers said I should stay out of there. But nobody has come through yet. No special forensic people, like with the car."

"I don't think that will be necessary. Trooper Morse . . . well let's just say he wants to level up, work as an investigator. You should feel free to have a look. You find anything, you let me know, okay?"

My paranoia acts up again — Ridley wants to see what I'll do. She's not telling me what the kids said and she wants to see how I'll behave in the next few hours, whether I've got some evidence to hide.

She offers a soft smile and goes out of the door. The dusk is settling as I watch her walk to the car, and we're expected to get a late spring snow shower tonight — I remember hearing that on the news some time during this long, insane day.

With Ridley driving away, I sit down at the table alone. One by one, the kids wander out of their rooms. Melody dumps her pasta bowl in the sink and sits down in the same seat Ridley was just occupying. I find it hard to look at her. "Everything go okay?"

"With the policewoman?"

I nod.

"Yeah. She was very nice."

"Yes she was," Russ pipes up as he walks in. "But I don't get why she was even here."

Stuck for a moment in indecision, I give Melody a meaningful look and get up from the table. "Let's get you some juice, honey," I say to him.

Melody must hear the tremble in my voice. Before I know it, she's up and has wrapped her arms around me, Russ joining her a moment later. I fight back tears. I want to ask them more about Ridley, what was discussed, but I'm either too tired or too scared. Russ's words are muffled against my arm.

"Hey, Mom? When's Dad coming home?"

CHAPTER FIFTEEN / LIES AND MISDEMEANORS

After taking a long hot shower I spend some time with the kids. I haven't decided what to tell Melody but I've got a plan for how to broach the subject with Russ.

I'm going to lie. Again.

"Dad left to go to a writer's conference. Do you know what that is?"

"No . . ."

A story that John has left town for a few days buys me a little time, and I'll get Melody to go along with it. Russ seems slightly confused that his father never said goodbye, but it's better than worrying him over the truth. We read three books and his eyelids are dropping.

Afterward, I sit beside the lump of covers in Melody's bed. I know she's not asleep but she won't look at me.

"Mel, honey. Can we talk?"

"It's fine."

I lean over her and stroke her hair. "Thank you for making dinner."

"I'm just trying to help."

"I know, honey, and I appreciate it. But everything's going to be okay. And you don't have to worry about keeping it together. Not for me, not for anyone."

She continues to show me her back. "Somebody's got to do it."

"No, that's my job. I'll keep us together. But I'm sorry this is all happening right now, right around your special time."

"It's not special." The resignation in her voice pierces my heart.

"Of course it's special, baby. And so are you. You are the best daugh—"

"Mom. Stop it."

"I'm just . . . I'm telling you that—"

"Please stop. Just don't. Don't try to do anything else."

It sparks me a little. "What did I do? I'm dealing with this thing the best I can. *I'm* not the one who's not home." I regret it the second it slips out.

"See?" She sits up in bed and stares at me in the dim lighting. "You *are* mad. You think it's all his fault."

I take her hand. "Honey, I don't mean it's his fault. We don't know what's happened. I'm just saying I'm trying to keep our family together and things are hard right now. I'm sorry."

"You don't even know why he's gone. You don't even understand." The last word dies wet in her throat, her eyes growing red.

"What do you mean? I'm trying to—"

"You're in your own world. And then you guys are fighting and you're angry at Dad . . ."

"Mel, what are you talking about? That we sometimes argue? Honey, all married couples argue — about their kids, about money, whatever. It's natural. And your father and I get along really well."

But she yanks her hand from me and buries herself in the covers. All that's visible is her honey-colored hair fanned out over the pillow.

An idea is forming in the back of my mind that I'm afraid to allow full shape. But when Melody continues to give me the silent treatment, it rounds out: maybe the best thing is to send Russ and Melody to John's dad. Put them on a plane to Arizona where they'll be far away from this — I won't have to keep lying to Russ and Melody won't be riding this roller coaster. She resents me for John's disappearance because there's no place else for her emotions to go.

And it might get worse. If John was intoxicated, maybe he hit his head and wandered off. The nights have been near or below freezing. If he's confused, in a fugue, managed to hitch a ride, there's no telling what could become of him without any ID or money or a phone. And the best case scenario? It's actually what Ridley suggested: that he left us. That, in a proper state of mind, he decided to go out for the proverbial pack of cigarettes and never returned.

I could ask his father and Delores to come and take over daily operations; that's another option. I can't accomplish much with the kids around. For one thing, I never followed up with RJ the bartender, and the police haven't said anything about him. That could mean they spoke to him and nothing came of it or they haven't yet. Ridley has her hands full. If I don't do something I'm going to lose my mind.

I have an address. I can drive over and talk to RJ early in the morning.

"Mom?"

"Yeah?"

"Do you think Dad committed suicide?"

I lean down and hug her and speak softly in her ear. "Absolutely not. Your father and I are happy."

I'm not depressed. I have joy in my life.

It's true — I know it is. Despite common struggles, we're blessed to get along and share a loving household. Something happened. I've got to stop turning it over in my mind. John didn't run from us. He didn't intentionally disappear like that.

Her voice is muffled by the bedding, plaintive. "Then what's happened?"

"I don't know, baby. But we'll find out."

I can smell the apple shampoo in her hair, feel the delicateness of her shoulders and bones. Sleep is going to be hard, if not impossible. There's so much to do. I'm going to have to contact the hospital and help reconfigure the schedule for the next week because I'm not going to be working.

"But what if it's because of what you said to him? How can you be sure?"

I feel the feet of something cold pound across my gut. "Honey, what do you think you heard me say to your father?"

"You said if . . . You said that if Dad didn't like what was happening, then he could just leave, that it probably would be for the best for him just to disappear."

"What? Melody I never said that." But my mind is searching, scanning.

"I heard you."

"When? When did you hear me?"

"The other night. At dinner."

"At dinner?"

"Yeah." Her voice is just a whisper.

"Melody, I don't know what you think you heard but I never said that to your father."

She huddles in deeper under the covers.

"Mel? You believe me right?"

But she won't respond.

* * *

At just before eleven o'clock, I'm standing in the door of John's study.

It's cooler in here because when it was remodeled it had its own heating system installed: baseboard electric that operates on a separate thermostat. I check the gauge on the wall, set for 65 degrees, but it feels colder than that, like the room is becoming a crypt.

John has one set of high shelves that holds mostly books, plus a row of DVDs and Blu-rays. We watch a variety of TV shows and movies together, usually my choice, but left to his own he likes his cop flicks and westerns.

Among his books are popular bestsellers from crime fiction authors, mostly hardcover, and there is a shelf of non-fiction: *Into the Kill Zone, Ghost, Making the Grade*. I know a lot of his research happens online, but occasionally he'll go somewhere, spend a few hours in a location he's writing about. Once, years ago in Troy, he did a ride-along with the local police.

Beside his laptop is a list of handwritten names. I recognize three of them as other popular authors: Paula Hawkins, Ernest Cline, Andy Weir.

His laptop is closed on the desk. Ridley said she's apt to go through it tomorrow. Like his phone, it's password protected. I lean forward and push around some of the other papers on his desk. None of it makes much sense and John's handwriting is messy — what little I can decipher is gibberish without context.

I ease away from the desk and stand up, mindful of my back. It's better, but I have to be careful.

The wall hosts several framed pictures including a black and white from our wedding. In it, the lake is behind us, the sun setting, and John holds me in his arms in a classic carry-the-bride-over-the-threshold pose. There's also a framed receipt from Juno's, the restaurant where we shared our first date. And another framed receipt of his first royalty payment, the humble sum of $900.

He loves you.

Selma's words have floated up from the depths of my mind.

We've been doing all right financially, haven't we? John handles most of the bills, but the last time I checked in, we still had plenty in savings. When was that, though? Maybe half a year ago, maybe longer. And according to Marty, *Edge of Night* didn't sell very well.

But I make a decent living as a nurse practitioner. Even if John's latest book underperformed, we should be okay.

But then there's our hefty mortgage, our massive student loans, insurance and monthly payments for two cars, taxes. Like a lot of people, our expenses have risen to meet our income: braces for Melody, remodeling the office, and John sunk quite a bit of dough into my mother's camp on Lake Ontario.

She could have sold the place when she needed money for her legal defense, but she didn't. Instead, she kept hold of it, and it's all still in her name. My half-brother and half-sister don't visit the place often enough to invest in it and Leland has no claim to it as the son of a man who violently abused her.

I glance beneath the long countertop desk. I've gone through everything in the room except the metal file cabinet wedged under the farthest end of the counter.

The first drawer sticks then opens with a slight squeal. I finger-walk through files containing the children's birth certificates, the deed on the house, Melody's adoption papers, and a file for our passports. I yank the passport file and go through it. My passport is there, but not John's. The hairs stiffen on the back of my neck.

The bottom drawer won't open. I squat down to get better leverage and give it a tug, muscles tightening in my back. No go. It's like the bottom drawer is still locked, even though the file cabinet has one mechanism for both drawers. The place for the key is in the upper right corner of the unit. It turns a rod or something that either holds the drawers shut or allows them to slide freely along their tracks.

There are bric-a-brac holders in the office: a coffee can with paperclips and a mini-flashlight; a small cigarillo tin atop the shelves with some screws and thumb tacks — but no file cabinet key. I feel along the edge of the cabinet in case one is taped against it. I shine the mini-flashlight between the back of the cabinet and the wall with no luck.

Fine. You want to play dirty? Let's play dirty.

John's got a small crowbar in the basement and I bring it back to the study. I'm trying to jam the sharp end behind the lip of the bottom drawer but I'm not having any luck, so I go back for a hammer and give the crowbar a couple of whacks on the curled end, but the sharp end just glances off.

I'm making a lot of noise but unable to break the connection: that metal rod in place that keeps the bottom drawer from sliding out. Winded, I sit back on the floor and brush hair out of my face. So how come the top drawer is free?

And then it's clear: a key was never used on the cabinet. The last time the top drawer was opened it was forced by someone much stronger than me.

CHAPTER SIXTEEN / BREAK-IN

Enough is enough. I can't sleep and it's a long way off before I can expect answers from Ridley.

A drill and a jigsaw should do it.

After scrounging around in John's toolbox for metal bits, I grab a coiled extension cord and take everything upstairs.

Melody is leaning against the wall outside her bedroom. "Mom, what are you doing?"

I'm still not sure I want to tell her, but I realize I can't do this alone, not with my back the way it is. "I need your help."

She's eager to get in on it. "What's up?"

We go to work shimmying the cabinet side to side until I can get my fingers around behind and pull. I touch the drill to the metal and press the trigger. The drill bit squeals on the metal and slides off. "Close Dad's door," I say to Mel. The second attempt is better — the bit catches and little pieces of metal shavings are flying as I make a hole next to the locking catch. I'm getting the hang of it and make three more holes, forming four points of a square. No idea what I'm doing, really, but it seems to be working. I can feel the vibration of the jigsaw in my teeth and smell hot metal as it squeals to connect the dots — the holes I've just made. Now the catch is free of the rod. When I pull on the handle, the drawer issues a wrenching scream, a small pop, and then—

"Bingo. We're in."

Melody laughs, a bright and genuine sound that flutters through me. "I feel like we're robbing a safe or something," she says. "What are we looking for?"

"I don't really know." As I pull out the files, my cat-burglar sense of accomplishment fades. John is a pack rat who holds onto tax returns for years before letting them go. Why would he lock them up? We file jointly so I already know what's there.

Melody yawns after I've flipped through a couple recent years. I glance up at her. "Why don't you go to bed, honey."

"Am I going to school tomorrow?"

I look over the scattered papers and then lift my arm. Melody helps me to my feet and into John's chair. "I don't know. What do you think?"

"I want to help you find Dad."

The tears are quick and unexpected, but I don't try to hide them. I stroke her cheek, tuck a tendril of hair behind her ear. "I know you do."

"I'm sorry about what I said."

"I wish I knew what you heard, why you think I would say something like that. It was at dinner?"

"I think so. On Saturday night, after you got mad at us about making noise. Then you and Dad were in his office."

"I didn't get mad at you . . . Dad and I were in his office? I'm not sure that's right." Thinking back to Saturday night, it's easy to get the order of things confused even though it was recent, because so much has happened since. We had our dinner, the awkward meal to end all awkward meals, but I don't recall being in his office alone with him.

Melody regards me with a sleepy face. "Where do you think he is?"

"That's what I'm going to find out." I pull her into an embrace. "You need to get some sleep."

"I can't," she says in a soft voice that's close to my ear. "I have bad dreams."

Her unease reminds me I still haven't talked to John's father or stepmother. They don't even know he's missing, unless Ridley has called them. But if she has, I would have heard from Frank by now. I check the clock on my phone: it's going on eleven, but in Arizona it's only eight. He might still be up.

Melody pulls back from me. "I dreamed about an old woman."

"An old woman?"

"Yeah. This, like, gray old woman."

It's as though Melody has peeled back the lid on my private thoughts. "What was her name?"

"I don't know. She didn't have one."

"What was she like?"

"She was, like, trying to talk, but then all that came out of her mouth was dirt." Melody is looking at me, then her gaze wanders. "Hey — a ladybug!"

I see what she's talking about. The round red beetle moves along the back of John's desk. It's getting to be that time of year when insects invade our home and flies buzz in the windows on warm days. Melody sticks out her finger and the ladybug climbs on. I watch her, caught in this delicate limbo between childhood and adulthood. She laughs as the bug tickles her; it follows the ridge of her hand and circles her wrist. "They smell if you squish them," she says.

"What else happened in your dream?"

"I'm going to take it into my room."

"Mel . . ."

She flicks me a look, having already left the subject behind for this new discovery. "It was just a dream, Mom."

Just a dream. I'm searching for coincidence again, thinking of Selma Ford, making connections where they don't exist. Just like my own mother did.

"Goodnight, Mom."

"Okay. Goodnight, honey."

With Melody gone, I ease myself onto the floor and continue going through the old tax files, bills, reports from auto mechanics on the car, and linger over the estimate on fixing the brakes, which John had done a few months before, like I told Ridley.

Maybe John's Subaru plays a bigger role than I've been seeing. I did suspect the license plate could be wrong, but that was just the shock of the moment. What else? Could there have been some other mechanical failure the police haven't figured out yet? Probably not. I keep going through the stack anyway, a growing pile of them on my left.

My phone vibrates in my pocket. I recognize the number.

"Bruce?"

"Jane — how are you?"

"Bruce, I, ah . . ."

"Can we talk? I know you probably have some things you want to ask me. And I'm sorry about earlier — about how I acted on the phone."

"This is a really hard time."

"I know, I know. I talked to the police — you still don't know where John is."

Whenever it's said aloud I feel vulnerable, like I've just given up some sort of protection.

"Let me help you," Bruce says. "Okay?"

"I'm not sure what you can do, Bruce." Talking to him is a bit awkward. I gain my feet and start to pace John's study, the floor creaking.

"Listen, I talked to the troopers and I spoke with someone named Ripley."

"Ridley."

"Yeah. So, I explained to her about John, about how he and I go way back and—"

"You got angry when I suggested you threatened John. You said maybe I didn't know him all that well, or maybe I didn't know everything about him. There's been a lot of that going around lately and, if you want to help, the best thing you can do is be specific with me."

"I know. I'm sorry, that was . . . everything from back then, you know — I was a little shit, okay? I know that. And I don't make any excuses. I just meant that John was going through something, that's what I know, but I expressed it poorly."

"What exactly, Bruce? What *exactly* did he say?"

Bruce sighs. "Jane, look . . . I mean, men go through these things."

"*What* things? Tell me what he said, Bruce, and please don't spare me."

"He just — you know. Well, we've been talking for a couple weeks, actually."

The blonde woman. Maybe that's who Melody heard. He had an affair after all.

"First he just said he felt smothered — suffocated, or something. And I suggested—"

"Suffocated? He said that?"

"I think so, yeah."

"Suffocated how?"

Another sigh, and Bruce jostles his phone, making scratching sounds. "Wife, kids, responsibility, routine."

I let that sit for a moment before I say, "Okay."

What more do you need in order to accept it? John left you for someone else.

"Bruce, did he tell you he was . . . Did John say anything about . . . about another . . ."

A long silence from Bruce, then, "Someone else? Another woman?"

"Maybe that." He seems to think about it. "We didn't get into specifics, Jane . . . but, maybe."

"You didn't get into specifics? He either said he was having an affair or he didn't."

"Here's the thing . . . I just feel guilty, like I had something to do with this."

"How could you have anything to do with this?"

"I want to help — let me help, okay? I'll do anything you need."

It's on the tip of my tongue to ask Bruce about Rainey's illness. Detective Ridley had no information on it. Or about her having a private conversation with John that Melody overheard. But despite the direness of the situation, social custom overrides. Am I really going to question the legitimacy of someone's sickness? Am I going to suggest some sort of conspiracy, something Rainey did to cause John's disappearance? I have to keep some sense of decorum or I'm lost.

"Bruce, I appreciate you calling and your willingness to help. But I think, right now . . ."

"Just keep it in mind, okay? You need someone on your side, Jane. I mean the cops are good but — you know, they have other cases. They're slow and methodical. You need someone helping you through this. If it were me, John would do it."

Well, until Saturday, I didn't even know you existed. "That's nice of you."

"Listen, you didn't let me finish. So it started with him talking about feeling smothered, but then he started acting — I don't know . . . paranoid."

"Paranoid about *what*?"

"It started when I came over that morning. And then afterward, after dinner that night, when we were on the phone."

I picture John at his desk, the way he was when I brought Russ in for his goodnight kiss, the look in John's eyes, like he was a stranger.

"He was scared, Jane."

"About what?"

"He wouldn't say. But he did tell me — well, he admitted he'd been drinking."

"He told you that."

"Yes."

"What was he scared about, Bruce? Please, just tell me."

"All I know is he thought he was being watched."

I see the SUV in my mind's eye. I think about John's intense reaction — the way he sped up, almost seeming to taunt the person tailgating us. "Bruce, you need to tell the police what you just told me. Have you told them?"

"I told Ripley. Uh . . . Ridley. But I don't think they're going to know what to do with it. I mean, the idea that John is acting paranoid? The way they see it, he's been drinking and he takes off. The cops aren't going to prioritize it. Especially if he was . . . well, if you think that's true about him and someone else. Like maybe it's a disgruntled husband or something — shit, I don't know. But my point is, without something solid, they're just not going to care enough. I know some of these guys and you need more help."

I pinch my forehead, close my eyes as my mind shifts gears. "Bruce, there was *blood* in the car. That's not solid? And guess what? I think John's file cabinet has been broken into."

I open my eyes when I hear something on the other side of the house — an engine winding down, as if a car is pulling up. Jolted into action, I leave the study and slip into Russ's room with its view of the driveway, just in time to see a set of headlights wink off and hear the engine die.

The flood lamps come on, bathing the vehicle in bright light. It's an SUV.

"Bruce . . ." My heart starts hammering. "Did you just pull up to my house?"

"What? I'm nowhere near you. Why? Jane, is someone there?"

Panicked, I move quickly out of Russ's room and cross the hallway. "Mel," I say, a bit breathless, "close your door and lock it."

She sits up in her bed, fear spreading across her small, pretty features. "Mom? What?"

"Just do it."

I move on toward the front door. I think it's locked already but want to check. Then there's the back door, the door to the basement — each secure, I think, but I need to make sure.

"Jane," Bruce says, unmistakable fear coming through. "Jane, call the cops."

"I'm going to." I check the front door — the lock is engaged. My heart thunders in my chest and my neck and scalp tingle. I hear a door slam shut in the driveway and risk a look through the window beside the door.

The driver must see me standing there because he stops halfway up the walk.

It's my stepbrother, Leland.

"Jane you there?" Bruce is still on the phone.

"I gotta go." I'm not sure if he hears me because my voice barely registers in my own ears. Just dirt coming out of my mouth, maybe.

I cancel the call and dial 911, not taking any chances. My mother nearly killed Leland's father. With everything that's happened, he could be dangerous.

The line is ringing as I hurry from the door to search my bedroom — John keeps a baseball bat at his side of the bed. It's cool and smooth in my grip.

"911 emergency response, can I have your—"

"My name is Jane Gable. I'm calling to report an intruder."

There's a delicate knock on the door. I enter the living room to see half of Leland's head in the door's semicircular window and let out an inadvertent scream.

"Mommy!" Melody wails from her bedroom.

"Ma'am, is the intruder in the house?"

I yell toward the front porch. "Get away from the door, Leland!"

"Do you know this person, ma'am?"

"He's outside. On the front porch. He's not welcome here."

"Jane!" Leland's muffled voice comes through. "Hey, Janie, come on . . ."

I run past the laundry room to the rear door and lock it, talking to the dispatcher in one long train of thought. "He came over uninvited. I haven't seen him in years and now my husband is missing and he's showing up — there's no restraining order or anything, but—"

"Ma'am, are your doors locked?"

I'm running downstairs to make sure the basement door is secure. The slide bolt is already engaged. "Yes."

"Is there any other way the intruder could get into the house?"

"He could break a window."

"Who else is there with you?"

"My children. Are you sending someone? Please send someone."

"Ma'am, I've alerted the police. Someone will be there in a matter of minutes. Just sit tight."

Returning to the first floor, I approach the front door slowly but don't see Leland's head. Bat in hand, I step to the window.

Leland has walked back toward his car. He looks over his shoulder, sees me and stops. Then he opens the SUV's passenger door and leans in.

The fear is like a paralyzing agent, freezing me in place as I imagine my mother aiming a gun at Leland's father and pulling the trigger. I envision Leland taking another gun from his car, one he plans to use on me and the kids.

Then I'm in Melody's room, sitting with her on the bed, the bat in one hand and the phone to my ear in the other, and the dispatcher is trying to reassure me. "Someone is coming, Jane. Sit tight — someone is coming . . ."

CHAPTER SEVENTEEN / LELAND

Plain Jane. Plain Jane's life is a runaway train!

When I was six, a man named Alfred Pinchot moved in with us. He had heavy-lidded eyes and scars on the backs of his long-fingered hands. He was a drug addict. When he became abusive, my mother didn't go to the police. Eventually, he moved on.

After Alfred Pinchot, Mom told me and my half-brother and half-sister that the Earth had been created by a race of alien beings. One day, in the delicatessen a few blocks from our First Avenue apartment, she had a public meltdown. She told strangers that a massive solar explosion would engulf the planet and bring the end of days.

Pretty soon, kids at my school heard about it.

Plain Jane, your mother is insane. Two girls would rap it like a hip-hop song. One of them, whose name I forget, would beat-box, pursing and popping her lips in rhythm with the singer, Dalia Dannon. Dalia would spit the words like she was on stage: *Plain Jane / your mother is insane / your motherfuckin life is a run-a-way train! What? Oh!*

My half-brother went into the military and ended up staying overseas. My half-sister lives in Iowa and is married to an Evangelical Christian accountant. I've never met my biological father, but their father, Pinchot, is around somewhere, likely sitting in someone else's living room with that spooky unfocused look, the TV on but he's not really watching. Pinchot would be unsurprised to hear of my mother finally turning on the next abusive lover, Daryl Chase.

Maybe Pinchot already knows. Maybe, when he saw the news reports of an attempted murder landing a Troy woman in a maximum-security penitentiary further upstate, he snapped out of his daze and took notice. Maybe he patted his chest for bullet holes and counted himself lucky.

When my mother was with Daryl Chase, I was already out of the house. So was Leland, who's about my age. I saw him only a few times after my mother pointed the small Glock pistol she'd taken from a friend and pulled the trigger — I saw Leland at the arraignment and again for sentencing. His father recovered, though still suffers breathing problems from the bullet that nicked his diaphragm.

Leland's problems, well, I always thought they were more mental in nature.

* * *

The troopers are back in my driveway, having arrived together in one car. Both men. One of them is outside, going through Leland's vehicle, a dark blue SUV with rust around the wheels.

Leland is in the back seat of the police car, behind the wire mesh. He could have left before the cops got there; it took them almost ten minutes to arrive yet he remained in the driveway.

The other trooper is inside the house, writing down what I've been saying as I watch out of the window. His radio crackles and a voice says, "Clean."

"Okay, ma'am," the trooper in front of me says. "We've had a look and there are no weapons in this individual's vehicle — he said he reached into his car to get a pack of cigarettes. That's what you saw. Anyway, he has no wants or warrants, so unless you wish to press charges, we can go ahead and—"

"What sort of charges could I press?"

"Well, trespassing on private property, that's about it. You say he didn't threaten you? Threaten to hurt you or the kids?"

"No. Not exactly."

"And there's no restraining order or injunction against him, nothing like that?"

"No. He just showed up. Maybe he has reason to . . . I don't know . . . maybe he . . ." I'm shaking again, questioning whether I've completely blown this out of all proportion.

Finished with the SUV, the trooper still outside gets into the front of the police car and shuts the door. I can see that he's talking to Leland.

I cradle my head for a moment. Melody stands beside me and gives me a squeeze. Her presence makes me feel guilty. *I'm* the adult, the one who's supposed to make sane, rational decisions, and yet she's the one showing adaptability, coming to comfort me even though she blames me for John's disappearance — even though I just freaked out and screamed and ran around the house checking the door locks when a not-entirely-strange man showed up.

"All right," the officer in my living room says. "Well, he says he's very sorry for it. Claims he knows nothing about your husband, except he heard about the disappearance and just wanted to talk to you."

"At eleven o'clock at night?"

"We'll warn him that if he sets foot on your property again uninvited, we will arrest him on sight. Okay?"

"Did he say how he heard about it?"

"I think a lot of people are talking, if you want the truth. It's a pretty tight-knit area."

"But he doesn't live around here."

"Correct, ma'am. We have his current address over in Cohoes. He was visiting his father today, he says, and he decided to stop by to see you, and he regrets it."

I'm looking at Leland still, who nods in the backseat at something the first trooper is saying. He then makes some strange gesture, orbiting a hand around his head with his finger pointed down. What does that mean? My mind is seizing on every abnormality now, every unexplained moment, as my life continues to disintegrate. I draw a deep breath and let it out slowly, feeling some of the tension release.

"I'll go talk to my colleague and we'll wrap this up. Just sit tight, ma'am."

People are always telling me that.

"All right. Thank you."

"Don't mention it." The trooper reaches for the door. "Detective Ridley will call you first thing in the morning." Then he leaves.

Melody draws even closer to me as we both press toward the window to watch as the second trooper reaches the police car, talks with the first one, and then opens the rear door for Leland. He steps out and glances in my direction, making me flinch.

"Mom, who is he?"

"Nobody, honey."

"You think he knows where Dad is?"

"I don't know. They'll keep an eye on him. Let's try to get some rest, okay?"

* * *

Fat chance. If I had trouble sleeping before, it's now impossible. My stomach gurgles and adrenaline crawls through my blood. I keep thinking about Leland, what he could be up to. Maybe I was wrong to put it past him — maybe he is capable of a kidnapping, taking John off somewhere in a bid for revenge. But it still feels too far-fetched, more likely that Leland is just dumb enough to drop by my house unannounced late at night, a capricious move that's very much in character.

And then there's the file cabinet in John's office. The top drawer wrenched open, the bottom one still locked. I was in the middle of going through it all when Leland showed up. I need to search every inch of my life if I'm going to understand what happened to my husband.

So I creep back to the office, like some pathological glutton for punishment. At least Melody has fallen asleep. The sight of my children gives me a hollow feeling, as if the world I knew — what I thought was my life — was just some kind of naïve illusion. As if some ancient and fundamental law of the universe has been upended.

I need to understand why.

The stack of files are where I left them in a pile on the floor — mostly those old tax returns. But the file cabinet is not the end of my hacking.

With the laptop up and running, I try *password* first, just to see. No dice. I try John's birthday in all numbers — 41880. Nothing. Russ's birthday next . . . Melody's . . . my own. Then names: mine, the kids'. John didn't have pets growing up, no obvious obsessions over a fictional character. Everything I try fails. In the movies, the person hacking a password is always on the brink of giving up and then lightning strikes. It's not happening, but my phone is vibrating. Again.

I dig it out for a look.

Everything okay???

I never called Bruce back. *I'm okay,* I type. *Talk tomorrow.*

I set it on John's desk where it jitters a few seconds later. And then again. Bruce is writing me *War and Peace,* apparently. He seems relentless, eager to help — and ply his trade.

Right now he's one component too many for me.

On the floor, I continue going through the files. John keeps thorough records of his expenses including printed spreadsheets. It'll take hours to look at every gas station fill-up, every meal or supply purchased in the service of writing books. Nothing jumps out.

I think of John as predictable, shy of the outside world. Have I been wrong? I've assumed he was home at his desk,

151

doing whatever writers do: typing away or pulling his hair out as he faced the blank page.

My heart skips a beat when I see a file marked *Canada*.

It only takes a few seconds flipping pages before I realize what it is: an application to restore a person's admissibility. The forms are blank but, as I continue through, I find copies of a completed version, filled out in John's identifiably messy handwriting. They're dated slightly under a year ago.

My mind spins. Trooper Morse theorized that John may have been detained in Canada because of harsher penalties for DUIs. Apparently, a person can restore their admissibility via paperwork and fines. From what I can tell, John has done just that.

Is that my answer? He left the country? If so, why? Just knowing that he is potentially legal to enter Canada doesn't mean anything on its own — it only feels significant because of Morse's theory. And if he went over there to research a book, there'd be records, a meticulous account of his expenses like always.

Unless it wasn't about a book but something else, something hidden. With Canada less than an hour away, he would have plenty of time to make surreptitious trips across the border.

And then destroy the evidence.

CHAPTER EIGHTEEN / MINDS ARE MADE UP

Tuesday, March 26th

Gorski stands in the doorway of the study. "Looks like a little B&E," she says about the mangled file cabinet. Her delivery is so deadpan that I hiccup a laugh. She nods at the mess. "You did that?"

"I did. But I think it was already jimmied open — the top drawer. You can see there the little catch has snapped off. I had to use a drill to get the second one free — Ridley said I could look around."

"No, I understand that. But it'll have to go in my report. And I'll need to see everything you removed or you'll be withholding evidence."

Her tone is like acid on my giddy sense of discovery. "Of course. I would want you to. And you'll include that the top drawer was already broken open?"

"I'll put in that it appeared broken open, yes."

She doesn't look at me, and my heart sinks. I know she's only doing her job, but she'll annotate what I've said, hopefully.

There are bigger fish to fry: the application to rehabilitate John's admissibility into Canada is going to add a layer of

153

complexity. Surely Ridley will seriously consider the idea that my husband has skipped the country. Such evidence may bring in federal investigators, though I'm not sure of that and no one has said so yet.

Gorski's gaze falls on the bottle of Jim Beam. A drunken writer alighting for Canada. That must be what she's thinking now. A drunken writer who hits the trail and his wife starts tearing through his office looking for God knows what: to find evidence of an affair; to get at stolen money; to throw away the drugs — such theories must be going a mile a minute. And yet, still no forensic technicians dusting for prints or shining special lights on things. The cops seem to be phoning it in, minds already made up.

Maybe they're right. Not about me, but about John. Maybe it's time I faced up to that at last. My husband isn't gone because of some halfwit stepbrother of mine seeking payback. He's gone because, like my daughter has indicated, I haven't been paying close enough attention. I've been phoning it in, too, while my husband lived a double life.

Russ is in the other room asking Morse about his gun. I couldn't send Russ to school believing his father is away at a writer's conference. It required another lie — not to the school, who understand the situation and are willing to excuse his absence — but to Russ. "Spring Break starts today," I told him. "They changed it." I could have said we were at nuclear war and he would have been just as thrilled, bounding off down the hallway with his hands in the air singing the praises of no school. He hasn't even questioned why there are police in the house again. That I'm getting better at lying makes me ill.

"Okay . . ." Gorski pulls a pair of latex gloves from her back pocket and gives me a sidelong look. "Are there any chemicals in here, any drugs, anything I should know about besides the bottle of liquor? I don't want to find something that means I have to get CCSERT down here."

Please. Get people down here. Check everything. "No, there's no chemicals."

"How about firearms."

"We don't own any weapons. I mean, he may have a knife or something, but I doubt there's anything like that in here."

She's just looking at me now, like she wants to ask something else. Then her eyes clear and she goes for the laptop, slips it into a large clear evidence bag.

"So what kind of stuff does your husband write about?"

"Huh?"

"He's a writer, I thought." She snaps open a smaller bag and picks up my husband's phone like someone would pick up a dog turd and drops it in.

"Yes. Um . . . crime fiction."

"That's interesting, huh?"

I'm not sure how to respond. Bags in hand, Gorski gives me a wan smile. "So, this should be it for now. Oh, Ridley said something about the taxes?"

"In that box right there. I put everything in there for the past six years. My husband keeps things longer than most."

"Let me send Trooper Morse in for those."

I watch Gorski move down the hall and listen to her speaking quietly to Morse. When he gives me a funny look, I realize I'm just standing there in the doorway, wringing my hands. I get out of his way and point out the file box. He grunts as he hefts it. As he's passing back out of the room he shows me a little concern. "You seem tired. Probably hard to sleep. You should try to get some rest."

"Do you handle a lot of missing person cases?"

"A few, yeah."

"How is this one? Is this how it typically goes?"

He considers it. "Most missing persons have some mental health issues, and, you know, they don't have family, don't have friends looking for them. In some cases people don't even remember their names or where they came from. Your husband has you."

* * *

The rest of the morning passes in a dreamy haze. Ridley calls around noon, not "first thing" like I was told, and Bruce's words echo in my thoughts: *There's nothing solid, and they're just not going to care enough.*

"So," Ridley says, "you had a bit of a scare last night."

"It was unexpected. I guess I panicked."

"I'm glad you made the emergency call. I did speak to Mr. Chase earlier today. At the moment he has an alibi for your husband's disappearance — he was miles away at his home in Cohoes, as corroborated by his live-in boyfriend."

Boyfriend. I had no idea.

"But it's still probably the right thing to be careful of him."

"What about Bruce Barnes?"

"I've spoken with him, too."

"And he told you John was worried that he was being watched?"

"He said something along those lines. But the impression I got was that he feels your husband was *unraveling.* I think that's how he put it."

"And what about Mr. Barnes himself being involved? Maybe having something to do with when they were younger?"

"You're talking about a motive? He claims he doesn't harbor any resentment from anything that happened. But I'm going to look at it — any police reports from back then. I'll talk to people. See if I can turn up anything. In the meantime, I want to talk a minute about the paperwork — the application for Canadian admission. What did you know about it?"

"He never mentioned it."

"Did he have any plans to leave the country?"

"No." I'm frustrated. "Not that I know of."

"Can you think of a reason? Work, maybe?"

"Work would be all I could think of. That he was working on a new book and needed to do some research."

"But he never told you. If he was traveling into Canada at any recent time, he didn't tell you about it."

"He did not."

"And this doesn't line up with what you've told me about your relationship with John, the openness of communication . . ."

I swallow my pride. "It doesn't line up, no."

"Also, I wanted you to know we have the tip-line going. And there's going to be a press conference this afternoon."

"I thought we still needed to decide about that?"

"The press conference is a must-do. But I can email you the statement beforehand, see what you think. It'll just stick to the basics . . . when he was last seen, that he has no known mental health issues, that his vehicle was found. We're not going to talk about the blood at this time — we're still waiting for a few things with that."

"Okay . . . yeah, that sounds okay to me."

"Would you like to be at the press conference? Say a few words?"

"I don't want to leave the kids and I don't want them there for that."

"I understand. It's not necessary, just check the statement and hit me back with any questions or concerns. Have you spoken to John's family?"

"I called Frank this morning. The conversation lasted about two minutes."

"I spoke to him, too. He says he hasn't heard from your husband in six months."

"Like I said, they're not close."

"How are you holding up?"

"I'm all right."

Ridley says, "Mmhmm," like she's been through this a hundred times, though I doubt she has. "It's a waiting game. You need to pace yourself. Your husband's laptop and phone are en route to the FIC in Albany so the techs can work on them, bypass security."

"Is that likely?"

"They're pretty good. And I'm going to keep the tax returns here and be going over them myself."

"Okay."

"Mrs. Gable, the best thing you can do at this point—"

"Sit tight. I know."

"I was going to say keep yourself up. In these situations it's easy to forget your own needs. Get plenty to eat and drink. Do your best to sleep. Don't forget to take care of yourself."

* * *

That afternoon, a depression falls so swift and fast I feel almost bullied by it. After a chaotic couple of days with everything at full speed, things have ground to a halt. All the activity that kept the dread at bay is gone. The depression seeks to settle in, wrap around my brain like a thick wet cloth.

I need to get a little sun on my face, so I step outside, but it's lost behind gray clouds. Karen texts and asks if I need anything. I can't leave the kids for the press conference. And I'm afraid I'd fall apart in front of all those cameras. Karen says she's coming over anyway; she won't take no for an answer.

Depression is unfamiliar to me. I used to be a happy person, giving people the benefit of the doubt, seeing the good in them. Now I don't know who anyone is or what they're after. I don't know if my husband fell victim to foul play or left us voluntarily. But we've been marooned in this strange land, outside the boundaries of normal life, where the lack of routine and familiarity reveals the utter frailty of our human condition.

The tears come and I search the sky for the sun, willing it to appear. It doesn't. Time to go back inside. Maybe take a glass down and fill it with some of John's bourbon.

Then I see it.

Pulled off the road and about 200 yards away is the SUV.

Not Leland's SUV, but *the* SUV, black with a brown stripe and tinted windows.

It's pointed towards me but almost hidden there against the trees, the gray light destroying shadows and depth, but there's no doubt in my mind that it's the one I've been seeing and I start toward the road as I pull out my cell phone.

The SUV jerks into motion as I fumble to get my phone into camera mode. I glance back at the house but Melody and Russ aren't near any of the windows. No one else is coming down the road at this point; it's after 1 p.m. on a Tuesday in March and everyone else is at work or school.

"Hey," I say, getting louder. "Hey! Hey!"

The SUV completes the turn — at this distance I'll be lucky to get much of anything but I take a few pictures as it gets up to speed, then it rounds the bend and retreats out of sight.

I check the pictures I've just taken, use my thumb and forefinger to zoom in. Dammit. The license plate is just a blur when magnified. Maybe Ridley's people have the means to enhance it.

As I'm standing there at the end of my driveway, another vehicle approaches: Karen's green car. She pulls in a moment later, giving me a curious look from behind the wheel as she rolls down the window.

"Whatcha doing?" She glances at my phone.

"Losing my mind."

I tell her about the SUV. The times I've seen it, that I've told the cops about it and that nothing has turned up. Just like John thought he was being watched, now I'm under surveillance, too.

I show Karen the picture and ask if she's seen anything like that around town.

"I can't say that I . . . well, I mean, the Everetts have a vehicle like that."

I look up the road, where my neighbors live, the corrections officer and his wife, just around the bend and out of sight. "The Everetts?"

"Think so." She gives me a look. "What do you want to do? You want to go up there? I'll stay with the kids."

"Maybe it was just one of them and they left something at home, turned around."

Karen keeps her eyes on me, similar to the other day in the kitchen, like I'm someone too timid to face my demons. I see shopping bags sitting on her passenger seat, full of food and drink. "Just a few things," she says. "I thought maybe you'd need a hot meal. There's a meatloaf in here — wait, do you eat meat?"

"This is very nice of you, Karen."

"Not a problem." She frowns. "I need to get it inside, so . . ."

"I'll help you."

She doesn't hide her disappointment well. Sighing, she opens the door and I step back out of her way.

"I'm going to go talk to RJ, from the Trailhead. On my way I'll stop at the Everetts' and have a look at their car."

"Good girl," she says. I help her carry the bags into the house.

Inside, we set the items on the counter. Karen has also brought a dish of mashed potatoes and one of steamed carrots together with milk, bread and eggs. "Just the basics," she says.

"I don't know how to thank you."

"Don't worry about it. Happy to do it." Then she blushes. "Well, I mean, I'm not *happy* . . ."

"Stop. I understand what you mean."

She takes a seat at the island and pulls a bottle of wine from a brown paper bag. "I also brought this — I don't know if it's appropriate . . ."

I must look uneasy because Karen suddenly slips it back into the bag. "I'm sorry. Probably a bad idea."

I hold her wrist and pull the bottle gently back out. "You know what? Let's have a glass right now. Middle of the day. Some liquid courage before I play private detective."

The corkscrew is buried in a kitchen drawer. After uncorking, I pour us each about half a glass and raise mine. My hand is trembling a little as I speak. "A toast to John —

that he's okay. That he comes back to us soon." I don't know why I even say it. I feel outside of my body, like I'm watching a stranger from the corner of the room.

"Amen," Karen says. We both take a drink. "I'm not sure you'll like this brand. I'm not much of a sommelier."

I can't really taste anything. "It's good."

I realize what's happening: despite the tenderness I feel toward John and the deep desire for his return and for my once normal life, there's that part of me, a survivor, a person who knows how to move on, how to start over when things go wrong. She's emerging.

My phone shudders on the counter and I check the number. "Karen, shit, I have to take this. Ridley? Hi, everything all right?"

"Jane," Ridley says. "How much do you know about your finances?"

Glancing at Karen, I walk a few steps away. "John does the books. I get a W-2, not much to it. But he has to file a bunch of different forms. Why? What's wrong?"

"Have you looked at the numbers?"

"Not lately, no."

"According to your tax returns, John's royalties from book writing have been on a steady decline. Last year he claimed $13,000 from writing. You pulled in much more. Do you and your husband pool your money?"

"We have a joint savings account. It still has some of our wedding money in there from nearly ten years ago, I think." I really wish I'd checked that account more recently.

"Well if you're not pooling your money, you're spending your own money on whatever you need?"

"I have things I pay for and things that come out of my paychecks. John pays the mortgage and utilities . . ."

I went through the mail the other day in a daze. There was something from the electric company that might've said *Urgent* on the envelope. I look for the pile, feeling Karen's eyes on me.

"I've been able to check into his bank account," Ridley says. "First, there's been no recent withdrawal on his debit cards. That was the first thing we wanted to look at — see if we could trace a withdrawal to a certain bank or ATM. There's nothing on the credit card, either, and no online purchases. So I don't know what he was living on then and if he's . . . nor what he could be using for money right now."

She was about to say *if he's alive*. Maybe that's what John wants. To be untraceable, lost, with no paper trail to follow, no use of digital money, looking like he's dead.

"Unless he has access to *your* account. But I'm not seeing that."

"He doesn't. They're separate."

"Okay, well . . . the subpoena came through and there have been no big cash withdrawals prior to his disappearance. Not that there was much to draw from."

"How much is in there?"

"In all three accounts — personal, business, and joint — there's a combined total of nine hundred and forty-six dollars. The last transaction was the debit card used five days ago for seventy-seven dollars and forty-two cents. Looks like a restaurant?"

"That was our date."

"Sorry?"

"We went out on a dinner date. That's the night we saw the SUV."

"Oh right. Okay. I have that in the timeline." She exhales loudly. "He could have gotten a credit card since then and be living on that."

The shock of it feels cold, numbing. We've never been money-driven people but this is stupefying. I usually have a rough figure in my head: a touch over twenty grand in savings. But it sounds like John has been using it to pay the mortgage and other bills. He's been buying groceries, getting gas, even paying for Melody's bi-weekly piano lessons. And then, apparently, he ran out. Or, came close — running on fumes. Just under a grand in the bank now, according to Ridley. Peanuts.

"Does he have any other bank accounts?" I ask.

"I haven't been able to find any. Just yours, with Fidelity Trust. You have six thousand, one hundred and fourteen dollars."

While John's been the one tending the nest egg, I've managed to squirrel a little away. Growing up with a mother living paycheck to paycheck, marrying a man whose future finances were uncertain, I took precautions. But it's not much. I'm burning through both my sick time and personal time. Unless I go back to work soon, the money supply shuts off. Six grand will last me a month, maybe two if I stretch every dollar.

"Does John have any wealthy relatives?"

"No."

"How about his father?"

"Frank and Delores live on his pension, which isn't much."

The more I think about it, the more I realize how in the dark I've been. For one thing, I'd thought *Edge of Night* had been more of a success. But since John's crime series wound down, nothing has hit big. It shouldn't be surprising, either; the average annual income of a fiction writer is something like $8000. Maybe I've taken certain things for granted.

What has he been doing all day when I'm at work and after he feeds the kids and puts them to bed? When I'm home, and he's enclosed in his study? Occasionally I'll pause outside his door, listen for the tapping of keys. Sometimes I'll hear them, lately not so much. He'll go out for a bit — "I'm just going to stretch my legs, see if I can work a few things out." What's he been up to? Or is this just more paranoia filling a vacuum of answers?

I tell Ridley about getting a cell pic of the SUV sitting up the road from my house. She'll see what she can do with it, she says. We hang up.

Karen has obviously overheard my end of the conversation about finances and put the rest together. She's looking grim, her head down as she stares into the wine glass and rotates it by the stem. I share Ridley's half of the conversation with her and Karen flicks little looks at me, nods, then finishes her wine.

She wipes the corner of her mouth with a thumb and fixes me with a look.

"I have to tell you something."

CHAPTER NINETEEN / TROUBLING
REVELATIONS

"Karen? What?"

Karen exudes a certain tension as she looks into her wine glass.

"Honestly? It upset me a little bit. I know we don't spend a lot of time together — I think we've talked more in the past couple of days than in the past three years."

"I'm sorry. I don't mean to be . . ."

She shakes her head and looks at me. "No, you don't have to say anything. I understand what it's like. Believe me. Matt and I see people coming in to the community. And it can be a little . . ."

"Provincial?"

"We're not the most well-off county in the state, right? I think there's some pride. It's hard."

Karen looks ready to choke on what she wants to say.

"Karen . . ."

"I hate gossip."

I have to stop myself from taking her by the shoulders and shaking it out of her. "What is it? Karen. Is it about . . . this?"

There's a spark in her eyes. "People have seen him."

"What do you mean?" I worry the kids might overhear me and lower my tone. "They've *seen* him? Where?"

"I don't . . . I'm sorry — I don't mean now. I mean before."

"Okay, so people have seen him. I don't understand."

"Walking around, talking on his phone, acting upset."

"Who? Who's seen him? Where?"

"Amy Dugan, for one. She lives on Grant Street, by the river."

Everything is jumbled together and for a few seconds I feel disassociated again, like I'm not even me, but slipped into this life by accident. The feeling passes and I remember my life, family routines. "John walks by the river sometimes — when he's writing and he needs to think, get some exercise. Sometimes he comes by the hospital and says hi to me if I'm available. Amy Dugan talked to you about seeing John?"

He loves you . . .

Karen still acts like she's got a secret she can't digest. Her face twists with the telling. "Seeing him, hearing him — he was sort of . . . Amy says he was yelling and swearing. And someone else, you know, someone else saw him, too. Darby Trestle lives in the—"

"Yelling and swearing?"

"Upset. He seemed upset, she said."

"I know Darby. I know where she lives."

"She told me about it — Darby — when we had the kids together. She saw him on a *separate* occasion, and he seemed just as distraught. And now you mention this thing with work, and the money thing, it makes sense maybe. That he was talking with this guy, his agent, right? And he's just been . . ."

Bruce's comments come to mind. That John was agitated, afraid. That he thought someone was watching him. It has to be the people in the SUV. Bookies or something? People he owes money to? Karen is right: I need to check it out.

"His agent says they haven't talked," I tell her.

166

She's looking down again, not really listening, and then our eyes connect.

"I think it's hard for men today," she says. "That's not making excuses. It's not that. But a lot has changed, right? I mean they're good things. More women in higher education, more jobs. There's still a pay gap, there's still harassment, but sometimes I think we forget how far we've come."

I bite my tongue, knowing that to the privileged, equality can feel like oppression. John has never whined, though. He's always seemed to fit as a domestic man working from home, unthreatened by my salary. If anything, I'd thought at one point his masculinity could have been threatened by Bruce Barnes. That's usually how it goes: men getting themselves into trouble over ideas of strength and honor.

"They have an instinct that doesn't just go away," Karen says. "They want to provide. I think their self-worth is attached to it. I hope I'm not offending you."

"No."

"But I believe you've got millions of years of evolution shaping men to be competitive, to take what they want. We're the gatherers. They're the hunters."

Better just to let her talk.

"But like I said, I'm not making excuses for any behavior — you have to get with the times. I'm just saying . . . well, it's something to look at."

Maybe. Maybe I've been wrong about John and he feels secretly oppressed, or at least underperforming as a provider. Then again, if he's kept his financial troubles a secret, then I guess there's no maybe about it.

A sense of betrayal slides through my heart like a length of lead pipe — John's been lying to me. Not directly, but by neglecting to communicate with me. By keeping it all to himself, bottling it up, he's been letting me believe we're okay. I might have a role to play; when you have happiness, you want to keep it. That might mean not looking at things too closely — like your husband's secret misery and financial fears. So what has he gotten himself into? Has he been trying to make money in some other way?

"What about you?" I ask Karen. "What about Matt? Do you think he's content?"

"He's got a — you know, he has a—"

"A man's job?"

"That's not what I was gonna say."

"It's okay. It follows from what you're saying. I mean, does he seem happy?"

She doesn't answer. It's an intimate question. Maybe I've asked too much.

Her voice lowers. "Let's just say I've found out a few things, over the years. But all around, yeah, he gets to drive his car fast and carry a gun."

John's not like that. Or am I kidding myself? Maybe he needs to conquer and compete and I've just been fooling myself it could ever be any different.

For the first time, I taste bitterness. I've been angry, I've been afraid for John — he's been on my mind every second since I found him gone. But I'm a little sick of being so preoccupied. It's selfish, but I'm just drained. The sleepless nights and all these endless worries and theories and being under the police microscope — skepticism, implications, questioning my own sanity. Now a woman from our community is talking to me about how boys just need to be boys, how men, at their core, are independent souls only tolerant of their modern trappings because they don't know what else to do.

John made his choices and withheld things from me. Either he's been secretly drinking and planning his escape or he's in trouble — with the law or someone else. Either way, it's his own doing. It seems less and less likely my husband is a victim, abducted or otherwise. The thought has a finality to it which makes my knees go rubbery, my chest hollow.

I finally manage to find my voice again. "Well, like I said, I know John hasn't been talking with his agent because I talked to him and he hasn't heard from John in nearly five months."

"No, you're right. I don't think he was talking to his agent."

It's a peculiar comment — how would she know? Just how keen are the eyes and ears of Hazleton? "Okay, well, if people are eavesdropping on my husband, maybe that's part of why he thinks he's being watched. I mean . . ." I stop short, reading her expression.

Karen looks like she has more to say, but this last bit is stuck in her throat and she avoids my gaze.

"Karen, *what*? What else?"

She faces the hallway like she's worried about the kids then takes a deep breath, studies her hands. "Maybe because we're not that close, I can tell you something other people wouldn't."

A bead of sweat works its way down my spine. "Like what?"

"People in this town know about you, and what happened with your mother."

There it is. My mother. Three years I've managed to avoid it. Then Sergeant Ferron questioned me, Ridley after that. Now there's town gossip. I can only imagine what looks people have been giving me in the grocery store behind my back, what they've been thinking.

"Okay," I say with a measure of defiance. "People know about my mother. So what."

"All I'm saying is that what happened with her, it's going to bias people. I'm sure you know that. They're going to get certain ideas."

"People like Amy Dugan."

"Well, yeah. Like her."

"There's more? Don't people have anything better to do?"

"Well when your husband is walking around acting upset, yelling into the phone, people assume it's marital, you know? That's natural." Karen shakes her head and looks out the window. "It's just talk, Jane. That's all it is."

"Tell me the talk, Karen. I can take it."

"Just that you and John . . . sometimes you get a little . . ." Her eyes dart around until she finally looks at me. "Physical."

"Physical?"

"Upset, and it turns physical."

"John has never laid a hand on me."

She's locked her eyes on me now. "Not John."

I actually have to stifle a laugh as the implication strikes. The notion of me hurting John is so bizarre after the stress of the past couple of days that the laugh would be a tension reliever. But it might not stop. "Karen. You've got to be kidding me. If John left, he did it to protect us."

"And not himself? That's what I'm telling you. Some people think he left because he thought you were going to . . . Well, there it is."

"That's insane."

"It's just people. They don't know you. They listen to news reports about women shooting their husbands, and that sort of—"

"Women who were probably fighting for their lives!"

Karen doesn't speak. It's in her eyes: my outburst is evidence that I'm possibly as unreliable and dangerous as my mother.

* * *

Ridley calls back while Karen is in the bathroom. "First, I thought you'd want to know we've been keeping an eye on your stepbrother. Leland returned to Cohoes late last night, according to the local police down there."

"All right." At some point I have to call him and apologize.

"So the vehicle you saw would not be his. I've managed to get a partial number from the plate and am running it through DMV. From what I can tell already, though, it looks like this is going to show up as a rented vehicle."

"A rental. Okay."

"Second, I checked into Bruce and Rainey Barnes some more. Turns out she's being seen by an oncologist at Albany Medical Center. She has cancer."

"I'm sorry to hear that."

"Bruce has offered us his own blood and tissue samples. He's been very cooperative. In fact — and I don't usually pass on messages like this — but he asked me to tell you he's available if you need anything."

"Okay. Thank you."

Bruce Barnes . . . Mr. Law Enforcement, with a cancer-stricken wife. Wants to help out so much it's driving him crazy. Maybe I can use the extra input? He's known John longer than I have, even if they had a falling out at one point. And he knows the area. I can have Bruce help me find John and he might also give me a heads-up about what the police are doing. He seems to have their ear.

But he's odd and he scares me a little, so it'll have to be on my terms.

"Jane?"

"Yes, sorry."

"The last thing . . . we're just having a little trouble here. Or, the lab is. They've sent me some preliminary findings that . . . Let me ask you, do you know your blood type?"

"A-positive."

"And how about your husband. Do you know what blood type he is?"

"John is O-positive."

"Okay."

I know this because I'm a nurse, but also because John and I have joked that I could receive blood from him if it was ever necessary, but not the other way around, so he needed to be the careful one.

"It's still going to take time for the DNA results, but preliminarily . . . Jane, the blood in your husband's car tests as A-positive. That's your blood type. Not his."

"What?"

"Your blood type is the one we've found in the Subaru, not—"

"I heard you, I just don't understand. It has to be from someone else with the same type, then."

Silence from Ridley. "Jane, you cut your hands, isn't that right? When you fell."

"I cut my . . . What? That can't . . . How does that matter?"

"We've got a serologist studying the pattern, determining projected versus passive blood stains. At first blush, it could be droplets from someone with cuts on their hands. Like we talked about."

"Right, that John fell. That he got hurt . . ." I walk backward a few steps so I can look down the hallway. The bathroom door is still closed, Karen hopefully out of earshot.

"Jane, consider it from my perspective for a minute, okay? Either your husband fell and injured himself in a way similar to you and somehow our lab messed up the ABO testing or—"

"Or what?" I feel cold. I'm shaking and I can't stop. Anger, bewilderment, or something else? Guilt? I ask Ridley if she thinks I'm lying.

"Maybe not lying, Jane, but perhaps confused."

That word again. Like *sit tight. Sit tight, Jane, as we make sense of your confusion.*

"Confused about *what?* I was at *work*, and I came home, and my—"

"Well your colleagues said it was a busy night and—"

"What does that mean?"

"And you left at one point to get a wallet or something. You went to the main hospital and were gone for a little while."

"This is ridiculous."

"It doesn't matter." Ridley's voice is cool, calm, distant, as if coming to me down a long tunnel. "Jane we're not saying you did something while at work."

The implication is deafening.

"My husband wasn't here when I got home. Period. We found his car miles away. How would I have . . . I don't understand this. Obviously there was some other person in the car. It wasn't *me*."

She's silent for a moment. "There's something else. It's early in the lab work but, as you'll know from your nursing experience, certain drugs can show up in the blood for one to two days after use, or longer, depending."

"Drugs?"

"From your blood draw, not from the car blood — we've only been able to get a type on that. But the blood you gave us . . . it tests positive for PCP."

I squeeze my eyes shut, try to find a clear line of thought amid the shifting pieces of my exploding life.

Ridley says, "I'd like to do a urine screen."

"Fine. I don't have anything to hide."

"And a lie detector test."

"This is insane!"

"Well, it may *seem* so, but as a medical person you'll understand we have to follow the facts, follow the science. It's about ruling things out. Let's rule out everything we can, okay?"

"Rule me out. As a murderer. That's what you're saying."

"Jane?" Her voice is hard now, like a stone.

"What?" I sound shrill.

"I'm going to ask you not to leave the area for a little while."

CHAPTER TWENTY / A CONFRONTATION

I don't tell Karen about the blood. Her heart is in the right place but my mother didn't raise a fool — Karen is only human and has no reason to be loyal or keep secrets. Nor would I want to put her in that position. Instead, I tell her what she wants to hear.

"I'm going to try RJ now. And I'll check the Everetts' place for that SUV."

"Now you're talking. I've got the kids. I'll watch their movie with them, make some snacks. You take your time."

"Thank you, Karen."

* * *

The Everetts are just up the road. I stop the car in their empty driveway and sit for a minute watching the house, thinking.

My blood? A lie detector test? Ridley warns me to stay in the area?

I need answers more than ever.

Straight ahead of me is the Everetts' garage, the windows reflecting the overcast sky. I get out of the Toyota and walk briskly but casually until I can see inside. There's a riding mower in there but no vehicles, no dark SUV. If they own one, it's in use. So much for that.

RJ lives ten minutes from the heart of town in a trailer park where he's built up his own double-wide trailer to be something bigger. There's no siding on the exterior but there are silvery insulation panels that say *Celotex*.

A TV blares inside. Footfalls approach the door after I knock and it swings open. A young guy with a sleepy look answers. "Hello?"

"RJ?"

"Yeah?" He's bearded and his hair sticks up at the back.

"I'm Jane, John Gable's wife." His eyes widen as he recognizes our names, either from the news or the local gossip. "Oh, hey."

"Can I talk to you for a minute?"

"Sure, yeah. Come on in." He holds the door open.

"Oh — okay, thanks." I smile and squeeze past him.

A dog clicks across the linoleum floor and gives me a sniff while wagging its tail.

"Candy," RJ says, "leave her alone."

"It's all right."

"Go on," RJ says to the dog. "Go on, lay down."

The copper-toned retriever bobs her head a few times then lowers it and lopes off into the living room, her paws silent over the carpet.

"Sorry about the mess," RJ says. The kitchen has a horseshoe-shaped counter dividing the living room from what looks like an office. There's a hallway that goes back presumably to bedrooms and a bathroom, the way littered with clothes and tools. The air smells like dog food and coffee.

"You should see my house," I say.

He nods toward the brew pot on the counter. "Can I get you a cup?"

"No, thank you."

He's barefoot and in a sleeveless blue T-shirt and either boxers or gym shorts, I can't tell. He grabs his own mug and looks at me. "You want to sit in the living room?"

175

"I'm okay right here. I just have a couple things I want to know if you can help me with and then I'll get out of your hair."

He scratches his neck. "It's no problem. I don't go in to the Head until four o'clock. This is sort of my morning."

"So you work at the Trailhead as your main job? As a bartender?"

"I worked for DPW for a while — highway maintenance, bridges — but then I hurt my shoulder and I had to stop. So I went full-time at the Trailhead. I help do maintenance there, too."

"A guy working on the roof gave me your name."

"Oh, Larry. Yeah. He comes and goes. Gets hired for minor repairs and whatnot."

"So the police spoke with you about my husband . . ."

"They did, yeah." RJ leans against the counter and regards me with soft blue eyes. "That has to be . . . I can't imagine what you're going through. Is there anything . . . Have they found anything?"

"They're trying."

He looks down and scratches his neck some more.

"RJ, have you ever met my husband?"

"Um, I think so — I mean I've seen him. Around town, and stuff. Maybe at the Fourth of July barbeque?"

"But never at your bar."

He takes a sip of coffee, shakes his head. "No. Never."

"The Knotty Pine . . . do you know who works there?"

"I pretty much know all the bartenders in town. Not many of us. There's me, there's Corey Reber, Kelly Ashton—"

"Could you write their names down for me? And if you have a number for them, could you write that down, too?"

He doesn't move for a moment.

"It would really help me out," I say.

"Yeah, sure. Of course." He moves deeper into the kitchen.

Candy lifts her head from her paws and cocks it to the side, watching. The flat screen beside her plays the morning news.

RJ scrolls through his phone contacts and scribbles down some numbers. "That should be everybody." He hands me the piece of paper.

"Thank you."

He sees me to the door. "Hey," he says. "Good luck."

* * *

There's one liquor store in town. I walk in and approach a woman about my age with a large mole on her cheek. I show her a picture on my phone. "Have you ever seen this man come in here?"

"You police?"

"I'm his wife."

She flips a hand. "I'm just jokin'."

She suppresses a grin as she looks at the photo. Maybe she doesn't watch the local news and thinks I'm a woman trying to catch her husband in the act of infidelity. Doesn't matter.

"I've never seen him in here," she says and glances up at me. "Just you."

It takes me aback. "Me?"

"You don't remember me. Just a couple of nights ago . . . you came in for some wine?"

"Oh." My heart is thudding. "Right, of course." I put the phone away and look at the camera in the corner. "How many people work here? Besides you?"

"Um, there's three of us. And the owner."

After convincing her to provide me their names and numbers, I'm looking at the camera again. Now I'm thinking about my own face captured on camera as much as John's. "How far back do your videos go?"

"Huh?" She follows my gaze. "Oh that. Yeah, that's just for show. Don't tell anybody." The smile still plays at the corners of her mouth.

"Your secret is safe with me," I tell her, relieved when I shouldn't be. "Do you sell Jim Beam?"

"Yeah. Think so, right over there."

I follow the aim of her finger and walk to the shelf. The bottles look like the same size as the one in John's office. Same label, too.

I spend the next ten minutes in the car outside the liquor store, watching the people come and go, some of them without a care in the world, some showing obvious signs of affliction — twitchy eyes, sallow complexions. There's no reason I should be feeling guilty about having been to the liquor store recently, but my chest is tight anyway.

Once I get home and relieve Karen I go through the numbers I've amassed between RJ and the clerk. Of the seven people, three answer. All three are aware of my husband's disappearance. None of them saw him either at a bar or purchasing a bottle of Jim Beam.

I leave four messages with my query and contact information then I send a single text.

It's to Bruce Barnes.

If you want to talk, I'll be home this afternoon.

* * *

Bruce's big pickup truck comes rolling into the driveway a half hour later. He's wearing a hockey jersey and jeans and boots and looks pleased as he nears the front stoop.

"Jane, I'm so glad you called."

"Hi, Bruce."

He leans in for an awkward hug, one hand on the small of my back. There's a smell on him I can't quite place, like he just came from a restaurant, perhaps. A little grease mixed with something sweet, like syrup. His face is open, his eyes shining.

"So are you okay? What happened last night?"

"I'm sorry about not responding to your texts."

"It's all right. I can come on a bit strong."

178

"It was my stepbrother, Leland Chase."

Bruce raises his eyebrows.

"They questioned him. Already eliminated him — he's got an alibi for the whole past week because he was miles away with his . . . ah — his partner. And he's back home now."

"Still, probably should keep an eye on him."

"Police say they are."

He doesn't look convinced. I tell him about visiting RJ and trying to get in touch with anyone serving John drinks or selling him bottles of liquor.

"That's a great idea. Cops should have been all over that. Jesus." He shakes his head.

"Bruce, I have to be honest with you . . ." I've been nervous since he pulled in, but I have to press forward. "Ridley said that you told her you didn't hold any grudges against John. Is that true? Did he do something? Hurt someone? I need to know."

Standing two steps below me, just off the stoop, Bruce has a wounded look. "Jane, I was a messed-up kid. I can own that, you know? I got a little . . . I guess defensive when it first came up. I felt like I was in a corner. And then when I talked to the cops it was, you know, pride, I guess. There I was talking to someone supposedly looking for your husband and I didn't want to get into how I was a bully, right? Because I was. And I've been trying to make up for that."

I take a deep breath and let it out slowly.

Bruce holds up his hands. "I also want to come clean about something. When I told you I was looking for property. It's true — it's just touchy right now. We don't know how things are going to go with Rainey. We're trying to stay positive. But getting mortgage preapproval and all that . . . she's, you know, she told me to back off of it."

"Bruce, I'm so sorry about Rainey."

"We're going to make it through. Okay? In the meantime, I just want to help you. Because let me tell you, from what I've heard, people think John had some kind of mental episode. Or got boozed up and had a plan to leave you guys. *That's* why I was careful about what I said to that detective. Because they've got nothing, and that's the problem. That's why we — you and me — need to figure this thing out."

I sniff a little, on the verge of crying. "They also think he could be running from something, some sort of debt, some kind of trouble."

Bruce's eyes lock on mine. "If he was in trouble, got to a safe distance, a safe place, he'd reach out and let you know."

"That's what I've told myself, but . . . he could still be lying low or something, you know?"

Bruce looks away and dips his head side to side. "Maybe."

"You really think he . . . These cops, Bruce, they're looking at me like I'm the cat that swallowed the canary. That my husband is a drunk, some high-maintenance celebrity type. Or they think I'm not telling them something. They're even asking me to take a lie detector. And when I went to the liquor store today, I . . ."

He faces me. "That's nuts. See? They don't know. They don't have anything, that's why they're doing all that. Making you question yourself. Christ! It's easier for them to just push it off, hang it on you, otherwise they've got to run out the suspects, follow all the leads, and they're paid by the hour, you know? That's why I was always in the private sector. I got paid because I did a good job, not because of taxes."

"There was blood in the car. First they assumed it was John's, now they're saying it's *my* type. They don't even seem to be considering the possibility of a third person, even though my blood type is fairly common."

"Then they don't know whose blood it was."

"No, but they tested the sample I gave them. I had no idea they were going to do that. Now they're saying it tested positive for drugs."

"Drugs? Like what?"

"I take medication. Tramadol for my back. And I've been using sleep aids. They can both be false positives for other drugs and Tramadol can even be a false positive for

PCP. They're running more tests to determine whether the blood is mine but right now they think I'm some drug addict who . . ." I sit down on the stoop, hard, because I can't stand up anymore.

When I look up at Bruce he's staring off at the ridge of mountains to the south. "Fuckin' cops. If this was my deal — I'm telling you I would've handled things differently from the get-go."

"Bruce, you can stop pitching to me. I need help."

He smiles but his eyes stay serious. "How much blood did they find?"

"Not much. A few drops. Like John could have been cut or scratched. But, they're saying it's not *his*, so . . ."

Bruce frowns. "Okay, so if it's not yours . . . whose do you think it could be?"

I answer with my eyes: at this point anything is possible.

"Well, I'll tell you what," Bruce says, "first things first. Let me go rummage around in John's office, give everything a fresh look. Fresh pair of eyes. And then I want you to give me the names and numbers you got. Let me follow up on that. The last thing you need is to be running around doing the job of the police."

"Thank you, Bruce."

"That's what I'm here for."

I'm about to say something else, something about the relief I feel having someone on my side, when the front door bangs open, causing me to jump. Russ comes bounding out, recognizes Bruce and his eyes light up. "Hey, hi!"

"Hi, bud. How you doing?"

"I'm good! How is your bullet hole?"

Bruce laughs.

I actually laugh, too, and it feels good.

* * *

A little later I have to take Melody to her piano lesson. Bruce has gone through my house, first with me, then on his own while I made the kids a late lunch. I heard him sitting and talking on the phone, chasing down the bartender and liquor store leads on my list, trying them again in the hope they'd pick up this time.

He asks me to step aside while they eat and we move back to the front stoop, our makeshift HQ.

"Okay, so, as for the stuff in John's office . . . I've come up with pretty much what you have — nothing really that indicates foul play, not overtly, and we're really short on any clues besides the entry into Canada thing. So that's that part. For the other thing, I managed to get two more of those folks on the record, and one of them — a liquor store clerk named Penny who saw the press conference — she told me John bought some liquor from her. At least twice. She works the day shift, so I guess that makes sense — it's happening while you're away at your job." He drops his head and pulls air through his nostrils. "I'm sorry to have to tell you that."

"Okay." It is what it is.

Bruce looks up. "I would do more but right now I've got to head down to Albany. We got Rainey in there with a specialist and we're going for our first appointment. I'm sorry I couldn't do more. But when I get back I'll take another run at this thing."

"Bruce, thank you. And I know you're all about staying positive, but I just want to say . . . you're both in my prayers."

He looks down and then glances up the walkway toward his truck. "Hey, we're fighters, right? Take care, Jane. I'll be back."

As Bruce pulls out of the driveway, my phone rings. I wave to him and answer.

"I've got something we need to talk about," Ridley says. I'm getting used to her voice in my ear by now. It's almost like she's become my mother, attempting to guide me down dubious paths.

"First, your husband's hard drive has been wiped."

"What does that mean? Someone tampered with it?"

"Maybe. More likely, your husband just got rid of everything."

"Everything?" I imagine all that he's been storing on his laptop: every one of his novels; personal things, like family photos and videos; paperwork from publishers; any non-fiction work he's doing.

"Everything," she confirms. "I can't find anything backed up either — no cloud. There are several attachments in his email accounts including documents from and to, I believe, his publisher."

"Those are John's manuscripts. They send them back and forth by email when they're editing."

"We got into his phone, but it's been wiped, too. No contacts, no text messages, no call log."

I get the familiar hollow feeling. Either my husband has taken extreme measures to cover his tracks or someone has tried to scrub him from existence. "Isn't there a way to recover the drive?"

"Not really. If a hard disk gets wiped and just sits there, sometimes recovery works. But if you add new data, then there's almost every chance the previous files will be permanently lost."

I try to follow the convoluted logic. "So is there new data on the computer?"

"Yes. A few new things. That kind of resets the—"

"What's on there?"

"What we call dummy files. Just enough new data to ensure the old data disappears completely. John knew what he was doing."

I wince at the comment. "Or someone else did."

Ridley is quiet.

"Why would he erase everything on his computer and phone?" It's not a question I really want an answer to.

"Because he's hiding something, Mrs. Gable. Or so it appears. With the state of your finances being what they are, your husband's mysterious disappearance, the permanent deletion of data on his personal devices — it looks like John might've been involved in illegal activity."

I feel the heat rising to my face. "What would it be? I mean, what are we even talking about?"

"Are you aware of your husband's arrest? When he was twenty-two?"

"His what?! No."

"He was arrested and charged with assault. He was in Florida."

"Um . . . well, John traveled a bit after college. He took a couple years off, traveled, then came back to New York to finish school. That's when we met. He was *arrested*?"

"And spent thirty days in Broward County Jail."

I sit down to absorb it, ignoring the protest in my lower back. "Who did he assault?"

"Two men outside a bar in Pompano Beach. One of them was the bouncer. The bouncer pressed the charges."

I breathe. "Okay. But what does—"

"He was arrested again in New York. Also assault. He stayed out of jail this time but paid a fine."

I obviously know John was a drinker — still is, apparently — but he never shared that he was a *brawler* too.

I consider his temper, his sudden flare-ups, the way he yelled at the SUV on the road that night. We don't argue much but there have been times he's frightened me, punched the wall or kicked a door. Then there are the accounts of him ranting and raving on the phone while walking the back streets of town.

"Chances are . . ." Ridley's voice sounds far away. "He's had more incidents like these, only they haven't been reported."

"Okay . . . so how does this tie in?"

"It's just another piece of the puzzle."

But I take it further: John had an altercation with someone. They were texting or emailing and eventually it escalated to a physical confrontation where someone — the other person if it's not John's blood in the car — got hurt. And if John fled, maybe it's because they were *badly* hurt, even dead. What if my husband wiped all proof of his correspondence, killed someone, dumped them and left for Canada?

That theory would be chilling if it didn't leave a gaping hole.

"He doesn't have any money. If something happened and John ran away to escape prosecution, he couldn't get far."

"Which is why, Mrs. Gable, you can understand our need to consider that your husband was . . . well that he may have given you reason to—"

"To hurt him? To stage something that made it look like . . . what? This is crazy."

Her voice gets flat and cold again. "The blood in your husband's Subaru is not his ABO type, Jane. It's yours. Your blood draw has tested positive for—"

"Tramadol. My *back* medication."

"We've spoken to witnesses who believe you and your husband were having problems."

"Oh God, this can't — these are just people in the neighborhood who—"

"Not just people in the neighborhood. I told you we also talked to the staff at the hospital."

"What? And?"

"I'll be blunt. You have a history of violence in your family. I understand your mother had more than one abuser. Just consider how it looks from our perspective. Every other possible theory behind your husband's disappearance requires a bit of a leap. And in most cases like this, it's a family member or someone close who's—"

I hang up.

CHAPTER TWENTY-ONE / BLOOD

Colette stands in front of the big red door of her house, hands folded primly in front of her, brow knitted with concern. My phone has been ringing — Ridley — but I ignore it. I'd power it off, but John could call — or Bruce with a lead.

"You sure about this, Mom?" Melody sits beside me in the front passenger seat. Russ giggles to himself in the back and adjusts his earbuds. He raises the tablet to better see the movie in the late afternoon sunlight.

"Huh?" I'm lost, just sitting in the car and not moving.

"I said are you sure about me going to my lesson?"

"She's got the extra practice scheduled for your concerto. And I think it will take your mind off things."

We need something normal. Our lives are spinning out of control, my thoughts like shattered mirror across a hard floor, each shard showing only a partial reflection of the person standing above it.

"I'm still going to do it?"

Aside from taking the kids out of school, the rest of our schedule has proceeded on automatic pilot — making meals, putting the kids to bed, even doing laundry; you just don't think about it. This is something extra, something bigger, and part of me protests: *We can't go without John*. But it would be terrible to miss it when she's worked so hard.

"We're going to do it. We have to live our lives."

Melody studies me a moment, knowing there's more I'm not saying. The idea that John and I have been getting "physical" has been buzzing in my head since Karen first said something. Then Ridley chimed in. At first I chalked up Melody's reaction, blaming me, to having nowhere else to direct her emotions. But what's that old rule? If three people tell you the same thing — Melody, Karen, Ridley — consider it's probably true.

There's the blood-type match, John's fear that he was in danger, his drinking, the sanitizing of his computer and phone. What's more likely: that John was doing something illegal for cash, that some mystery person shows up out of nowhere and John has to confront him, or that I did something and then blocked it out?

What if I'm as delusional as my mother?

"Mom?"

"Sorry."

"I'm going in." Melody opens the door.

"Mel . . ." But it's not the time or place to grill her any further about her feelings, or about what she thought she overheard me say. I'll find a better time to bring it out of her.

Or you're just stalling. Afraid.

My daughter steps out into the afternoon and I follow, steeling myself to greet Colette.

Colette keeps her hands to herself as if I might be contagious. She doesn't want to catch a case of missing husband or whatever else I have. She focuses on Melody. "Come on in, honey. So good to see you."

"Hello," Melody says.

"How are you doing, sweetheart?"

"Good."

Melody gives me one last glance and steps inside. Colette lingers at the door and looks at me with that mixture of pity and reservation. But she's discreet, saying nothing about John, and for that I'm grateful.

I clear my throat. "Be back in an hour, okay? The usual."

She looks around me at Russ in the car. I follow her gaze and say, "We'll have to get him started soon."

Colette puts on a smile that betrays her disbelief. My son taking piano lessons? Fat chance.

* * *

Two minutes later, we're pulling into the hospital parking lot.

If the blood is really mine, how is it in my husband's car?

One possible answer: I have blood in storage at the hospital. A lot of nurses do it. It was so long ago I forget the protocol, and it may just get mixed up into a general bank. Or, it's been kept separately and someone took it, put drops of it in John's car. Everything assumed so far could be wrong — maybe John was never even at the rest area. Someone drove his car there, added my blood, and left it. But why *my* blood? Why not John's? Because they meant to frame me.

I'm getting ahead of myself. The police have found a blood *type* that matches mine but not my actual DNA.

Not yet, anyway.

"Jane?" It's Caitlin, standing in the smokers' area, a patch of worn grass around a birch tree, one of those genie-lamp cigarette disposals listing to one side. Caitlin has an arm across her chest, the other holding out her Parliament cigarette in front of her chin. She pushes it into the disposal and walks closer.

"Hi, Cate . . ."

We go through it. I explain everything I know while pity fills up in her eyes and then she admits to the cops coming around — Gorski, mainly, asking questions about me.

I search her hazel eyes. "Did anyone say anything about . . . I don't know — I don't even know what they would say. Well — I know that someone said I left for a while Sunday night."

Caitlin bites her lower lip and glances away. "I think Patti told them that. And she might have told them — I don't know for sure it was her — that thing you had about six months ago. When you and John were fighting."

"That was nothing."

"I know it was. And I know you were just blowing off steam."

"What did I even do? Did I say something, or . . .?"

But as soon as Caitlin reiterates it, I'm remembering.

"Just that you said sometimes John could use a good ass-kicking. You were joking. I know you were joking. So did everyone else. It's just Patti. She likes the drama. You should have seen her with that state trooper . . . you'd think she was on TV."

"Cate . . . is it possible someone took my blood out of storage?"

"Um, I mean, they would have had to break in. The cooler is always locked up."

"It's not mixed, though?"

"I'm not sure. I can check for you. You want me to check? Or do you want to come in?" She leans down and smiles at Russ. "Hey, handsome."

Russ looks up from his tablet and blinks. When he sees her he grins and waves. "Hi, Caitlin."

She leans on the car door, her face a few inches from mine and I can smell the cigarette on her breath and traces of her perfume. Caitlin is young and pretty and prefers large earrings. Today's are a bluish-silver set of faux seashells, wiggling with her head movements. She's a good kid. She grew up in the area, never saw much of the outside world, but she's got a toughness some people seem to have, like she can take whatever life throws at her.

Like I used to have.

"You know," she says quietly, "maybe the silver lining to all of this is that John was never injured. Someone else's blood, so . . ."

"Maybe, yeah."

"And these blood-type tests. Did they have someone do it on site? Like field test it right there?"

"I don't know."

Caitlin scrunches her nose. "They're not reliable."

The hospital is squat and gray with blacked-out windows fronting the street. Selma could be sitting behind one of them as we speak. I lower my voice so Russ can't hear. "What if it was John? He comes in, signs something, gets a hold of it?"

Her eyes acquire a conspiratorial look. "Is he hiding from someone? Maybe wants it to look like he's, you know . . . What do the police think?"

"That he got lit up and slipped into Canada. That he left us. Or that I did something to him. They're asking me questions. They've got my blood and they want my pee."

"Oh my God."

I keep looking at the dark windows. "Selma Ford said something to me the last night I was here."

"What'd she say?"

"She said, 'He loves you.' She looked right at me, Cate, and she was lucid when she said it. I know how it sounds. I, of all people, know how crazy it is. I'm probably just looking for answers and ah . . ."

Caitlin stops my ramble when she reaches into the car and touches my shoulder. "I'll see what I can find out."

"I'm just thinking if . . . it's so far-fetched but . . . if there was any way John came by, said something to her. Like a message for me. A warning."

Caitlin wears a sympathetic smile. It takes me a few seconds to realize she's not just feeling sorry for my plight, she's feeling sorry for me. Maybe because here I am, showing up with wild stories about my missing husband and my blood in his car while wondering aloud if the little old lady with Alzheimer's has anything to do with it. The idea that my husband would entrust a secret to a woman with a disease-ravaged memory is the most idiotic thing I've come up with yet. And if anything it only reinforces the idea I'm trying to cover something up.

This could be it. This could be rock bottom.

We talk a little more and she has to get back to her shift. Everyone misses me (except for Patti, probably). Everyone's pulling for me and hopes John gets back home safe and sound. Caitlin is sure it's going to be okay; there will be a perfectly reasonable explanation. She waves goodbye before using her ID badge to slip in the side door.

I stare at the large tinted windows before I put my car in gear and roll out of the parking lot.

* * *

The van parked in front of my house says *News Channel 5*. A reporter waits at the end of my driveway. When she sees me, she slaps her cameraman on the chest and he hefts the rig onto his shoulder. I pull in and park without making eye contact and say to Russ, "Honey we're here. We've got to be quick. I'll race you to the front door!"

He's old enough to use a standard seatbelt with a booster in the backseat. I lean back and click the button to free him and glance out the rear window of the car. The reporter and cameraman are staying back by the road, which is public property.

My door feels heavy and everything moves in slow motion. I've never liked being in the spotlight. Russ jumps down after I open his door and barrels toward the house.

"Mrs. Gable?"

My raised hand is something between a wave and a *don't-come-any-closer*.

"Can we have a few quick words?"

Just a few more steps to the door and I'm home. The spot where I tripped on the uneven brick is right in front of me.

"Is there anything you'd like to say, Mrs. Gable? Do you think your husband has been kidnapped?"

Don't stop. Don't talk to them.

"Did he have any sort of mental issues you're concerned with?"

Russ stands on the stoop and faces the road. "Mom, who's that? Is that TV people?"

"Go on inside, Russ."

"Mom, but they're—"

"Russ — go *inside*."

He tries the front door. "It's locked."

I dig for my keys.

"Mrs. Gable, there is a lot of law enforcement working on this — volunteer crews are searching — are you prepared to accept the possibility your husband left of his own volition?"

Don't do it.

I turn on my heel and stride toward the reporter, talking as I come. "My husband is in trouble. Whatever happened to him was not his fault, or mine. Now if you'll—"

They're straining toward me, her microphone outstretched, the blank eye of the camera fixed on me, but my phone is thrumming in my pocket. I check the incoming number, turn my back quickly to the TV crew and head inside, answering as I go.

"Ridley?"

"I've spoken to FIC — to the lab. They've been able to move pretty quickly on this."

"Okay. I'm sorry that I—"

"Jane, the blood in your husband's Subaru, we've been able to eliminate you. You're not a match."

I'm too stunned to speak.

"It's ABO-similar but the Rh type is wrong. We're still working on the DNA, of course. But we know from the ABO typing that the blood is not John's. And now we know from the Rh that it's not yours either."

On the stoop, Russ sticks his thumbs in his ears and wiggles his fingers at the TV crew.

Ridley says, "So your idea that the blood is from an unknown third party, we're checking into that. We're checking your children . . ."

My brain doesn't seem to be working quite efficiently enough to grasp what she's saying. "There's no way it's the kids!"

But, wildly, crazily, I'm thinking of Melody getting her period, even though it has to be impossible her menstrual blood would be in the car. Just a warped thought that passes through my mind in the absence of something definitive as I step to my front door and push Russ's arms down. Or perhaps it's because I don't want to consider the much more likely scenario: that John had another person's blood on him when he abandoned the Subaru.

"I'm sure it's not your children," Ridley says, "but we're going to be thorough. In the meantime, can you think of anyone?"

I look back at the TV crew, still filming and aiming the mike at me over the distance, as if they can capture some of this.

"Maybe John was never even in the Subaru?" I say to Ridley. "Could someone else have just driven it and left it there? If he was abducted it could be the kidnapper's blood on the wheel."

"Mrs. Gable, is there really no one you can think of?"

"I don't understand. No—"

"Marcus Gainsborough is the biological father of your daughter, Melody, is that correct?"

My hand is on the door but I'm stuck, unable to move. "What?"

"Mom," Russ says, looking up at me. "Did you know a bullet can still move around when it's inside a person's body?"

Ridley finally answers. "Marcus Gainsborough. And from the information I have, Mr. Gainsborough is currently listed as missing."

CHAPTER TWENTY-TWO / PANIC

I can barely hear Ridley's voice beneath the roar of my maternal instinct. From the moment she said my ex's name my heart cranked and my palms started to sweat. After dragging Russ back to the car and putting him in, I throw open the driver's side door and sink into the seat.

I can't believe I never considered this. I ask Ridley what kind of car Marcus drives.

"There's a Chevy Tahoe registered to him."

An SUV. Does anyone not drive an SUV these days? Although, I did say to Sergeant Ferron I thought it might be a Tahoe . . .

The news reporter and her cameraman are daring to get closer, filming me while I sit behind the wheel on the phone to Ridley. For a split second I see how it all looks from a bird's-eye view: the harried celebrity and the relentless paparazzi.

Melody!

"Ridley, I have to call you right back."

"We need to talk about this, Jane. What's the—"

"I'll call you right back." I cancel the call and flip through my contacts, hands shaking. Russ is saying something with growing concern — he's picking up on my anxiety. The camera looms in my window, the mike aims at my head on the other side of the glass.

I've got Colette's contact up and make the call.

The line rings and rings. It makes sense that she doesn't pick up if she's in the midst of a piano lesson, but that doesn't melt the ice shards in my veins. I drop the phone, my call to Colette unanswered, and hit the gas, reversing out of the driveway so fast the reporter and cameraman have to jump out of my way.

* * *

I hear the piano playing before I'm all the way to the red door. But I want to see my daughter; I need to be convinced she's okay. After a couple of whacks with the side of my fist, the music stops.

The door opens and Colette stands there with a mildly concerned, mildly perturbed look on her face. "Jane?"

I yell past her. "Mel? Honey? You in there?" It's irrational but I don't care.

"Jane, what—"

Melody shuffles into the hall in bewilderment. "Mom? What's the matter?"

I reach for her but stay put. "Come on, honey. I need you to come with me."

"Jane, you're scaring me. Do you need help?" Colette's voice lowers at the same time she pales. "Do you need me to call the police?"

Melody hasn't moved yet and we lock eyes. "Mel, I need you to get in the car."

"Why?"

"Just do it, please." One more second and I'm barging in and grabbing her.

"You never tell me anything. Is it Dad?"

"Honey. Now. We'll talk in a minute."

She stalks down the hall toward me with extra stiffness and speed for effect. I touch her as she pushes past me — I just need to have my hands on my daughter, confirm that she's solid and unharmed — but she shrugs me off and pounds down the steps to the driveway.

"I got a call from the detective on John's case," I tell Colette.

"What happened?"

Melody encloses herself in the Toyota with a slap of the door. "It's about Marcus," I say.

"Jane . . . here, you need to sit down."

She's right. I'm shaking again — shuddering, really — like I've suddenly got low blood sugar or my screws are coming loose.

On the porch is a white wicker loveseat and two chairs with red cushions the same lipstick shade as the door. A wicker table stands between them, some type of Easter flower arrangement in a vase. Colette sits while I remain standing.

"Jane . . ."

"He's missing."

Her face turns up to mine and the softness she carries, the sweet piano-teacher-lady façade, falls away. In its place, that imperial Gainsborough demeanor shines through, the kind that inhabits her nephew, Marcus, my ex. Melody's father.

"Well, that's not official," she says. "We don't know anything yet. We just know that . . . that woman — she likes to create a controversy."

She's talking about Marcus's girlfriend. "Have you heard from him?"

"No. I'm just his aunt, Jane. The last I saw Marcus was at a wedding eighteen months ago. I don't even get a Christmas card."

I take a step closer. "Here's what we know . . . we know that the police are thinking about him because there's unknown blood in my husband's car."

She's calm. Her mouth is a thin line, eyes hunting for any sign that I'm a threat to her or her family name. "Marcus wouldn't have anything to do with that."

196

"It's not my blood and it's not John's," I tell her. The shakes are subsiding. I'm feeling more confident. "They're thinking about Marcus because he apparently hasn't been seen or heard from in three days. And because he's Melody's father. And, well . . ."

Colette places her hands on her knees and looks out into the overcast afternoon. A light rain has begun.

"You haven't heard from him?"

Her sharp eyes catch me. "Of course not. I don't know anything about this. And if I did, why wouldn't I say so? Jane, I've only been kind to you." Her hazel eyes are wrapped in wrinkles. Her crisp white hair is pulled back into her usual tidy bun. I calculate the expense of her stylishly casual clothes, like she dresses as if she saw a piano teacher in a film and decided to copy the look, complete with the sweater over her shoulders.

"I know you've been kind to me, Colette. I know what you've done. But right now I just need to keep Melody with me, okay? Until we figure out what's going on. I'll pay you for today. Full lesson."

"I don't care about the money. That's not why I teach her. She's family."

The words make me cringe. "I know," I tell her. "And thank you."

My lingering look says the rest of what I can't say: *But the second you know something about your nephew, you need to tell me. And until I know where he is, you're a threat.*

Her eyes talk right back: *This isn't the first family controversy I've been through. It won't be the last.*

I turn down the steps and walk into the driveway. When I get back behind the wheel I glance through the windshield and see Colette now standing in front of the red door, watching.

Melody says, "Mom, you're freaking out."

"No I'm not. I'm okay."

"Freak out!" Russ calls from the back seat. "Le freak, c'est chic. Freak out!"

Melody crosses her arms and turns her head away. "This is what you do."

I turn the car around in the wide driveway without responding to her and get going. The mansion shrinks in the rearview mirror.

* * *

Melody is in her room on lockdown. Russ plays video games in his own room — that kid has had too much screen time lately but I've never needed the artificial babysitting so much. I pace the house while talking on the phone with my old pal Ridley.

"Tell me about your relationship to Marcus Gainsborough," she says.

Plain Jane. Plain Jane is insane. Just like her mother.

"He was abusive, controlling, and an addict. So I left him."

"Physically abusive?"

"Emotionally. Verbally."

You're a runaway train.

"Uh-huh. I have here a domestic violence report. Filed by Gainsborough. He didn't press charges against you but it names you as the aggressor. Punches to the head, neck and ribs."

"That's a lie."

"It's a *lie*? It's a pretty detailed report."

I sigh. I lean against the wall, touch my forehead to it, feel the smooth coolness.

Plain Jane . . .

"Marcus was out partying and got into a fight with some guy," I explain to Ridley. "I told him we were through, we were done, and he threatened to go to the police and say I did that to him. Okay? I told him to go ahead. He said he was gonna press charges. I said there was no way it was going to stick and he chickened out. This is going back fifteen years. *Fifteen years.* We were young and stupid."

198

"And you have sole custody of Melody? Or joint?"

"Marcus never sought custody of any kind. He knew he couldn't be a father. Melody is my husband's daughter, he adopted her — Marcus never showed any interest. None. Not a birthday card, nothing. He hasn't seen her since she was eighteen months old."

"Yet you ran to get her, like you're afraid of him."

I move from the wall to the couch. The room is spinning and I close my eyes.

"Jane?"

"Colette gives Melody piano lessons. She's Marcus's aunt on his father's side. They don't have much to do with each other. Not anymore. Marcus has been going downhill. I rushed to pick up Melody — it was instinct. It just brought back old fears . . ." I leave the tears to dry on my face. I don't know how much longer I can do this. "I've kept tabs on Marcus a little bit. I mean, I just hear things about him — secondhand . . . mutual acquaintances. I've never talked to him directly. Not since he called me one night."

"When?"

"It was after John and I were married. John had adopted Melody. Marcus told me congratulations. He said he was happy for me. He'd been drinking, was slurring his words."

"Did he know about the adoption?"

"Yes. And recently I heard from some people that, though he'd been stable for a while, he was wrecking his life again. He has more kids with another woman and he's just screwing it up I guess."

"So . . ."

"When you told me he was missing I assumed the worst."

"Because you thought after all these years, with him never filing for custody, never trying to reunite with Melody, never contacting her, he was suddenly going to kidnap her . . ."

"With everything that's going on? I mean, do you have kids, Detective Ridley?"

She pauses. "No."

"So how do you—" I stop myself. No point digging an even deeper hole. When you've been with a man like Marcus Gainsborough, it never really leaves you. The instability, the looming threat never goes away. You can't let your guard down.

Ridley is saying something but I talk over her. "How did you find out that he was missing? Did it just come to you or . . . ?"

"Sort of. It was inputted into the state police system. I've been crawling through your list of acquaintances — that's what we do in a situation like this: we start with people closest to the victim and we work our way out."

I rub a hand over my face and try to settle down. I used to always be the steady one. I was Plain Jane. Nothing too remarkable about that Jane. She's steady. She's efficient. You can trust her. Now my strengths are a liability: I'm seen as pushy and aggressive, a suspect for spousal murder.

You can't win.

Ridley says, "Your ex-husband was on my list. I tried to call him. I emailed him. I heard nothing for twenty-four hours. Usually when the police call you, you pick up, you call back. So I sent a trooper around. His place was a mess. During the process of that wellness check, it came to our attention that he was entered into the missing person's database three days ago. In fact I talked to the woman you mentioned, Stacy Ray, the one he has two other children with — she was the one who filed the report. She hasn't seen him in a week."

It's Stacy who Colette was sneering at and dismissed as melodramatic.

"Maybe he took off," I say. "He's the type — always had the means to escape at his leisure. He'd go to New York, fly out to LA, run away to the Caribbean. Whenever. Just if he felt the need."

I used to think it was a great perk — travel to exotic places, our child would never lack. I didn't have anything growing up. Neither did John. I guess in the end you wind up with people of your own kind. If you're from the street then they're from the street. That's how it works.

"You were married to Marcus for three years."

"It fell apart." I don't tell Ridley that the Cinderella dream was subsumed by Marcus's dark moods, caused by stuff disappearing up his nose off of glass tables and pocket mirrors, or how exotic trips turned out to be neurotic episodes of Marcus trying to dry himself out.

"And you lived in the Troy area when you were with him?"

"Yes."

"But Marcus's only family are his aunt and uncle who live in Hazleton. Where you live."

I know where she's going. Of course I do. It looks too coincidental — I must be hiding something again.

"Colette reached out to me after the divorce. Said if I ever needed anything . . . She sits on the board at Hazleton Hospital and she helped me get my job. That's how we wound up here three years ago."

Something whips through my mind silver-quick and I barely catch it: *The blood. Access to storage.* But it feels like grasping at straws and I have to dismiss it as more paranoiac thinking.

Plain Jane is insane.

"Why would she do that?" Ridley asked.

"People do nice things. She knows Marcus is . . . she understood what I went through. And I'd met her a few times when he and I were together. Sometimes you lose the guy, keep the family."

At the same time, I wasn't going to go from one messed-up relationship to the next after I divorced Marcus. Expecting each one to be different but following the same pattern is pathological behavior. I knew I needed to change everything. I was twenty-four, a divorced single mother to a baby girl, when I started going to college. I would've qualified for all sorts of financial aid if I hadn't married Marcus — because of his wealth I had to pay for everything with loans. Colette understood that, too.

"With all of Marcus's family money," Ridley says, right on cue, "you never sought child support payments?"

"I wanted to be done with him. I didn't want to go to court, didn't want to see him. I just wanted to move on. After I left him I stayed at our family camp that first summer."

"The one on Lake Ontario? Henderson Harbor?"

"It was originally my grandfather's. My mom took it over when he died. She was the only one of his children who showed any interest. Melody was my responsibility. It was something *I* did — no one forced me to have a child, so I took care of her."

"But the divorce — it was Marcus who filed."

I tell Ridley that it wasn't such a clean break. I had one of the first cell phones I ever owned back then, and Marcus would call me up at night. The conversations always went the same until I finally stopped answering: he'd be remorseful and apologetic; he would tell me how much he loved me, how much he wished he'd never initiated our divorce, how he wanted to take it all back. I would tell him he needed to get help and then he'd get defensive, angry. *What do I need you for?* Eventually the calls stopped and I was able to move on.

"The camp isn't winterized, so I moved back in with my mother in Troy."

Worried that I'd made a complete mess of my life and determined to put it back together, I vowed to never let a man bust it up again.

"My half-brother and half-sister were still living in the apartment and they helped with the baby while I went to classes."

"And then you met John."

"Yeah. Then I met John. We dated for a long time because I was skeptical. I didn't want to get married again, but he convinced me. He'd been sober two years. He had his head together. He wanted to adopt Melody so we could be a family. It was a fresh start for both of us."

Ridley grows quiet, perhaps absorbing everything I've told her. "I'm not questioning you, Jane. Not as a person or as a mother. I'm trying to fit the pieces together, just like you are. That's why we need to be honest with each other."

"I'm being honest with you."

A long pause. "Okay."

"I don't need to take a lie detector test."

She's so silent I think the call might've dropped. But there's a slight din in the background, police scanners and other cop voices, phones ringing. "Do you think Marcus could be involved in what happened to your husband?"

It's my turn to hesitate. Finally, "Yes."

"Why?"

"To make me look guilty of something so that I lose custody of Melody and he gets her back. Make it look like I . . . like my mother, I . . ."

The words get lost because I'm suddenly envisioning it so clearly: Marcus coming over to the house, either by taxi or some other way, talking to John, somehow convincing him to take a ride in the Subaru. They get into a fight. Marcus does something to John, hurts him, dumps his body somewhere, and inadvertently leaves a bit of his own blood behind before abandoning the car at the rest area.

With Leland, I can't imagine such an elaborate, sinister scenario, even if he has the ostensibly greater motive. I can see Marcus for it, though. Marcus is smart, devious, and has the means.

"Okay," Ridley says, "we're going to stay on top of it."

"Thank you." It's my turn to ask a question, something I've been burning to know since I first saw the Subaru. "Can you . . . what was in John's notebook?"

"Jane. I can't discuss that with you."

"All right."

"But I do have something to ask you — does the name *Olympia* mean anything to you?"

"No. Was it in the notebook?"

"Again, I'm just going to keep certain information with me for now. It's better for you and for me. This way when I ask you about certain things we avoid any sort of contamination. So, nothing comes to mind?"

"Olympia? No."

"Okay. I'll get back to you when I know more about Marcus. And with definitive blood results."

CHAPTER TWENTY-THREE / THE BODY

Wednesday, March 27th

I swing my legs over the cushions and the floor feels cool beneath my bare feet. The events of the past days are a blur of faces and a cacophony of voices. Not sleeping at night, fatigue forces me to nap during the day.

I wake my laptop at the kitchen island and it suddenly occurs to me that I don't hear my kids.

"Russ? Melody?"

Melody appears first, blinking at me from the mouth of the hallway. "Yeah?"

Then Russ scoots into view. "What is it, Mom?"

"What time is it?"

Melody scowls at me, walks a ways into the kitchen, looks and points. There's a digital clock on the stove in plain view. "Um, it's two-thirty, Mom."

"Okay."

She holds her gaze on me. Russ has already dismissed my apparent lack of observation. "Can I have a snack, Mom?"

"In a minute."

The kids don't move and I wave them off with the back of my hand. "Go on. I'll get you guys something to eat in a little bit."

Russ leaps off to his room. Melody backs away more slowly. I need to get them outside to play; the weather has improved some. Neither of my kids have been to school all week — have they been getting any exercise or have I relegated them to their rooms like prisoners? The kitchen smells funky, like spoiled milk. I give my armpits a sniff and notice that I'm a little rank as well. I have a headache. But my attention wanders back to the computer before I do anything about it.

Olympia.

My research is still there from before I zonked out: Olympia is a sports company. It's the capital city in Washington State. It's a Greek sanctuary, site of the Olympic Games in ancient times. It's also a men's bodybuilding competition and the name for a zillion other things, including some people. But what holds my fascination is the painting by Édouard Manet.

The original is kept at the Musée d'Orsay and depicts a nude woman reclined on a chaise longue, propped up on some pillows while a dark-skinned servant brings her flowers. According to a few different sites I visit, the painting caused a scandal when it was exhibited at the Academy of Fine Arts in Paris, 1865. Manet was criticized for "crude" work, lacking the dignified and almost mythological depiction of nudity in such paintings as Titian's *Venus of Urbino.*

I check out the latter and see the similarities and contrasts: Manet's figure is less voluptuous, the image is darker and flatter and, if it weren't for the black servant delivering the bouquet of flowers, she could be mistaken for a prostitute. I'm no art history major, but it strikes me that Manet might have been an early feminist. Was my husband writing about some controversial piece of art or am I completely off my rocker?

I'm transfixed by the black cat at the foot of the woman's bed. The woman and her servant are realistic, but the cartoonish cat leers with large, crooked eyes and has an arched back and mangy fur. I feel like I'm that cat — an odd version of myself, perpetually alarmed and bug-eyed as my life makes less and less sense. Then again, maybe I'm the woman. Plain, hard to read.

John, where are you?

I ask this in the doorway of his study. Reaching over to touch the cold place in the bed beside me, I close my eyes and try to sense the answer. Nights are spent googling about missing spouses, eager to hear from anyone who's been through this how they coped. I devour stories of reunited loved ones, but the world of missing persons is mostly an abandoned place of unanswered prayers and isolated, lonely people. Most of the missing are either located within seventy-two hours or not until years later. If ever.

This is the fourth day that John has been missing, if you include Sunday. In a strange and bittersweet way, I'm becoming accustomed to it.

Since we were married, we've never been apart more than two nights in a row. I've been to nursing conferences overnight, spent a night or two alone with the kids at the lake house. This is a record.

Olympia. Meaning what? I have to know what was in John's notebook, what he was working on last. What if he really was doing some sort of book research when something happened?

I'm so tired. Limping around like a three-legged dog with too many scents on its mind. When my phone rings I can't find it right away. It jiggles against the coffee maker and I answer an unfamiliar caller. "Hello?"

"Jane Gable? It's Eve Sheppard with Channel Five News."

I leave the kitchen. I've installed drapes over the window beside the front door and I push one back. The news van is in the road; the cameraman and reporter are on my lawn. I see the woman's mouth move, just out of sync with the words in my ear.

"Mrs. Gable, we'd appreciate an update from you on the status of your husband and the ongoing search."

"You're on my property."

"If we could just have a quick—"

"Call Detective Ridley," I say, and hang up.

Eve Sheppard looks at her phone, then at the house, and I duck out of sight.

I'm back in the kitchen when someone knocks on the front door.

"I'll get it!" Russ yells. He pounds down the hallway and I rush to intercept him. The activity traumatizes my lower back. *Shit*. Not again.

"Leave it," I tell Russ with a clenched jaw.

"But, Mom . . ."

"*Russell.* It's a TV reporter, milking this for ratings. Just ignore the door."

"Milking what? Why do they want to film us? Maybe I want to be on TV!"

"*Russell!*"

He gives me a puppy-dog look and skulks back to his bedroom. Eve Sheppard's head shows in the door window. Part of me wants to storm outside and give her a piece of my mind, but that wouldn't help anything. Plus I need to take it easy now — any more aggravation and I'm going to wind up immobile. And I just got my back sorted out, too.

"Mrs. Gable? Please open up." Her muffled voice sounds plaintive, like her life depends on my giving an on-camera statement. How I love my husband and wish for his safe return and want to thank all the men and women of law enforcement — don't forget the local community — for their support. Fine, if that's what it takes to get rid of her.

I waddle painfully to the door, unlock and yank it open.

The camera light blasts on as soon as I'm standing on the threshold and Sheppard sticks a microphone in my face.

"Mrs. Gable, Channel Five News has learned that police have found an unidentified body of a male in his thirties. Do you have any comment on this?"

* * *

"The body is a man named Carl Dixon," Ridley tells me an hour later. "A known drug dealer."

"A drug dealer?"

"Multiple felon. Connected to some pretty scary people."

"So not Marcus?"

"Correct. As of less than an hour ago, Marcus Gainsborough is no longer missing."

"Wait — what?"

"We've located him. He booked a flight to Belize three days ago. Local authorities there have made contact with him."

"Is he returning to the States? What's he saying — is he saying he talked to John at any point?"

"We can't force Mr. Gainsborough to return home. The local authorities found him in good health and he's willing to answer more questions. But so far he's said he knows nothing about your husband."

Melody is safe. It's something solid, at least, something I can rely on.

A drug dealer is dead, his body found in a hasty woodland grave by a couple of hikers and their curious dog. Then there's an abandoned vehicle, a black BMW, stripped of plates and sitting in a Walmart parking lot about twenty miles away. What does it all add up to?

"The trail where the hikers found Carl Dixon isn't far from where John's car was parked at the rest area," Ridley says. She doesn't come right out and say it, but I can hear it in the space between her words: the police are checking down any possible link between my husband and the dead man.

John. Oh God, John. Getting into drugs? Then something went horribly, horribly wrong?

I feel like a pincushion of emotions.

Ridley understands and we end the conversation.

"Russ?"

I hear something thud and then a crash. "Yeah, Mom?"

"You okay?"

209

"Uh-huh!"

"Where's your sister?"

"In her room!"

After ten minutes rumbling around in the kitchen I call them in to eat. My laptop is sitting open on the island. I was researching Olympia before the reporter interrupted with her bombshell news. Once the kids are seated at the table I sit back down on the stool and check my email for the tenth time that day — I just can't help it.

There's nothing new, but before logging off I feel a pulse of inspiration and check my spam folder. It's the usual junk advertisements and newsletters I never signed up for.

And a message from LBarnes409 that stops my breath.

It's just one line: *Remember your wedding.*

LBarnes. That has to be Rainey. AKA Lorraine Barnes. But why is she writing me and what does she mean? I'm practically shivering with adrenaline as I type a response.

Rainey — is this you?

I hit *Send* and stare at the kids gobbling down their mac and cheese like I haven't fed them for days. I was sitting at this very same table when Rainey asked how John and I met, and he told her, "the old-fashioned way," and then I briefly described our humble little wedding at the lake house.

"Can I have some juice?" Russ asks.

"You know where to find it." It feels like I can't move. If I do, I might begin to disintegrate.

He gives me a look, shrugs, and heads for the fridge.

"Get me some too, Russy," Melody says.

"Every man for himself."

"I'm not a man. I'm a woman."

The laptop chimes with a new message.

It's been automatically delivered, it says, from the mail server host — a failed delivery notice. My reply to LBarnes409 has bounced back. Either she deleted the email account in the past seven hours or it was configured to reject anything incoming. I don't even know whether that's possible or not, but in my heightened state of paranoia, it seems like something Rainey would do. After all, she ran a security company in Florida, didn't she?

The kids are still bickering as I walk down the hall to John's study and stand in the doorway.

Remember your wedding.

Did Bruce figure something out? If so, why not contact me directly? Why have his wife do it? Unless maybe he's using her email. I bring up his contact on my phone and make the call.

After a few rings, his same outgoing message: "Hi, it's Bruce . . ."

I look around John's office with fresh eyes, seeing it for the man-cave that it is, the secrets it harbors.

The cops have John's computer, phone, and tax records. I've pored over his books and notes. I find myself looking at our wedding picture, the one with John holding me up. There's another one beside it: after getting the formal shots, the photographer had us loosen up and do something goofy. In my simple white dress, I hold up a sign that reads *He cooks!* and John, looking dapper in his dark blue suit, holds one up saying *She has insurance!*

Behind us, framed by poplar trees, is Lake Ontario.

Seeing John's smiling face wipes out all the bitterness. He can be a total pain in the ass, but he's my husband, my partner. He's always treated me with respect.

Selma's voice floats up from my memories: *He loves you.*

They're telling me something. Selma and Rainey. Selma has a degenerative disease and she could have been talking about anything, probably her own tangled memories — it's just random coincidence. But Rainey is a different story. Her husband has been trying to help me, taking my side when the cops seemed more suspicious of me than worried about John.

I step back from the picture and my weight causes the floor to creak.

After staring at the wedding picture some more, I ease my weight onto my back foot and then onto my front foot, listening to the sound. When John remodeled this room, he had to level the floor. I remember the construction process — John showed me how he put down sleepers and added insulation between the old and new floors. The floor in this room is solid, but there's this one spot where it creaks beneath the braided area rug.

I lower myself down carefully and roll up the rug. Pergo flooring is laid down in a staggered pattern so that there aren't any long seams between the slats, but there's one section where the seams form a square. And the edges of the square are a little ragged, the Pergo slightly chipped as if someone made a cut.

Heart beating harder, I slide my fingertips over the seams. I need something — like a butter knife. A moment later I'm digging in and lifting out a corner. Beneath the laminate flooring is a square of plywood. It's a little harder to leverage out and I'm starting to sweat. I can't seem to pry it up because it's an inch thick. The cat's paw and hammer do the trick: they splinter the plywood and I'm able to lever it back and pop it out.

Beneath is a space about six inches deep. Inside is a metal box.

I pull it out, my arms rippling with goosebumps, adrenaline prickling around my ears. The box is unlocked.

CHAPTER TWENTY-FOUR / THE GUN

Nothing makes any sense. John has never owned a gun. Maybe he used a rifle when he was younger for hunting, but we've never had a gun in our house.

I look at it, spit gone from my throat, fingers tingling with a sudden numbness.

Don't touch it.

I don't even know what kind it is or whether it's loaded or not.

Though it does look familiar.

I look up at the wedding picture again. Rainey's message was a ray of hope, now it seems like an omen — I'm already certain that this gun will match to the drug dealer's body and that John's fingerprints will be all over it.

The next idea seizes me so fully and forcibly I feel choked for air: *Mom shot Daryl Chase with a 9mm Glock.*

The name of a caliber and brand I heard repeatedly for several weeks during her trial. A weapon I saw pictures of during my deposition. This is it.

Leland snuck into the house and put it here. That's the only explanation. It's Leland, not Marcus, setting this whole thing up — Leland, having his revenge after all. I've underestimated him.

I start looking around the office, but I'm not seeing anything. Temporary blindness, they call it — only my vision is intact, but objects have lost all meaning. I've finally arrived in that alien world that mirrors my own; the parallel reality rubbing up against mine has now taken over.

Only the sound of my children brings me back: plates dropped into the sink, the pounding of feet, the squeak of Russ's voice and the frustrated mumble of his older sister.

My children, my home. Invaded by these hostile elements. My mother was right: there are dark forces at work, people behind things, pulling the strings, lying to the public about anything and everything and reality is an illusion crafted by Hollywood and Madison Avenue. In truth, we're all lost.

Plain Jane. She's insane. Her life is a mutha-fuckin runaway train! Oh!

No it's not. I can handle this. I can take the gun and I can hide it somewhere else. Or destroy it. Guns can be destroyed, right? Because the cops will never believe me. No way. Not after everything that's happened. Not when my mother nearly killed a man with the very weapon in my floorboards, not when they've been looking at me hot-eyed with suspicion all along . . .

No.

It's impossible. My mother is in jail and the gun she used to fend off the abusive, wife-beating Daryl Chase would have been impounded. Put in an evidence locker — whatever they do.

It's a cop plant, then, a salting of the mine shaft. Did Gorski stick this in my floor to screw with me? How deep does this thing go?

I see Karen's face, feel the knowing vibes coming off of her in waves as she watches me pace around on the phone with Ridley. How much of what Karen has told me is true? Any of it? John walking around, yelling into his phone, or Patti from work telling police I threatened to hurt him? They could be making it up, or at least embellishing — part of a conspiracy to sink me and my husband. Why? Because we don't belong here. Because we're different. Because—

Stop it.

The words ring as if they were spoken aloud, so clear and direct that I look around the office, wondering who's there.

Stop it, Jane. This has gone on long enough.

I'm on my backside, palms down, the open floor between my splayed legs. Like I just gave birth to a baby Glock. The kids could walk in any moment.

Jane.

The voice again, it's in my head, but now it rings familiar.

Janie . . .

Only one person besides my mother has ever called me Janie, and that's John. I listen for more, some detached part of my mind noting that yes, now I am listening to voices in my head.

There's nothing else.

Just a feeling. A feeling that John is reaching out to me, trying to communicate something to me from wherever he is. Maybe there is no such thing as telepathy, maybe there's no spooky dark force manipulating my world, but there's intuition, right?

Snapping into action at last, I cover the floor with the loose Pergo tiles and roll the braided rug back over it. Then I stand, sweating, as Melody appears in the doorway.

"Mom? What are you doing?"

I brush a sweaty lock from my forehead, a smile jittering on my face as if there's electricity running through my lips. "Nothing, honey. Everything's okay. Need something?"

She observes me a moment longer — Melody is so sharp, with so much complexity already at twelve years old — and then looks away. She's just decided I'm unstable. I know it. Feel it deep in my stomach.

"Can I go outside?"

The blinds are drawn and anyway John's view is over the backyard and forest — if there are reporters still parked out front or some dark SUV idling up the street, I can't tell. But I say, "Honey I don't think that's a good idea right now."

Melody's eyes track across the room until she's staring at where I'm standing. She looks right down at the rug beneath my feet and says, "What did you find?"

In the end, I guess, it was the idea of telling my children one more lie that finally broke me.

* * *

"Don't touch anything," Ridley says, sounding slightly out of breath. "I'm going to send a crew over right now. I'll be along as soon as I can. Don't . . . Just don't—"

"I won't touch anything. I'm done in here."

Ignoring the finality of my words, or perhaps because of them, Ridley adds, "You did good. You did the right thing, Jane."

Maybe. Maybe I did the right thing. But if so, I did it for me. I did it for my kids. I didn't do it for Ridley, who either thinks I finally cracked and came clean, or I just delivered evidence that my husband is a murderer.

The next few hours are surreal. Despite what I said about not going outside, I let Melody and Russ play around in the yard in winter coats and woolen hats while I supervise. And despite my worry, there's no SUV up the road and no news van — though I'm sure they'll be back. One or the other.

The yard is free of snow and ice; the grass is yellow and brown and bent over in bunches, stiff to the touch. I can see my breath but there's a warm sun penetrating the puffy white clouds. For the first time in many months it truly feels like spring is in the air.

* * *

Once the forensic crew (two men and one woman in full-body suits) have gone through John's office, taken the gun out in an evidence baggie and dusted everything in there for prints, things get quiet again. Melody and I make dinner. We do it together, working to a recipe from one of my mother's cookbooks, with me giving her gentle instruction here and there. Melody doesn't really need it but permits me the role with a kind of preternatural grace.

Afterward, we even bake some cupcakes. Russ is eager to run the spatula around the frosting bowl until his mouth is smeared with brown sugary paste. He looks like some kind of mad clown, and when we tell him, he does a little dance, a combination of ballerina and crazy monkey that has us laughing until there are tears.

At some point, I guess, your children take on a life of their own. They've picked up on things — characteristics — not just from you, but other children, other adults, TV shows and the rest. It all gets synthesized into their own unique selves.

Maybe that's all we do: pick up the pieces of life and make something out of them, and that's our gift, that's our human soul, something that throughout eternity will never be replicated.

It almost feels like a normal evening when the kids park themselves in front of a movie in Russ's room. It doesn't feel like I'm farming them out to an artificial babysitter. They're actually getting along. They've chosen some mutually interesting entertainment (they both like *Moana*) and are content.

But when Ridley's car pulls into the driveway, it's back to business as usual. A familiar weight settles over my shoulders and it's like I'm stepping back into the role I've had to play this past week: the helpful but misunderstood housewife.

Only now, the role has a new dimension: the scrutiny is no longer directed at me. I can sense it in Ridley's body language as I open the front door for her, can see it in the directness of her gaze as we sit down at the family table. The freight has shifted. John carries it now, even in his absence.

"We went quickly on this," she says, and pulls out some papers from her valise. "I had the gun sent straight to our ballistics unit and they did a rifling test on it. That's when you shoot a weapon into a target so you see the marks made as it explodes out of the barrel. With the autopsy performed on Carl Dixon already, we had the projectile that killed him and were able to compare the two — compare that bullet to ones fired from the gun you found in John's study." She folds her hands on the table and draws a breath through her nose. "They're a match."

If she's waiting for shock or dismay, I'm all out.

"Okay."

"Okay. And since we had your husband's prints on file it was a quick look at a lifted print from the weapon and it's also a match. So, right now, this is the deal . . . you've found a gun hidden in your husband's study, with his prints on it, that was used to kill Carl Dixon."

Again she waits, but rather than get emotional, I seek confirmation. "And Dixon was a drug dealer. You said connected to some scary people?"

"Well, that part of it we're still getting into, but yes, he has a long list of offenses and known associates, and some of those KAs are people connected to a criminal organization. A drug cartel." She looks away for a moment and then her eyes wander back. "I mean, every drug on the street connects up to some cartel or organization in one way or another. It's just a case of degrees of separation. And Dixon wasn't quite a street-level thug but a bit higher up the chain. Not much, but enough. Which probably means that whatever he was selling was more than nickel and dime. If there was a transaction, there'd be some decent money involved."

"Which could explain how John is funded even though our savings are depleted."

For the first time, I see something like compassion in Ridley's small eyes. Even sorrow. For me. "That's right. It could be that John thought this was a way out of his financial problems. Or, it could be something that just happened

218

spontaneously — something escalated, there was an exchange of fire. We don't know. And then maybe, to buy himself some time, John steals money off of Dixon and hightails it."

"What about the blood in the Subaru, then. Is it Dixon's?"

Ridley's look of concern dissipates with a furrowing of her brow. "At this point we still have yet to determine whose blood is in John's car."

I'm about to ask why on earth she thinks John would bring the gun back to the house, but I halt when Ridley raises a finger and then opens a file on the table.

"I've also been following up with CBSA," she says.

"That's the Canadian border patrol?"

"Right. For a long time we had no evidence that John crossed into the country by land or air — but then I also checked with CBSA on their Marine Reporting hotline. I looked at the period since your husband was last known to be at your home. During that time, a number of boats and personal watercraft checked in with Border Services after entering Canadian waters on Lake Ontario."

She pushes a document toward me.

"Your husband showed up in Prince Edward County in Ontario, Canada, two days ago."

CHAPTER TWENTY-FIVE / THE JIG IS UP

John is in Canada.

It plays on a loop in my mind, like before: *That's John's car, and he's not in it.*

John is in Canada.

He's alive and in Canada.

Even if John is a murderer and a fugitive from justice, he's *alive*. The hope surges in me but I'm hesitant. Fool me twice, right?

"Is there a picture of him? Can we be sure it's him?"

"Well, there are over four hundred designated marine reporting sites," Ridley says. "Most are located at marinas and yacht clubs — there's a special telephone in a room that connects to a border agent. Or, you can use a cellular phone, and connect to that same Border Services hotline. We're still determining the origin of the call."

"So it's just a phone call. There's got to be a recording then. Of John's voice." I want to believe it. More than anything I want to believe my husband is okay and just hopped over the border — even if it reinforces the idea that he shot and killed someone, abandoned his family and ran to another country. I just want to see his face. Hear his voice.

Something. Anything. My gaze seeks some photo evidence in Ridley's open file.

"The man who actually placed the call to Border Patrol is not your husband," Ridley says.

"Who is he?"

"Right now I need to keep that information confidential. The person is a US citizen and has protected rights."

It makes some sense. We don't own any boats that could cross the thirty-mile width of upper Lake Ontario. John's not a sailor, and while he might be capable of driving a big boat or yacht, he'd be a complete novice at it. Lake Ontario is more like a sea, with waves that can scrape along at ten feet high.

Marcus, I think. Marcus has money. The last I knew, he owned a boat, too.

But Marcus is in Belize — apparently. "Still," I ask Ridley, "wouldn't Border Patrol get a — what's it called — a hull identification number? Did they give that to you? Who owns the boat?"

"Again, I'm not at liberty to disclose that."

It's getting exhausting, and my reserve of good feeling from an evening with the kids is already almost drained away. "Why? I don't understand. I mean I understand about protecting privacy—"

"It's not relevant. And I need to protect this person's privacy, yes. This is someone likely hired to take John across Lake Ontario, because the boat then returned to U.S. waters later that same day."

"Well — are you questioning the driver?"

"I'm coordinating with U.S. Customs and Border Patrol on it."

"And this person definitely says he took John across the lake, dropped him at Prince Edward County."

"That's about as much as I can say, yes." She gives me a flat look.

"So," I say, feeling irked, "John rehabilitates his right to enter Canada, then murders a drug dealer named Carl Dixon and charters a boat across the nearest Great Lake. It still doesn't explain the Subaru or the blood."

"Unless he's trying to make it look like something bad happened to him. But it could also turn out to be blood from anywhere — a motorist John was helping who was bleeding and drove his car briefly for some reason, or just sat behind the wheel. We don't know. We won't know until we have the DNA testing completed, and only then if there's a match for DNA already in the system. Listen, Jane . . ." She reaches out and places her hand on mine. She's never touched me before and I have to keep from recoiling. What is she hiding? What isn't she saying besides the obviously confidential?

Remember your wedding.

"Maybe it would help to see this as good news," Ridley says.

I have no idea how to possibly agree with that statement.

"We know that John is alive. And whatever he got mixed up in, maybe there's an explanation for it. Like you point out, we have some loose ends, but I'm confident we'll get the full picture very soon and we'll all be able to sleep a little better."

"Are the Canadian police going to pick him up? How do I reach him?"

She tries to conceal a sigh as she withdraws her hand. She wants me to just accept her leadership with minimal response.

"Of course I've contacted both the Ontario Provincial Police and the Royal Canadian Mounted Police. They've each been kind enough to extend that courtesy. They'll keep an eye out for your husband and—"

"Keep an eye out?"

"And if they find him, they'll keep tabs on him." Ridley's tone gets even drier. "Jane, at this point your husband has entered the country of Canada legally. We haven't brought any formal charges yet. The DA is looking everything over and will likely issue the complaint first thing tomorrow. John will be indicted, but the United States has an extradition treaty with Canada — in most instances, they would not force John's return until there's—"

"So they wouldn't let my husband into the country because of a DUI from over ten years ago, but they won't send him home if he's committed a crime here?"

"The DUI was a crime that was *prosecuted*, and there is dual criminality for that offense. He was punished here, but not there — that's why he had to rehabilitate his admissibility. If dual criminality is found in this case by two or more years of incarceration — and it will be — then we notify the Minister of Justice and then there could be an extradition hearing. John will either hire a Canadian lawyer or have one appointed. There is a chance that such a hearing can be waived in the hope it leads to leniency or sympathy from U.S. prosecutors. A good lawyer will probably try to play that hand. This is the process."

The emotions churn and conflict. My husband appears to have simply boated over to Canada, but the only way he can be forced to return home is through a bunch of legal gobbledygook.

There's something else bothering me though: why hasn't he phoned me? Why not reach out and tell me he's there and he's all right? Even if he did something horrible, the man I married was never so secretive.

"Can we ask the Ontario police to screen him?"

"Mental health? We can. I can ask. But I can't—"

"I know, you can't force them."

"That's right." She pauses. "I know this must be difficult. We're so close, yet—"

"Is he okay? Is he sick? Was Border Patrol able to give you *any* more information?"

"All I know is what I told you. A third party notified CBSA two days ago that they had entered Canadian waters and with them—"

"But is that really all you have to do? Just pick up the phone and say, 'Hey, I'm coming in. Thanks.'"

"The agent checks the status of the individuals, makes a determination. If they're ineligible to enter the country, they're turned around. If they don't comply, a marine patrol intercepts them. In this case, both parties were deemed eligible for admission."

"And then that's it."

"That's it."

"What about where they arrive?"

"Port Milford was the destination CBSA was given."

"And was that verified? By someone at the port? Or cameras?"

There's mounting frustration visible in Ridley's face. I can't blame her; I'm being pushy. But it's my husband, not hers. It's the father of my children. While she seems like a good detective, I'm sure there's part of her looking to make a big case, a boozy writer-turned-drug-thief who killed a man and fled for Canada. It's within her sights, she can practically taste it, and I keep trying to take it away.

"Port Milford was the destination given by the boaters," she says. "It's in Prince Edward County. That's a fairly rural, touristy area known for its wines and beaches, not for its closed-circuit cameras."

I know a little about Prince Edward County, though I've never been. Henderson Harbor probably rides the same latitude line as Milford. John, with whomever he hired, must have made a due west trip across Lake Ontario. I need to look at a map but, if memory serves, he would've bypassed two large islands before crossing the international border. We talked about boating across the lake someday — we talked about a lot of things. And now he's made the trip without us. As a murderer on the run.

My God.

"You never told me what you found out — Olympia."

"I didn't? I'm sorry." She flips through some more papers. "Among the many possibilities, I did look into Olympia & York, which was a massive Canadian-based international property development firm that went bankrupt in the early nineties. The company re-emerged as Olympia & York Properties Corporation. They still own properties all over the world, but there's a concentration in Toronto, Canada."

Naturally I looked into it a bit more when we discovered John's application to rehabilitate his admissibility, but I can't find any connections to your husband or any members of that company or their shareholders or properties. The other pertinent findings were a bank called Olympia Trust and a law firm, Grazer and Olympia."

I think about it for a minute. "Are they nearby?"

She gives me a look with half-lidded eyes. "Sorry?"

"Are they close — is there either a branch for that bank or the law firm located on or near Prince Ed—"

"Well, banking can be done remotely, of course. And the law firm? No. That's located in Quebec City, so quite a ways away. But still not beyond the realm of possibility."

"That John contacted a lawyer ahead of time, before traveling over? With the expectation or maybe the concern that he'd be found out?"

By you, by the way. You were the one to find the gun and call the cops and turn him in.

Ridley is nodding. "I said that whatever happened between your husband and Carl Dixon could've been spontaneous, and that's possible. This is all speculative, but, with the application to renew admissibility made in advance, together with this possible link to a law firm — and we'll know more in the coming days if John hires someone from there — it supports a theory of premeditation. That John planned this out and executed his plan. That leads to a charge of murder in the first degree, the charge to include premeditation, and that's what the DA will seek."

I feel dizzy with uncertainty, my armor cracked at last. "Do you think he did it?"

Her eyes are cool, the compassion and sorrow long gone. "It doesn't matter what I think. It's what the evidence shows. And, Jane . . . there's one last thing we need to consider."

There always is. I wait.

"As we discussed, Dixon is connected to some dangerous people."

"You think someone might come for the money?"

"Or they might want to get to John. And they might think the best way to do that is through you."

I'm already picturing the SUV as it sat up the road, windows dark, engine idling, its hidden occupants watching me.

"I want to post someone to your house. I think we need to start taking some extra precautions."

CHAPTER TWENTY-SIX / INTUITION

Sometimes you don't know what you're doing while you're doing it but you understand it afterward. This is not the same thing as the "automatic pilot" of doing laundry or making dinner in the midst of a missing husband, but a different kind of subliminal force altogether. It's like this: you're not ready to fully realize something but some part of you goes through certain motions anyway. It's as if there are two of you — the one taking orders and the one with a much higher security clearance.

I asked Karen to sit with the kids one more time so I could go out for some groceries and she was happy to oblige. The trooper posted to my house didn't like it, but I looked into Morse's eyes with those big curly lashes and said that unless he wanted to do my shopping for me (and if he wouldn't mind swinging past the drug store to pick up some feminine hygiene products, thanks), he ought to let me go. After he blushed and looked away, I got into the Toyota and took off.

I never told Ridley about the email. Sure, I was overwhelmed. Finding the gun, hearing about John's entry into Canada and the first-degree murder charge was a lot to cope with. But I could have said something. I just didn't. I had other orders.

And now I'm sitting here outside the hospital, parked beneath an elm tree. Caitlin emerges from the side door. She looks around the parking lot as if she's Deep Throat before pulling her jacket tight across her nurse's uniform. I flash the headlights and she trots over.

"Brrr," she says, and I can feel the cold air emanating from her, smell her perfume as she warms her hands against the heater. When she faces me I notice that this evening's earrings are two large crescent moons, each with a dangling star in the gibbous space between the horns. Pretty.

"So," Caitlin says, "I talked to them."

"Thank you. And?"

"Well, it wasn't easy. But, Lorraine Barnes is definitely checked in to Albany Medical Center."

"When?"

"Two days ago." Caitlin continues to feather her hands over the vents. "I had to lie, basically."

"I'm sorry."

She gives me a sidelong look and a cockeyed smile. "No — I don't care about that. I love this cloak-and-dagger shit. But what I'm saying is, they wouldn't go for the straight request. I had to tell them we had an amnesic patient claiming Lorraine Barnes was her daughter and that I needed verifying information."

"Who'd you use?"

"I told them it was Selma Ford."

"And they went for it?"

Her grin widens. "Hey, I know how to work it, baby. Yeah, they went for it." Her eyes linger on me a moment before she hands over the envelope.

I called Caitlin the moment Ridley left the house. The papers were faxed just twenty minutes ago — medical information on Lorraine Barnes, suffering from Stage 3 lung cancer, who has known allergies to penicillin and three other antibiotics, who is thirty-eight years of age, Caucasian, with brown hair and brown eyes. Blood type A-positive.

Same as mine.

"Holy shit," I say softly.

"Did I do good?"

Unable to take my eyes from the paperwork I reach over and touch the back of Caitlin's neck and give a light squeeze. "You did great."

"So what's it mean? It's her blood in John's car?"

I swallow over a lump in my throat. A quiet excitement builds inside of me.

"It could be."

* * *

Ridley is not happy to hear from me. It's the apogee of her investigation, and I, the unrelenting wife, am back with more questions and concerns, throwing more wrenches into the works.

She's also calling me Mrs. Gable again.

"Mrs. Gable, the notebook is at the lab, still undergoing analysis. We found only your husband's fingerprints on it so far. Yes, I can get it back and go through it with you."

"I'm just confirming that it's where you found the word *Olympia*."

"You're just . . . Are you running this investigation, Mrs. Gable? Or am I?"

Calm, cool Ridley has finally snapped. I'm not trying to upset her. I truly respect her and feel grateful for all she's done.

"I'm not running my own investigation," I say, knowing full well that I am, "I just can't sleep. I'm sorry. If you could just tell me what else you found . . ."

"And you think that's going to help you sleep? I've spent hours — days — following the blind alleys of words and phrases in your husband's notebook. *Olympia* was the only salient bit. Unless you think there's some profound meaning to the words *cooking* or *insurance* . . ."

* * *

229

Moments later, I'm back in John's office, my ears still ringing with those two words as I stare at the framed photograph on the wall. That Ridley missed this is understandable — who studies a silly wedding picture and tries to connect it to words scrawled in a notebook from an abandoned car?

No one. Maybe not even me, not without Rainey sending me that email: *Remember your wedding.*

And even so, now that I'm here, it feels like two steps back instead of one step ahead. I already know about the gun in the floor. What else is Rainey trying to tell me? And why is she reaching out at all? Is it her blood in the Subaru?

The obvious next move is to call Albany Medical Center and speak to her, but she's a patient in the midst of surgery. So, then I should tell Ridley. I should tell her about Rainey's blood type — but there are two problems there. First, maybe the cops already know. They should've tested Rainey and Bruce. I was under the impression they had done so. It's going to make them look bad and cause more trouble for me if they never did. But second, and far more importantly, I've done an end-run around the police and asked a member of my nursing staff to do something illegal: solicit private, HIPAA-protected information on a patient. Caitlin could go to jail and so could I. Coming to my senses about turning in a handgun in my husband's floor was one thing, but inciting a lawsuit against my hospital and staff is something else. Plus, roughly thirty-three percent of the population is A-positive; on its own, it means nothing. Only in conjunction with the email might Ridley and her team think there's something substantive — and then we're back to the idea of someone questioning a woman undergoing cancer surgery.

I look deep into the photo, searching for anything hidden, something Rainey had seen when she was in this room, when she'd studied it herself.

There's me, grinning in my wedding dress and holding the sign above my head: *He cooks!* And then there's John, his sign at chest-level: *She has insurance!*

Behind us is the lake, and part of the house, and just off to the other side, the edge of the storage shed where we keep the watercraft and lawn equipment.

What are you telling me, Rainey?

The obvious answer is, again, the gun in the floor. Perhaps, facing her mortality, she's seen the light. Whatever is going on between John and Bruce, while Bruce may be covering it up, Rainey peeled back a corner to show me what's underneath.

But then there's the notebook itself. When I asked Ridley if the handwriting for *cooking* and *insurance* was the same as John's, she reiterated that it was at the lab and they were looking into it — but I'll bet my life it's not his flinty chicken-scratch. Which means if Rainey was in the car, if it's her blood from some unexpected cuts or scrapes and she jotted those notes on John's for-the-car writing notepad, then she was working against Bruce from at least that point.

Bruce.

Mr. Law Enforcement Wannabe, who hasn't answered any one of my calls or texts in the past twenty-four hours. Whose phone, when I try him one final time, doesn't even go to voicemail any more — there's only an automated message that tells me *the cellular number you're trying to reach has been disconnected . . .*

Bruce.

What did you do to my husband, you son of a bitch? What did you get John into?

I've exhausted all the possibilities here at home. I went over every inch of John's office before the crime scene technicians got in there. I've jumped through all of the hoops — blood and tissue samples, endless questions. I've dealt with the media, tried to keep my home a stable environment for my kids despite the turmoil. Now I've got a round-the-clock police presence — he's sitting out there in his cruiser, sweet and simple Trooper Morse who floated the whole idea of John absconding into Canada in the first place because of a missing passport and a half-drunk bottle of liquor. Not bad, Morse. You were in the gym but punching the wrong bag.

Still peering at the photo, it occurs to me that maybe there's no hidden message there, nothing to learn from the silly antics of our wedding day because maybe Rainey didn't even know about the gun in the floor and perhaps it's not the photo itself she was alluding to.

Remember your wedding.

Okay, I'll remember: My wedding was simple. Neither John nor I wanted a big, splashy affair. We invited his parents; Katherine was alive then, and John and Frank were still on speaking terms. My own mother brought Daryl Chase and his son, Leland. My half-siblings were there, too. Melody was three years old; Russ wasn't yet a twinkle in John's eye. That was it. The officiator was a woman named Marcy Landaker, her ample bosom pressing against a sharp-looking pantsuit as she stood in the heat, her back to the water, and we exchanged vows that we'd written ourselves. Simple stuff but beautiful in that way, the words still resonating in my heart. We promised to love and to cherish in sickness and in health and I promised to guard my husband's solitude, and he promised to become a famous author and make us a million bucks. Then he smiled, his eyes reddened and shone as he said, more quietly, he would do everything to support and protect me.

That was it. Refreshments were light and simple and we spent the rest of the day lounging by the water and grinning at Melody, who was a little dynamo, always on the go, flipping and singing and dancing and managing to be the center of attention at all times.

Frank and Katherine stayed at a nearby hotel that night. Leland left, as did my half-brother and sister, and only my mother and Daryl remained in the house with Melody. John and I had our brief honeymoon — two nights in Alexandria Bay. Neither one of us could stand to be away from Melody for any longer than that and we were saving money. Two brief but wonderful days walking hand in hand, exploring the Saint Lawrence River and its old castles while planning our lives together.

Funny to think now, as we rode the ferry along the seaway and could look across to Canada, that John would charter a boat to cross into that country all these years later, that he would re-establish his access, rob and murder a drug dealer, then escape abroad.

Funny.

I know my husband. I can read him. I always could. He was more than uncomfortable when the SUV showed up on the highway. He was afraid. And then with Bruce — his reluctance went beyond social angst: he hated it when Bruce was around. And now Rainey's blood is probably in John's car, a woman close to death who sent me a message. A warning. A clue.

My phone rings, displaying an unfamiliar number.

"Hello?"

There's silence for a moment and then, "Jane?" A woman's voice, but not Rainey's.

"Who is this?"

"We should talk."

My stomach clenches as I move to leave the office and notify Trooper Morse, but then I hold firm.

"About what?"

"We have mutual interests, for one thing. And I think the time has come to do something about those interests."

Though the words are ominous, she has a pleasant voice, almost smoky, like a seasoned actress.

I repeat my question. "Who are you?"

"My name is Olympia," she says.

CHAPTER TWENTY-SEVEN / DISCLOSURE

Thursday, March 28th

Tonight is Melody's piano recital. We're not cancelling, whether Ridley likes it or not. Morse decides the best thing for him to do is stick by the house. He doesn't say it, but the logic is tacit in his decision — no one is going to come for us in a public place, not even hardened drug dealers. But they might attempt a break-in while we're away.

I can't believe this has become my life.

And I can't believe what I'm now planning to do, using Melody's event as the perfect cover.

She's part of a group of five of Colette's students and she's billed to play last. We crowd into the small community center that smells of mildew and sweet baked goods. With us are Karen and her two boys. After finding our seats and sitting through the first two timid renderings of Mozart and Chopin, Melody prepares to leave us to go backstage and get herself ready. I hold her against me briefly, whisper into her ear that I love her and am proud of her. Slightly blushing and with downcast eyes, she moves off through the room so she can wait in the dusty stage wing with Colette.

I tell Karen that I have to go and make a call. She gives me a look like she knows I'm up to something, and watches while I kiss the top of Russ's head before hurrying away.

Outside, I text Olympia that I'm ready. Her reply comes back seconds later: *You'll see me. Be there in five.*

My teeth chatter as I wait. I tell myself that until we had police protection, there was nothing to ward off an aggrieved group of drug dealers; if they intended to do something, they would have done it already. I'm safe.

Maybe I'm a fool. I could tell Ridley right now what I've done and let the chips fall where they may. I don't have to implicate Caitlin or say anything about Rainey's blood type — I can make something up. Anyway, what do I think Olympia has to offer? If she's who I think she is — if she's connected to Dixon and the dark forces behind him — what's she going to do? Offer me my husband in exchange for information I don't have?

But I can't convince myself to talk to Ridley. I can't believe that my husband murdered someone and left the country. Something happened to him and I'm going to find out what.

* * *

The SUV pulls off the road fifty yards from the social center. Unsure of what to do next, I start walking. I've got my phone in my right hand, my thumb hovering over the *Call* button, Ridley's number on the screen.

I cross the road and walk along the shoulder, close enough now to see the woman behind the wheel. She jerks her head, indicating that I come up along the passenger side.

As I do, a dump truck rumbles past, followed by a blue sedan. My eyes connect with the sedan driver — he's a potential witness to this moment.

The woman behind the wheel lowers the window on the passenger side. She's blonde and supremely attractive, like someone from a movie — I had it right with the voice. And now I have sudden visions of her and John rolling together in a hotel bed.

This isn't a person who's connected to Carl Dixon; this is someone else entirely — a mistress, a lover. Possibly the woman Russ saw at our house. She looks strong; I can imagine her throwing a frying pan when things get tense. I can imagine that, after a stormy few months, John tells her they have to end it. She gets upset, won't let it go, sends him angry texts and emails, maybe launches a couple of those frying pans at his head.

She's emotionally unstable — she toys with us as we drive home from dinner one night — can't stand the sight of him with his wife, the "other woman." She's so volatile and unrelenting that he has to disappear, wipe his hard drives of all traces of her, make it look like he's dead, just in order to be free.

The entire scenario passes through my mind in about two seconds.

"I have the police on standby on my phone," I tell her.

She's wearing jeans and a sleek leather jacket with clean lines that hangs to her thighs. She's got her hands sitting atop the steering wheel, palms out, as if to demonstrate she's unarmed.

She looked like a superhero, Russ said. *I heard them talking in the driveway when I was in my bed. Dad and the lady.*

"Do what you got to do." Her tone is matter-of-fact. She's more beautiful the longer I look and it tiptoes across my thoughts: she's out of John's league. A ridiculous thing to think, but it's there nonetheless. John is handsome, intelligent — this woman looks like she could command an audience of thousands.

"Why have you been following me?"

She dips her head and looks up at me with big blue eyes. "I know how it must seem. And after the other night — seeing me down the road from your house—"

"And outside the grocery store."

"I've been watching you, yeah." She glances at the community center. The music of the third student drifts out, the discordant notes tinkling through the night.

"Why? Who are you?"

Keeping one hand in the air, she pulls a wallet from an inside jacket pocket and lets it drop open to reveal an ID. "I'm out of Jacksonville, Florida. And I've got power of attorney to arrest Bruce Barnes, who jumped bail down there two weeks ago. I'm a bounty hunter."

There is something sincere in her voice, but the past week has been so twisted, so scary, I've layered on the emotional armor. "How do I know that's true?"

"Take it. Have a closer look." She sets the wallet on the passenger seat.

Like a child warned not to get into the stranger's car, I stand my ground. "I'm fine right here."

She shrugs and returns the wallet to her inner pocket. "Suit yourself. I believe Mr. Barnes has used your husband to escape the country — to travel into Canada under a stolen identity: your husband's."

I'm too stunned to speak and dimly aware my phone is vibrating in my hand. I turn it over to see Karen's number.

"That the investigator on your husband's missing person's case?"

"No."

My hand shakes as I consider taking Karen's call. But I just need another minute.

"Bruce used John's passport to get into Canada. He got away with it because he traveled by boat."

"Then if Bruce is in Canada — where is John?"

She sighs. "There's a good chance that he didn't make it."

The first sense is a blow to my stomach — almost real, almost physical. The second is mental rejection. I have no idea who this person is, no matter what she claims.

"I think you should go," I say, weak in the knees. "I gotta get back inside."

She looks at the community center again. The piano music ends. From here the applause sounds like the babbling of a brook. One more performer, then Melody is up.

Olympia's gaze slides back to me. "I understand you've gone through a lot and you're not ready to just take all this at face value. I get that."

"If you work for a bail bondsman, why did you . . . On the interstate . . . Why were you driving like that? You sped up behind us and then slowed down and even shut off your headlights at one point. Why not just come to us sooner, before anything happened, warn us about Bruce?" My voice is on the edge of cracking.

"I put a tracker on your husband's Subaru. Two days before that night."

"Why not just come to us?"

"Catching Bruce Barnes was my original objective. But then I received information he was planning to leave the country. He was going to use someone's identity and travel by boat."

"How do you know for sure?"

"Because someone close to Mr. Barnes expressed it to me."

It all starts to fall into place.

"Rainey."

Olympia nods, once. "And when I learned it was going to be your husband, I followed you. It was an opportunity to catch Barnes in the act. And I'm sorry that I failed."

"But why drive like that? If you were following us, wanted to warn us, get us to stop, you flash your lights, beep the horn or—"

Another car is coming down the road. After it passes, something seems to have changed in Olympia's demeanor. She's losing patience. "Listen, Mrs. Gable, the only person who knows what happened to your husband is Bruce Barnes. And he's in another country, where my jurisdiction runs out."

"What about Rainey?"

Olympia shakes her head. "Rainey's part in this ended with her driving your husband's car to that rest area to make it look like he just vanished. This whole thing was set up by Bruce to put the murder of Carl Dixon on your husband."

I'm regretting now that I didn't take a closer look at her ID. If she's a bounty hunter . . . "Why not go to Detective Ridley with this? We can do it now. We can talk to her together."

"That's not how this works. If Barnes committed murder, this is out of my hands. I'm here for you."

It takes me a second. "For *me*? What does that mean? Why would you be here for me?" I'm so afraid that I'm not even sure I've spoken intelligibly; the words are a nervous vibrato, as if my throat contains a bubble.

She thinks John is dead. She's here to deliver the message because she feels she owes me something.

The wind picks up and scrapes some of last year's leaves across the road.

"Because I messed up," she says. "I found out where Bruce was pretty quick — he grew up here, so when he jumped bail it was a no-brainer. I figured he'd run out of state and I was right that he came up here. I got cocky — or greedy, I guess. Trying to catch him in the act of fleeing."

"How did you find out for sure he was here?"

"Facebook, actually. There was a picture that was posted and taken down in the same day — someone in his extended family — a half-sister or cousin or something. The photo had a geotag and that was it. I took a flight, rented this vehicle and then contacted the District Attorney. A state judge issued a bench warrant. But once I was up here I couldn't get a bead on Barnes. That's when I reached out to Rainey. She was reluctant at first but then she told me Bruce had gotten into something way over his head. And she mentioned your husband, that he was involved. Your husband was a lot easier to locate." She gives me a look that's hard to discern — there's almost a longing in her eyes. "You guys pretty much stick to home. To routine. You have a beautiful family."

"Please don't talk about my family."

I feel like I need to sit down, but I stay where I am, keeping a few feet between me and the SUV. A bench warrant? Doesn't that mean the cops would have been looking for Bruce? If so, why wouldn't Ridley have told me?

Olympia stares ahead as she finishes her story. "Then I followed you up to Plattsburgh, seeing if you were maybe meeting with Barnes. You weren't . . . you were having a date. I got frustrated. I wanted to get close, make sure I hadn't missed something — like Barnes riding with you. You have to understand, at this point I didn't know if you and your husband were abetting Barnes or what."

I remember it like it just happened — the SUV riding up behind us at a good clip, then shutting down its headlights.

"I was taunting you," she admits. "Wanted to see if — I don't know — if Barnes's head would pop up. If your husband would react, pull over or something. At that point it felt to me like Barnes had slipped through my fingers."

My mouth is dry. If I'm to believe her, then Bruce used my husband to escape the law. Used him and threw him away — even killed him in order to accomplish his goal.

Without thinking I grab onto the SUV door and lower my head. The whole ordeal has become a weight around my neck that gets heavier with every step I take. I need to slough the noose. I can't breathe.

"Jane, I'm sorry about all of this."

My phone is vibrating again. Karen is wondering where the hell I am.

I look up at Olympia. "You said you're here for me?"

"Yes."

"Then go to the cops with me, talk to Ridley with me. We can tell her about Lorraine Barnes, everything she—"

Olympia is shaking her head. "Can't do that."

"Why?"

"For one thing, Lorraine Barnes died in surgery about two hours ago, just before I called you. It was adenocarcinoma, and they thought they could get it. There were complications, I guess."

It's terrible news, and not just because of how it affects me, but because someone died. My heart goes out to her and anyone who cares about her. But I don't have time to think about it for long.

"Jane?"

Karen is back on the edge of the community center parking lot. My phone has been vibrating non-stop — I can see it in her hand from here. I wave, my arm trembling, and call out. "I'm okay — be right there."

Even from a distance it's clear that Karen is worried. I look back in at Olympia.

"Go watch your daughter's recital," she says. "I'll wait."

* * *

On the small stage, Melody plays Chopin on a rustic-looking upright piano. She could've chosen MacDowell's *To a Wild Rose*, Beethoven's *Moonlight Sonata*, or even Debussy's *Clair de Lune*, but she chose Chopin. And she's good.

It's *Prelude in E Minor, Opus 28, No. 4*. The melancholy piece dances through the room and my palms are sweating. Karen keeps giving me looks — I haven't explained to her who I was talking to yet or what was said.

I try to focus on the music. Melody has been playing for just two years and while the short classical piece has simple notes for the right hand and basic chords for the left, she's nailing it, and the effect is haunting. For a sublime moment I forget everything, lost in the performance.

John is dead.

It's the second time I've had to face it. Seeing the Subaru in the unused rest area nearly knocked me over, but I recovered — there was hope. Things have gotten worse. The possibility that I'm a widow, that my children have lost their father for good, looms larger than ever. I can feel the tears slipping down as I think about what I'm going to say to Ridley.

Just had a chat with a bounty hunter who says Bruce Barnes is behind the whole thing.

Why did John get hooked up with Bruce? Were the two of them out doing drugs? Selling drugs?

I need to know more. I have to know what happened.

Remember your wedding.

I do. I remember how that first night in our hotel room overlooking the bay we listened to a duet between Johnny Cash and Bob Dylan called "Girl from the North Country." I remember how he smiled and his eyes wandered the room; how, like the music, we humans do this sort of dance, a peekaboo game of seeing each other, of recognizing the light and eternity in the other person. It's a dance, but I saw my husband, I know who he is.

I don't know Olympia, though.

I go over it again: even if she's not official law enforcement, she must work with them all the time. She'd have a license to practice. She said a bench warrant — wouldn't the state police know about that? Bruce gave DNA samples, for God's sake — Ridley would have been aware he'd jumped bail.

As the crowd breaks up into applause and Melody stands and takes her bow, I can feel the truth pushing through.

* * *

"We've been through the lake house," Ridley says on the phone. "There's nothing there. No signs of break-in, no signs of struggle. No sign your husband was there — not since he last visited."

"Did you take fingerprints?"

I'm back in John's office, at his desk. The SUV was gone when we left. Olympia might've gotten impatient. Though I was anxious, I stayed for about fifteen minutes of socializing and drinking punch. For Melody.

"No, Mrs. Gable, we didn't dust for fingerprints at the lake house. What's going on? Did something happen?"

I want to tell her everything. In fact I planned to, but I can guess the response: I face charges for violating HIPAA medical privacy laws and I'm in trouble for withholding evidence or obstructing justice, one of those, because I didn't disclose Rainey's email right away.

I think of John's Subaru sitting in the weedy rest area, drops of blood on the steering wheel and gear-shift.

Jump back a little in time: Rainey parks the vehicle in the middle of the night and her hands are bloody. Or, maybe she's not bleeding from her hands; the drops were fine-grained, more of a spatter or a spray, like someone coughing. Olympia said adenocarcinoma, a common lung cancer, affecting the outer lungs. You don't always cough, but if you do, late stage, you might expectorate blood. It's only a day later that she's checked into Albany Medical.

Bruce knows Rainey has been sick for some time. They don't have insurance. They need money for an expensive procedure. So he rips off a drug dealer named Carl Dixon, kills him then tries to frame John for it by leaving a crumb trail of clues. The clues lead to a gun in the floor of John's office and his boat ride to Canada.

But Rainey talks. Somehow Olympia connects with her, Rainey tells her the truth. And Olympia, looking for Bruce, watches us, watches John.

"Mrs. Gable?"

"I talked with someone who said they were a bounty hunter."

"Who?"

"From Florida. Where Bruce apparently jumped bail. She said her name was Olympia."

"Olympia what?"

I never even got the woman's last name, didn't look closely enough at her ID. After I explain to Ridley how it came to pass, she hurries to get off the phone. "I've never heard anything about this — *nothing*. What's she doing up here chasing a bail fugitive and not checking in with us? We're the *state police*. I never saw anything about it. Listen, I'm going to look into this tonight and I'll call you back first thing in the morning."

CHAPTER TWENTY-EIGHT / MY ALTER EGO

After the call with Ridley, I stand next to Melody in the living room, trying to keep my composure as I beam at my daughter, swelling with love, pride, a sadness that's all mashed together.

"You were amazing, honey."

"Thanks, Mom."

"Really something."

"I was okay."

The tears sting my eyes — she hasn't mentioned her father's absence but it's there between the words.

"Where's Russ?"

Melody turns her head and shouts in an ear-splitting voice. "Russ! Mom wants you!"

I smile through the crying and hear Russ in the distance. "What?"

"Mom wants you! Come *here*!" She shakes her head and looks at me. "What a dope."

"Be nice."

Footfalls pounding through the house precede my son's blustery entrance. "Huh? What? I'm right here, Mom."

"Come here."

Once he's close enough I get my arms around him, draw him in. His odor mixes fresh air and greasy hair.

"You need a bath. Let me look at your hands."

As I suspect, rinds of dirt caked beneath the fingernails. I let his hand drop and reach beyond him, get a handful of Melody's shirt and yank her toward me. I can feel the flutter of their hearts. Melody has a more pleasant scent than Russ, like citrus. Her fine hair tickles my cheek. Neither of them tries to wriggle free, which is unusual.

"I love you, Mom," Russ says in his light voice.

"I love you, too." I sense someone and look over the heads of my children. Karen stands in the bedroom doorway, tears swimming in her own eyes.

"What a week," she says, lip trembling. "Huh?"

"Yeah." My word is just a breath.

And then my phone rings again.

* * *

It's 11 p.m., shift change for the state troopers. Morse anticipated a half-hour gap in coverage for the transition tonight. He was right. At the moment, no one is watching me.

The rules I gave Olympia were to park in my driveway, and that my friend Karen observes from the house — the second anything looks wrong, she dials 911.

The sleek black SUV idles, waiting. I first check to make sure Olympia is alone, then slip into the passenger seat. I've spent the past two hours psyching myself up for this but I'm my mother's daughter; I can handle anything.

"You're not a bounty hunter," I say to Olympia. "You work for someone else."

"There's a black bag behind you in the seat. Can you get it?"

I reach for it, noticing the flexibility I've regained since my back trouble improved.

"This bag?" I set it on my lap.

"Open it."

I unzip the bag, expecting anything at this point. Another gun. A million in cash. A severed head. Instead there's a few assorted tools, lots of wires, and something I recognize as a camera. We had one like it when Russ was a baby so I could watch him from my phone.

"See the little case inside there? The little hard case."

It's slim and black, as if for cigarettes.

"Open it up. Take out the flash drive that's — there you go. Now stick it in here."

She points to the dashboard, which resembles the control panel of a spaceship, with more lights and buttons than I can figure out. But I see the small GPS screen and the USB port.

"Pop it in there. Now, click on the file that says 'Gable 3' when it shows — yup, that's it. Now hit play. Enjoy the show."

Within a few seconds, I'm watching my husband's office on the screen, the view from the corner of the room, near a set of bookshelves.

"When was this?"

"Just watch."

Bruce steps into view. He bends and lifts the loose flooring, takes a gun out of the bag he's holding and puts it inside. I can hear my own voice in the background, faint, talking to the kids in the other room.

This was when Bruce came over. The last time I saw him. He said he wanted to help. I can't believe I left him alone in John's office. What was I thinking?

Olympia talks while I watch. "Bruce Barnes convinced your husband to come with him on a drug deal. A kind of ride-along. Maybe for one of his books. And you know how it is with men, daring each other. Anyway, when they get there, it's a deal between Barnes and Carl Dixon. Barnes shoots and kills Dixon, who is employed by the same people who employ me." She turns her face to mine and the smile is gone. "My employer is one of the biggest cartels in North America."

My stomach sinks. John's angst. Crawling out of his skin at dinner. The dark cloud hanging over him for at least a week prior. *Why would you do such a thing?*

On the video screen, Bruce has left the room. The screen turns blue when the file ends.

"You lied to me once already. How do I know you're telling me the truth now?"

"You don't."

I nod at the thumb drive, still plugged in. "What do I do with this? Give it to the police and say it's from Carl Dixon's people?" I'm past nerves and fears at this point — the words just flow.

"I gave that camera to your husband," Olympia says. "I've been to your house, never in it." She pulls out the drive and hands it to me. "It's yours. Proof your husband isn't a murderer. And there's another clip on there that shows Bruce planting the bottle of liquor."

I roll the small drive between my fingers. "You told me you screwed up. You said you thought John had done something."

"The only information I had to work with at first was Dixon's death, a hundred and fifty thousand stolen, plus the product. So, three hundred large. I was contacted, put into motion. I knew that the exchange had been set up, I knew who the buyer was."

She tucks a lock of hair behind her ear with a gloved hand. "But I'm a professional. I gathered more information to make sure I had all my bases covered — no surprises. There was a text from Dixon that went out to my employers just prior to the exchange, said that there was another guy with the buyer."

"John."

She nods. "So, here's the deal with Barnes . . . he got started on this down in Florida. He worked for a security company in Jacksonville—"

"Night Watch."

"Mmhmm. Barnes and his wife started out small, rolled up a stake and took it wider, started to think they were bigger players, but they stepped on some toes down there so they decided to relocate up here. After being in the region about six months, Bruce found his way to my employer, made a connection. It's mostly heroin."

She dials up the heat, increasing the warm air blowing from the vents. "Where was I . . . so — you don't smoke, do you?"

"No."

"Good. If you were holding — you know — I can be weak when it comes to cigarettes. All right, so Dixon says there's another guy there, and he's not happy about it. Maybe it escalated and Barnes protected himself. Or, maybe he planned this — to get the money for his sick wife."

"That's what I think."

"They're trying some Hail Mary pass, some last-ditch attempt to help her. Like anyone would. And these are freelancers, you know — no health insurance. So, there's an idea among my people that Barnes had this all planned out, but I don't think so. I think he brings your husband there to show off. But then the thing escalates and now he's got a witness to a murder he committed. And then after all the macho dust settles, it probably starts to sink in that Dixon's absence is going to be noticed. The missing money is going to be noticed, and now Barnes is panicking. About the time he's going through these motions is about the time I figure out who the guy in the car was — your husband. Barnes keeps a low profile but Rainey is a bit more outgoing and I'm able to find her. So about a week ago I roll up on her. Barnes doesn't know. But she and I have a little talk and she tells me about your husband."

"And then you tracked us."

"Figuring Barnes is going to come around eventually, yeah, I put the tracker on your car Thursday night. Friday, you guys went and had your dinner date. From there it's like I told you."

"But why follow *us*? You knew Bruce was the buyer, you said you talked to Rainey — what did John do? He was just there."

"We don't just go around half-cocked, Jane. In my business you have to be certain. Barnes isn't the only guy out there. We have rivals, competitors. We thought it was Barnes but I needed to be sure. I needed to talk to your husband. I believed John — he was in the wrong place at the wrong time. He gave me Barnes's cell number, let me set up the camera. Barnes was coming around your place, testing John, seeing if he was going to keep quiet. Probably threatening him. Then the night John disappeared, it came to a head."

"I still don't understand why you didn't . . . Why didn't you stop Bruce before he did this to my family?" I'm past the tears, but still have to clasp my hands together to stop them from shaking with anger.

She gives me another look with her bright eyes. If she wasn't working for an international drug cartel I could see her as one of those sexy gladiators on TV. One I'd like to strangle for being part of this whole sordid business. "I tried, Jane. Barnes is slippery. He kept to public places, he dropped off my radar here and there."

I stare back and it slips through my thoughts that I'm having a psychotic episode. That to Karen, watching from the window, I'm just standing in the driveway, talking to myself. No SUV, no Olympia, no drug deal, just a missing husband who tottered off on a drunken whim and met with trouble.

I'm not who I think I am when I look in the mirror. I'm not who I've pretended to be all of these years.

That the fantasy of being mentally unhinged and delusional is preferable to the reality that speaks to just how low and dark things have gotten.

When I talk again, my words are almost inaudible. "What happened to my husband?"

She glances at the thumb drive in my hand. "There's another file on there. It's from the night they took John. On that one Bruce is sticking the bottle of Jim Beam in the cabinet — just his way of adding to the narrative that your husband was going downhill, likely to do something like this. But he put the gun in later, with you in the house. Why? Because he needed to hang onto the gun for another night. Because — and I'm sorry to say this — he used it on your husband."

CHAPTER TWENTY-NINE / AFTERSHOCKS

The days that follow are like a dream. I answer all police questions about Olympia, including an intense session with a drug enforcement agent. I take the lie detector test Ridley once promised. Karen recommends a lawyer willing to work pro bono. None of it fazes me.

Karen helps field the endless calls, most from reporters. They've set up camp outside my house. Eventually Karen has her husband Matt intervene. He gives Channel 5 a stern talking-to and they leave. After a little more time, the lawn is clear.

Karen tries to cook for me, but I like to be in the kitchen. It keeps my mind off of the things I don't want to think about — like holding a memorial service for John, or answering the questions that burn in Melody's eyes, that Russ doesn't have words for. We've all fallen into the routine — that's the saddest part, really; even the kids are functioning a bit more like subdued clones of their former selves. I actually miss their bickering.

After three more days of police protection, I convince Ridley to stand down. No one is coming for us because Bruce is in Canada and John is dead. We're not in any danger.

No one knows who Olympia really is — or at least, they're not telling me. I haven't heard about any apprehensions of a drug cartel employee, but maybe it's gone above Ridley's pay grade. Perhaps the Major Crimes Division or DEA play things like this closer to the vest. But, I don't know. Something tells me Olympia wouldn't have stuck out her neck the way she did if she was afraid of the police.

The only silver lining is that her gift to me had the intended effect — Ridley viewed the video files and submitted them to the DA, who withdrew the charges against John. All that remains for her to close the case is to find John's body and match the bullet that killed him with the gun Bruce put in my floor.

I ache at times, full body aches that make my back pain seem like a distant twinge. My heart doesn't beat the way it did — or so it seems. I'll place my hand to my chest and can't feel its rhythm. We can't keep living like this. At some point the kids have to return to school. At some point we need to say goodbye to John and move on with our lives.

* * *

Melody sounds sleepy when I knock on her door at six in the morning. "What?"

"Honey, pack your things."

"Why?"

"We're going to the lake house."

"What? Really?" She's more alert now, even excited.

Russ's door is open. He's overheard. "Will Dad be there?"

"No, honey. Just us. Pack some pajamas, your toothbrush, a couple changes of underwear, okay?" I'll have to repack everything, but it'll keep him busy for a minute.

Melody opens her door. "Are we going to stay there, like, for a while? Like the whole spring break, like we said? Or are we moving there?"

"Just pack enough for the week. Spring break is almost over. If we need more stuff we'll go into Watertown and go clothes shopping, okay?"

The prospect of new clothes cracks her armor. She smiles as she opens a dresser drawer and starts riffling through it. "Good, because I have *nothing*."

The lake is a three and a half hour drive. If we leave within the hour we'll be there in time for lunch. I can already see myself shopping at the little grocery store near the bay marina. I can smell the fishy air and imagine cooking on the ancient gas stove in the kitchen while the kids play in the yard overlooking the clear water.

At least, that's what I tell Ridley on the phone.

"Mrs. Gable, I'm not really sure about this."

"I need to get away," I confess to her from the porch. "I have to talk to my children. I don't want . . . not here. I don't want to do it here."

She's quiet. "You haven't told them."

"Could you?" I've gone numb to my own pain. What stings is when I think about them.

"Okay," she says at last. "Okay. But you have good cell service there? I need to be able to reach you at all times."

The service at Henderson Harbor is spotty and unreliable. But I know places where I can get a good signal. I don't tell Ridley it'll be intermittent; I can do without the obstruction.

"Yes. It'll be fine."

The sun has come out and is warming the day as I carry two bags to my car and pop the hatch. I sense the SUV up the street before I even turn to see it. It's in the same spot. I can just hear the sound of its engine idling. A dark figure sits behind the wheel.

I shut the hatch. I walk down to the end of the driveway — there's no vehicle there, just my imagination.

* * *

We take the scenic route; Sackets Harbor is where the Saint Lawrence Seaway meets Lake Ontario. In the warmer months, ivy climbs the brick buildings that frame the open-air eatery of Tin Pan Galley, its amber lights festooned above the outdoor tables. Men drive silver sport convertibles with their fifty-something wives, each in polo shirts and his and hers black sunglasses. More ivy swarms the power lines crossing the road of the charming little downtown area as seagulls swoop and scree, scavenging from hidden dumpsters.

But in early spring the town is subdued, minds still frozen in the grip of winter and dumps of lake-effect snow. Many seasonal houses remain dark and buttoned up. Elm trees, with their saw-tooth leaves, line the streets amid oaks and maples. The cedars edging the water take the shape of the wind.

Henderson Harbor is even quieter. There's no real downtown area. The road going in begins with big houses and large estates with names like Turra-Murra and Castle Bluff, then the road gets closer to the lake and the properties smaller until we're passing the marina and bait shop. This is where the poorer people live — essentially in the boat parking lot for the big sailboats and yachts. This is where my grandfather built his modest little lake house, which was then inherited by my mother.

* * *

We get out of the car and I pull the key from my pocket and open the door. The inside smells like it usually does: musty and unused. I click on the lights and remind the kids not to drink the water from the tap — the sulfur content is too high. "Bottled water is in the garage."

I look around at the old furniture: embroidered couches, thin-legged end tables, my grandfather's taxidermy fish adorning the walls. Some are my mother's catches, too. It's been over two months since I've been here — just the one time in mid-January to check on the place with John — but there's evidence of his more recent visits: a tool bag sits on the front porch and the extension ladder lies on the gravel floor of the garage, not up against the wall.

After we unload groceries and luggage, Melody and Russ head out to play. It's a warm afternoon and the lake is calm and softly lapping, foam sliding over the smooth pebbles. A glow has come back into my daughter since we arrived and it's the best thing I've seen all week. The kids chase each other in circles around the house then launch over the containment wall and scramble down to the water's edge to skip rocks.

"Be careful!"

I hug myself as the wind pushes off the lake bringing fishy scents and I walk back to the road. We're the only people around; just about every single place in this little neighborhood of a couple hundred people is not habitable in winter. The most eager arrive late April, but it's not until the Fourth of July that it gets the most active. The height of summer, like when John and I got married.

I face the lake house the way the wedding photographer was facing when she took the picture of John and me holding up our humorous signs. I raise my arms and use my hands in front of my face to form a makeshift frame. I've been over it in my mind a million times, piecing together the timeline for the night John disappeared, poking and prodding it to see what makes sense and what doesn't.

Olympia believes that the timing of Bruce stashing the gun means he held onto it long enough to kill John, otherwise he could have planted it earlier with the Jim Beam. Maybe so.

In some ways I guess you could say Bruce fits the profile of a killer: he's got that affinity for law enforcement you hear about some killers having, wishing they were cops; he's a bit of a narcissist, certainly prideful; and circumstances made him desperate.

But I have a hard time believing it. It feels more accurate that while he's a hothead, maybe an opportunist, he's not a cold-blooded killer. And if the drug-deal murder was unplanned, if Bruce has just been making this up as he's gone along, it's more likely he let John live. He just needed to stick John somewhere long enough to make his escape. And if he has a heart — and I think he does — he'd want John found eventually. So without the ability to send emails or texts or anything the police could track, he has Rainey leave a message in a notebook, something I would understand when the lights finally turned on in my mind.

Cooking.

Insurance.

Clues to a photograph that showed John and I on our wedding day, showed the lake, part of the house and part of the shed.

It's made of corrugated iron, a long rectangle that resembles a storage unit on a cargo ship. That's because my grandfather was a sailor and used to work the transatlantic ocean liners that came across the Erie Canal, up through the Great Lakes and all the way into the Saint Lawrence River.

There are no windows and one end is a door with two bars intersecting at ninety-degree angles, padlocked where they meet.

I pull out the keys again.

The padlock disengaged, I drop it into the grass, grab the lever of the vertical bar and swing it back. The door makes a familiar *clunk* and then gives off a squeal as I pull it back and swing it out of the way. The smell emitted is instant and overpowering — dust and mildew and darker things, too.

I grope for the dangling string and pull on the light. There are two kayaks, several bicycles, lawn furniture, yard equipment, life vests hanging from hooks in the ceiling, a stack of lumber, scattered tools, piles of boxes and stacks of old magazines.

And at the very back, lying on a blanket and unmoving, is my husband.

CHAPTER THIRTY / THEN

Tuesday, March 5th

"You need to go through something."

"Yeah," John said. "Right."

"No," Bruce said. "I mean it."

"What are you talking about?"

"You need to have a first-hand experience. Something authentic. And then you can write about it."

John looked at his old high school classmate with the ruddy complexion, gut gone soft in the middle — it looked like he was drinking too much. But his eyes had energy.

John shook his head and turned away. "Dude, I have — you know, it hasn't been easy lately."

"You got money problems?"

It was the last thing he wanted to talk to Bruce about. "We're okay. Jane makes a good living."

"But you could be doing better . . ."

"My monthly income hasn't hit four figures for over a year."

"Ouch."

"I mean, it's the money, but it's—"

"No," Bruce said, "I totally understand."

John was uncomfortable with that out in the open. But there was a sense of relief, too, unburdening. Besides, was he still in competition with Bruce? High school had ended twenty years ago. For God's sake, it was time to let it go. Time to shrug the inferiority complex. They'd all just been kids — Bruce hadn't known any better. Kids didn't know the effects of shame. It was in the past, more distant every day.

Besides, Bruce was no big success story. For all his bravado and boastfulness as a kid, here he was, approaching middle age and starting over, a new relationship, a return to his roots. People were just people.

"How about you?" John asked.

Bruce nodded his head and looked to the side. "Yeah. It's been up and down, man. Life on the high seas." He uttered a smoker's cackle. "Mostly down, though. Mostly down."

A silence developed. John studied his hands and looked out of the window.

"I'm serious, though," Bruce said.

"What? About having an experience?"

Bruce nodded.

It was awkward. "Yeah, well, that's what I'm saying. I can't just pick up and go climb Everest, you know." He tried to laugh away his nerves.

"I'm not talking about that. It wouldn't cost you any money."

"Okay. I don't understand."

Bruce folded his arms, leaned back against John's desk and fixed him with a matter-of-fact gaze. "I got something going up here — security gig. It's something I think you could . . . well you could do like a ride-along."

"What kind of security?"

"Let me put it to you this way . . . When we had the crash in 2008, you know what the smart economists said? What they knew? If it wasn't for the black markets, the whole country's economy would have just collapsed. I mean, rubble."

"Black markets."

"A whole underground economy that props this country up, keeps it liquid. You have countries where drugs are legal. And if people get too deep into it, you know, they go to a hospital, they see their doctor. Meantime, the money is flowing. It's all perspective."

John didn't know what to say. He wasn't sure whether Bruce was putting him on, whether he should just laugh it off — something about security and black markets and drug running? But Bruce looked serious. He'd always been a little edgy, but it was possible his mental health had taken a dive. Now, how to back out of this conversation and get him out of the house without it being too unpleasant.

But Bruce held up a hand. "I know what you're thinking . . . you'd be perfectly safe. Perfectly safe. For one thing, I'm strapped. Got a Glock 19 concealed carry and a SIG Sauer I keep on my ankle. And I know what I'm doing — been doing it for ten years. I know there's a stigma, you know — all of that. But you wouldn't be doing anything illegal, right? You're just there in the car. You get a little taste of the life. And I guaran-fucking-tee you it will turn on all the lights in your head. Think about it. Here you sit, at your desk, day in and day out. What's your life? Your life is taking the kids to school, making dinner — how are you going to write anything like that? You need to live, bro. And this . . . man, the fucking adrenaline you'd feel, the ideas you'd get."

The room felt cold. "Yeah," John said, "that would be something." *Try a smile. Might be Bruce just has one hell of a poker face and this thing really is some weird joke.*

"Just think about it." The same light played in Bruce's eyes. "It's a quick deal, in and out. It's all outdoors — you can just chill in the car. But you get the scope of it, you get the feel. None of these books in here — these cop books — are gonna do that for you. And I've been doing this for a while, too, like I said. Doing it in Florida. I can tell you some stories while we make the drive."

"Where?"

"Not far, man, not far." He got more animated, excited. "You could just tell the wife and kids something — I dunno, you got an overnight writer's conference or something. You come with me, we do the thing, and boom!" He clapped his hands, making John jump. "I'm telling you — you'd be off and running. And then when your book comes out, all your other books start selling like gangbusters. What do they call that — you know, the rising tide? And, listen . . . the experts encourage this shit. You've got to think outside the box. Ninety-seven percent of people just do the same shit over and over. They all end up working for the few who shatter the norms."

There were two options, John figured. One, say yeah, sure, sounds great — and get Bruce out of the house. The kids were going to be getting off the bus soon, for one thing. Two, just confront it right now, say no thanks and get him out.

"Yeah but, man, it sounds like what you're talking about makes me a party to something. I mean, that's the bottom line. I couldn't write about anything like that — not if it was illegal . . ."

"You fictionalize everything, man. You know how to do that. And then I'd be reading your book someday — man that would be fucking awesome."

"I can't lie to Jane. I mean, I just physically can't."

Bruce stared at John for a moment, something almost like pity in his face, then he shrugged. "All right, bro — well, whatever. You just keep going the way you're going, man. I'm sure you're a good stay-at-home dad and house-husband. Anyway, you know, it's not like you'd have to worry about the legality, because *nothing is going to happen*. It's just business as usual. Something I've done a thousand times. But it will fill your head full of real-life shit you can draw on for years. No more of this bullshit about psychological thrillers, women questioning their sanity or whatever."

John stood up from his desk, feeling more than a little uneasy. It was too much — Bruce was insistent. Whatever had broken in his brain was bad. The guy needed help.

But calling him out on his insanity right here, right now — it wasn't John's place.

Bruce moved closer and clamped a hand on his shoulder. "Listen, man. I want you to know something. All that shit, from back in the day, you know — water under the bridge. I don't hold any grudges, man. Life's too short. I hope you don't either."

John searched Bruce's gaze for as long as social comfort allowed. Was he crazy? Was this whole proposal just some long, strange goof? Or was there some latent narcissism in it? This idea of Bruce having him tag along as he went around to sell drugs or whatever else, talking about himself like he was some kind of celebrity. Like he was El Chapo. It was a fantasy Bruce harbored, to have some sort of scribe write his memoir, and he lacked the internal censorship to keep it to himself.

"I don't hold any grudges either," John said.

Bruce surprised him with a hug and gave him a few hearty pats on the back. Up close and personal, there were trace scents of alcohol.

"That's my man," Bruce said softly. Then he pulled back and gave a serious look that quickly fell apart. He stepped back and laughed, slapped his thigh. "You should see your face, man. You think I'm nuts!"

John just stood, unsure of how to respond. The relief, tentative at first, started to flood through. It was so powerful that for a moment he needed to sit down. Bruce was "out there," he was a different sort of guy with no real external reference points to help him navigate relationships, but he wasn't full-on psychotic. He just had a terrible sense of humor.

John smiled anyway. The pitch was over and Bruce pulled himself together. "Of course you're right," he said. "You're absolutely right. It's too much for you. If you were single, I'd say let's do it, right? But, no, it would be too much. With all you got going on — nice little family here. Even if you'd be a millionaire by the time the whole thing was over." He winked.

John cleared his throat again. "Yeah, sorry, Oprah."

"Oh, Oprah, Dr. Phil — the whole bit. You see that woman on *Dr. Phil* who was kept in a storage container for a week? Man, that was crazy. That guy who took her — what a fucking thing."

John pushed aside the grisly thoughts and moved toward the door. "All right, man, well . . ."

"Sorry — I've been taking up all of your time. You've probably got to get back to writing. What are you working on, anyway?"

John held the doorknob, feeling the weight of the question. "I got a few irons in the fire."

"Uh-huh. Well, better hurry up with those."

"Yeah." John opened the door. "I know."

And then he thought about it some more.

CHAPTER THIRTY-ONE / ALL HELL

Call everyone. Call 911. Get an ambulance here. Get Ridley. Call everyone.

While I've been trying to restore John to consciousness, shaking him, crying, holding him against my chest and gagging on the stench of human depravity, I managed to get my phone out, but it's no use in here — the metal walls block the already poor signal.

He's gaunt. His color is terrible, pale and sickly. He's been in here for almost two weeks, living on nothing but water and whatever scant food he was left — I see a few granola bar wrappers and empty pretzel bags, bottles full of dark urine, corners holding excrement.

I'm choking on emotion when suddenly everything inside me falls dead quiet — except for one lone thought:

You did this.

And I see it all, projected on the walls of the shed as if on a movie screen: arguing with John, angry mouths and spit flying. Arguing over money, over Melody — her development and her needs and the fact she takes her piano lessons from my ex's aunt. Fighting over his drinking, because I found the bottle when I was cleaning and he lied to me about it and I scream at him that I'm not going to go down this road again, not going to let another addict drain me of resources and patience and love, and I hit him, not expecting to, just hit him with the baseball bat beside the bed and it takes him just the right way, knocking him out.

I see an image of Bruce, firing a weapon into a darkened car, and then it changes to me, standing over John as he lies on the floor of our bedroom on the Sunday night after I came home from work, the start of a period of time for which I've since invented an alternate reality to explain things, an opportunist using whatever was around me: Bruce, an old friend showing up; Canada, because of John's application to regain admissibility; drug dealers, because of something I probably read in the newspaper — all to cobble together a story that makes sense out of my own heinous act.

"Melody!"

My voice is swallowed by the shed and its contents. Probably for the best; I don't want her in here anyway, seeing her father like this. I look at John and shake him some more and lightly slap his cheek. My tears fall on his sweaty face. If it were summer he'd be dead from the heat. But he's perspiring because he's alive. I didn't kill him. I've never hurt anyone.

Easing his head back down I get up and start making my way back toward the mouth of the shed, shoving aside the toys and equipment. I trip and tumble forward and bang knees and elbows and get back to my feet, lurch toward the open door at the same time I'm staring at my phone and punching in 9-1-1.

Finally outside, gasping in the fresh air as the call connects, I look around for Melody and Russ. They were last down by the water and I shout their names as the dispatcher answers.

"911 — what's your emergency?"

I give her my name and the address, tell her that my husband is in bad shape — malnourished, dehydrated — and I can't rouse him. I hurriedly tell her we need police, too, that my husband was abducted and filed as a missing person. Though she assures me someone is on the way, I stumble toward the road to see if anyone else is around that might help.

The only sign of life is about a hundred yards away: a black SUV riding a cloud of dust and headed this way.

* * *

At first I wave my arms — it doesn't even occur to me who this could be; I'm too overwhelmed by the need to help John — and then I let my arms drop.

Cooking and *Insurance* weren't the only things written in John's notebook.

Olympia.

As if a warning, from him to me.

I pull up Ridley's contact. The call goes to voicemail. "Ridley it's Jane Gable. She's here. Olympia is at the lake house."

I have no weapons, no guns. I fight the urge to run for the kids — they're better off where they are. Keeping my eyes on the SUV, I shout in the direction of their voices. "Melody! Someone is here! Run up toward the Hayberrys' and hide!"

I can't be sure if she hears me, though their voices go quiet. The SUV hits the brakes and skids to a stop on the dirt road, sending out a plume of dust. There's nowhere else to go, nothing else to do but stand my ground in the haze.

I see Olympia's boots first as she steps out of the dark vehicle, then the gun pointing at me when she shuts the door. Her blonde hair has been drawn back into a tight ponytail — she's in business-mode now, apparently. The whole thing — coming to me, acting like she owed me something — she has an agenda.

"Hi, Jane."

With hindsight, it seems obvious: would Bruce Barnes enter Canada with a hundred and fifty thousand dollars' worth of drugs on his person? What does that even look like?

Bruce may have spared John, but he'd always planned to come back, get the rest of the drugs and maybe the money that he'd stolen from Dixon. It was Rainey who was afraid John wouldn't survive the wait.

"How is everything?" Olympia asks. She nears, boots crunching through the grit, everything loud and vivid to me, as if some primitive part of my brain knows these are the last few seconds of my life.

"John is alive," I say quickly. "He's in the shed behind me. I called the police — they'll be here any second."

Olympia glances at the phone, checks the area, looks back at me. She seems to understand that emergency response will be slowed by the narrow dirt roads and the distance from modern civilization. These camps and lake houses like mine hold a common purpose: to leave the rest of the world behind.

"You know what I'm here for," she says.

"I don't want to get in your way. I don't care about any of that — money, none of it. I just want to get him to a hospital."

She looks past me at the shed. "In there, huh?"

"Yes."

Her eyes slide back. "And the kids?"

"Please . . ."

"You've seen my face."

"I won't say anything."

"Your son has seen me, too."

I strain to hear my kids, hoping Melody went to the neighbors' place to hide, but my addled mind sees imagined headlines about *Three Slain in Henderson Harbor*. The crime scene photos show small red sneakers at the end of a seven-year-old boy's legs as he lies dead on the beach.

I take a lurching step forward. "Don't hurt them."

"You've seen *their* faces, too," she says, and the rear doors of the SUV swing open. A man gets out from each side, one brown-skinned and the other white, each holding a gun — only theirs are bigger.

She talks to them over her shoulder. "Try the toilet tank, under the sink. Basic places. And be quick — what's the response time?"

"Just came over the scanner — first responder is six miles north. We got ten minutes."

"Go on," she says, and the men move toward the house.

Looking at me again, a mix of curiosity and sympathy in her eyes, Olympia asks, "Got an attic in this place? Crawl space?"

I nod, quickly. "Just outside the bathroom. Drawstring in the ceiling — stairs fold down. There's just old photo albums up there, things like that."

"Where else?" She wags the large pistol at the shed. "In there? With him?"

There's moaning behind me — John regaining consciousness. I take a few steps back, holding out my arms, as if to protect him. "Let me look."

"It would be in a black case marked C.R.D.," she says. "Carl Robert Dixon."

My phone vibrates in my grip. Ridley is calling back.

Olympia notices and holds out her hand, palm up. "Toss it."

I do as she says and she snatches it out of the air, checks the screen. Then she drops it to the ground and smashes it under her boot heel, twisting her leg back and forth to grind it down. "Now get in there. Look. Black case."

I'm about to, until I think ahead to Olympia closing me in with John while she finishes her search and goes after Melody and Russ. So I stop, look her in the face from five yards away. "You do it."

She points the gun at my head. Her expression is slack. The kind eyes and smiles are long gone. There's just the muscle-memory of a killer at work. "Jane, get in there and look for my property or I'm going to shoot and kill you."

I don't move a muscle.

"We don't care about Carl Dixon. We don't care about you or your family. We want our product back and we'll get it with or without you."

"What if he took it with him?"

"Even Barnes isn't that stupid. You're stalling. Get in there."

Something smashes inside the house, momentarily distracting the both of us, followed by the pounding of footsteps. A few seconds later, the door swings open and one of the men comes out with a heavy-looking grocery bag, dripping wet. "In the toilet tank, just like you said."

Olympia jerks her head at the SUV and the man gets in with the drugs. The other emerges from the house. He gives me a look and starts for the vehicle. If there's something human in Olympia, it reappears for just an instant. Her head tilts slightly to the side and her arm stiffens as she re-aims at my chest. "Sorry, Jane."

The sound of an approaching engine surprises us both. The way Hacksaw Road goes is by looping from two points that connect to the main road beyond. Olympia approached from the north, same way I came in, probably because she was tracking me. But I'd taken the scenic route through Sackets Harbor — the quicker way is to come from the south, the way the Jefferson County cop car comes barreling in, lights flashing, siren silent. I hope the ambulance isn't far behind.

Olympia walks into the road with an easy gait, like she's greeting a postal worker delivering her a package. The cop car hits the brakes. She takes aim and unloads a clip into its front windshield. The sound is deafening.

My last image of Olympia is her in shooter-stance, arm extended with the giant pistol in her hand. She disappears into the raised silt and then I'm running, sprinting across the lawn, vaulting the containment wall like a gymnast and hitting the rocky beach on its far side with both feet planted. My back seizes but doesn't give out.

The kids are nowhere in sight. Melody must have heard me after all. I move up the beach toward the Hayberry place as more gunfire erupts from behind me.

CHAPTER THIRTY-TWO / MARRIAGE

The Hayberry house is pretty. Years of sunshine have baked the cedar shakes charcoal and russet-brown with flares of pink. It has no basement and sits raised on cinderblocks. My children are hidden beneath.

I don't know how long we stay there — maybe six, seven minutes. The shooting ended before I even climbed up from the beach, heard my son chirp, "Mom!" in his best whisper-but-not-really-a-whisper voice, and then there were unintelligible shouts and the slamming of doors, the scrape of boots over dirt and gravel, more shouts, more doors and, finally, the wailing of an ambulance siren as it turned down Hacksaw Road.

While we hide, I explain to the kids what is happening as best I can. I tell them that their father is in the storage shed, alive but badly injured. As the voices and footsteps come closer and people call my name, my kids are at least prepared for what they are about to see.

Jefferson County deputies and New York State Troopers envelop the scene. An ambulance is parked in the dirt road by the metal shed. "Are you hurt, ma'am?" The paramedic reaches for us. "Are your children all right?"

After she looks us all over, a pickup truck with an orange light bar over the cab roars down the road, more vehicles behind it, and a state trooper is urging us toward his vehicle. But I need to see in the shed and I won't let go of my children.

Much of the items in storage have been cleared out, leaving a view inside. Paramedics place an oxygen mask over John's mouth and pick him up on a stretcher. They work their way out of the shed and Melody is crying.

I squeeze her tight but I'm all cried out.

Russ just watches. "That's Dad?"

"Yes, honey."

"He was in there?"

"Yes."

"Why?"

"Someone put him there."

"The guy with the bullet hole?"

"Right."

We step back to let them through and as the stretcher passes with John on it, he sees me and reaches out. I take his hand and he squeezes mine back. The kids are touching him. The paramedics and police are trying to keep us back but we're crowding around, all moving as one unit toward the open doors of the ambulance.

"Russ," I say, though I'm looking into John's eyes. "You're going to ride to the hospital in a police car, okay?"

"Okay."

Melody grips me tighter. "Mom I'm coming with you and Dad."

"I need you to stay with your brother. Make sure he's all right."

Melody falls over her father and hugs him and he runs his fingers through the tangles of her hair. Then he's lifted up into the back of the ambulance and I kiss Melody on the cheek, rub my hand on the side of Russ's face and get in with my husband. The doors close and I watch the kids through the rear windows as two troopers fall in beside them and lead them to one of the vehicles. I wave and each of them waves back.

* * *

John has trouble speaking at first. They pump a lot of fluids into him and set him on a course of antibiotics for his infected sores. When he's better and he's spent an hour or more with the kids, hugging and smiling at them and not saying much, I send them down to the hospital cafeteria and his eyes roll over to look at me, gone pink, filling with tears.

"I'm sorry," he says.

Most of it falls into place with what I've put together. Struggling for months to get a project off the ground, he was tempted to do something completely outside the norm.

"Honestly I was thinking about Bruce, about writing something more literary — two grown men who'd had trouble in school and where their lives had led them — you know, something like that — what happened when they ended up back in each other's lives. I thought he was going to buy some pot to sell. *Maybe* coke. I'd just get a sense of it, maybe feel a little scared. I'd use it. Break out of this rut."

They met Carl Dixon in Massena during a weekend John was supposed to be doing repairs at the lake house, two weeks before our date in Plattsburgh. Behind an abandoned factory, like something out of a movie, John sat there in Bruce's truck while Bruce carried over a backpack full of cash. He'd started drug dealing in Florida, like Olympia said, but things had gotten too hot for him and then Rainey was diagnosed, so they left.

"It was going to be his last deal, he said. A hundred and fifty thousand's worth and he was going to triple it — he told me this only afterward. Enough to pay for anything Rainey needed for her recovery, he said. But he got greedy, scared — I don't know. I'm sitting there and I see the flashes of light inside this guy's car and hear the shots. Then Bruce gets out and he's got another bag with him, a briefcase or something, and he jumps in and we hightail it out of there. I didn't even know what to think. I was in shock. I think Bruce was, too. He didn't say anything almost the whole way back to Henderson. He drops me off and he just looks at me and he says, 'We good?'"

"John, you don't have to."

"I never thought you and the kids were in danger. I didn't know what he was doing when he came to the house. I hadn't seen him in almost two weeks. I didn't know what to tell you — I thought he was trying to be my friend, trying to act like nothing happened. I was going to say something to you — I was, Jane. I wanted us to decide together if I should go to the police. And then she came to the house, that woman — Olympia — and asked me about him. I knew who she was — I could tell or something. She was one of the . . . she was behind the guy Bruce shot. She was cleaning up. She wanted to look around and see if I had anything — any money, any of the drugs. I didn't. And then she left. And that night they came back. Bruce and Rainey. Rainey looked terrible, like she'd taken a turn for the worse. She drove my car and Bruce put me in his truck and I fought with him, tried to get away. And he said, 'Calm down. I'm not going to kill you.'" The last word dies in his throat. John swallows and knuckles away a tear, pulls himself together. "They got the idea at dinner — about what to do with me. When we had them over and talked about where we got married."

I'm sitting beside the bed and have my hand in his. I feel calmer, more in control than I've felt in several days.

When our eyes connect again he says, "I will spend the rest of my life making it up to you. Everything you've gone through. You and the kids . . . nothing matters but the three of you. Nothing."

I've thought about it long and hard. During the ride in the ambulance, over the long hours since his admittance to the hospital, with the adrenaline settled and John returned to me, my mind has been going non-stop. I've questioned everything, looked into every corner of myself, wondered if this was what forgiveness felt like or if, instead, I was still numb and could no longer feel the trust I'd felt with John all these years.

He's not a saint. Just because he took on a single mother and her infant daughter doesn't win him any medals. In a relationship, in a marriage, it never ends. You can't rest on your laurels. You put in the work and the love and you maintain the trust every day.

Every day.

I thought about ending it, Mom.

But I didn't. If this was one of those novels you read about a woman going through all this kind of upheaval, she'd probably wind up with the cop on the case or the handsome stranger at the exotic place she'd gone off to while contending with the mystery. But this is real life. John isn't a Marcus Gainsborough. He's not a Daryl Chase. He's a good man.

He just really, really screwed up.

And I'm not perfect. You of all people know that, Mom.

So I stand up and lean over John and give him a soft kiss on the lips. "I'm going to go check on the kids."

He squeezes my hand and gives me a smile. Before I step out of the hospital room he calls over to me. "Hey, so how much currency does this give you in the relationship bank?"

I hold onto the door frame and look down to conceal my grin while I consider it. "I'd say I'm a millionaire at this point."

"That's fair," he says.

"I love you," I tell him.

"I love you, too."

Halfway down the hall to the cafeteria I can hear my children bickering about something.

EPILOGUE

Sunday, May 19th

One last thing, Mom — I thought you'd like this.

So about six weeks later as I'm coming to the end of writing all of this to you (it came out of me in a torrent, like I'm suddenly Jack Kerouac, and I've never written anything, really), I popped online to check John's book stats.

All the media attention has launched his book sales into the stratosphere. Even *Edge of Night* is finally having its day in the sun.

And though this started out as a letter to you, John encouraged me to send it to Marty, his agent, who wants to publish it as a book. So after you read this, and after some intense editing, I'm sure, it will be out there in the world, with all sorts of people reading it.

They'll probably want to know what happened to Bruce.

It was on the news about a week after finding John in the shed: Bruce was killed in Canada in what was "believed to be part of a wide-ranging drug operation," they said. So, that's that.

Anyway, John is outside in the spring blossoms, playing with the kids. Next year I guess for spring break we're going to go to Arizona to visit Frank and Delores.

Oh and we had the storage shed removed from the lake house. I'm sure Grandpa would understand.

Love you, Mom.

THE END

ALSO BY T.J. BREARTON

HABIT
SURVIVORS
DAYBREAK
BLACK SOUL

DEAD GONE
TRUTH OR DEAD

DARK WEB
DARK KILLS
GONE

Please join our mailing list for free kindle crime thriller, detective, mysteries and new releases.
http://www.joffebooks.com/contact/

ACKNOWLEDGEMENTS

I want to thank Lisa Regan Prodorutti for having an early look at this and helping me to unearth the whole story. John Ramirez and Bob Sirrine for spotting the snares and for their unwavering encouragement. Troopers Kristy Wilson and Sean Kane for lending their law enforcement knowledge and for their service and protection. To Korey Shumway — you've inspired a great character here and I thank you — much love to you, brother. Thanks to Ed Handyside for excellent edits and handling business like a pro; to Jasper Joffe for taking on yet another one of my projects in the midst of his amazing growth. And thank you, my wife and kids, for leaving the door to my office closed when I needed it, and for opening it up when I needed it more.

Thank you for reading this book. If you enjoyed it please leave feedback on Amazon, and if there is anything we missed or you have a question about then please get in touch. The author and publishing team appreciate your feedback and time reading this book.

Our email is office@joffebooks.com

http://joffebooks.com

find out more about T.J. Brearton
http://tjbrearton.net/

We hate typos but sometimes they slip through.
Please send any errors you find to
corrections@joffebooks.com
We'll get them fixed ASAP. We're very grateful to
eagle-eyed readers who take the time to contact us.

Made in United States
Orlando, FL
25 May 2024

47197298R00171